Laurien Berenson
joins the ranks of today's most
celebrated mystery authors with the
outstanding debut of the
Melanie Travis mystery series!

"Delightful . . . Melanie Travis copes with murder, single par-
enthood and the world of poodles with charm and stubborn
honesty. Four paws for this one."
—Carolyn Hart, author of the *Death on Demand*
and the *Henrie O* mystery series

"A promising first novel involving the dog-eat-dog world of
championship breeding."
—Mostly Murder

". . . an enjoyable read and a fascinating look at the world of
the competitive dog showing. HIGHLY RECOMMENDED."
—*I Love a Mystery*

"You don't have to love dogs to appreciate Berenson's wit,
clean writing style, and engaging, down-to-earth characters."
—*The Advocate/Greenwich Times*

"Fun reading."
—*Dog News*

"The writing is smooth, the charaters three-dimensional.
Watch for future books by this author."
—*Deadly Pleasures*

". . . this book is a delight."
AKC Gazette

"Written with a casual and inviting style . . . this is a sound
start to a mystery series."
Murder & Mayhem

Books by Laurien Berenson

A PEDIGREE TO DIE FOR

UNDERDOG

DOG EAT DOG

HAIR OF THE DOG

WATCHDOG

HUSH PUPPY

UNLEASHED

ONCE BITTEN

HOT DOG

BEST IN SHOW

JINGLE BELL BARK

Published by Kensington Publishing Corporation

A PEDIGREE TO DIE FOR

Laurien Berenson

KENSINGTON BOOKS
KENSINGTON PUBLISHING CORP.

http://www.kensingtonbooks.com

KENSINGTON BOOKS are published by

Kensington Publishing Corp.
850 Third Avenue
New York, NY 10022

First Kensington Hardcover Printing: February, 1995
First Kensington Paperback Printing: February, 1996
10 9

Printed in the United States of America

⟐❋ *One* ❋⟐

There's a lot to be said for dying in the midst of something you love. But fond as Uncle Max was of his Poodles, I doubt that he'd ever envisioned himself being found dead on the cold, hard kennel floor, his curled fingers grasping at the open door of an empty pen.

For their part, the Poodles didn't seem to think much of the idea either. All seven of the big black dogs were scratching at their doors and whining when Aunt Peg came out the next morning looking for Max, who was inexplicably missing from her bed when she woke up. The moment she saw him, she knew what had happened. The Turnbull men weren't known for their strong hearts; the doctor had warned Max more than once to slow down. But in the end, all the things they'd done together—giving up smoking, taking up walking, watching their cholesterol—hadn't made the slightest bit of difference.

Not one to panic when composure served better, Aunt Peg had closed her husband's eyes, then covered him with a blanket before picking up the phone and calling for an ambulance.

I learned all this from my brother Frank, whose name she'd supplied when asked by the police if there was someone they could call. One look at Aunt Peg and they must have realized that the sedatives the paramedics had so thoughtfully left behind were going to go to waste. That's when they started making comforting noises about next of kin.

We've never been the type of family to advertise our emotions. Aunt Peg would no sooner keen and wail than join the chorus line of the Rockettes. Nevertheless Frank had arrived prepared to offer whatever support was needed. That none was soon became apparent when Aunt Peg declared that his hovering was making her nervous and sent him home.

Now, three days later, Frank was kneeling beside me in the front pew of Saint Mary's Church in Greenwich. He looked every bit as uncomfortable as I felt when the rest of the funeral party trooped up to the altar to receive communion. It was painfully obvious that we were the only two to remain behind.

Thanks to my Aunt Rose, Max's sister and a member of the order of the Sisters of Divine Mercy, the church was full. As the priest began dispensing hosts from the golden chalice, I pushed aside the missals that littered the pew, sat back, and resigned myself to a long wait. Two by two, the sisters glided by, their rubber-soled shoes noiseless on the church floor. Many, I noted absently, were of the old school, which meant that they still wore the dark habits and crisp white wimples I remembered so vividly from my youth.

The soft rustle of cloth, the muted clacking of polished rosary beads that swung from the sisters' waists, both were sounds from the past. For a moment, I found myself transported back to the narrow halls of the convent school where I'd been raised. It wasn't a trip I enjoyed. Some Catholics refer to their faith as something that has lapsed. I tend to think of mine as expired.

Until that afternoon, it had been years since I'd been inside a church. Five years, to be exact, since an icy patch of road had sent my parents' car careening down a steep embankment and into a river, leaving me—newly married and newly pregnant—also newly orphaned. Bob, my husband then, ex now, maintained at the time that anyone who had reached the age of twenty-five was simply too old to qualify for orphan status.

"I know what I feel!" I wanted to shout at him. In later years, I wouldn't have been so reticent. Later we shouted about a lot of things.

Still, I had Bob to thank for my son, and in my mind, that more than evened the score. Davey was home now with a sitter, no doubt spurning the glorious May weather to watch Oprah Winfrey on TV. There'd be plenty of time later for him to learn about funerals—and about people who die long before you're ready to say goodbye.

A throat cleared scratchily, and I looked up to find Aunt Peg standing above me. One of the first to go to the altar, she was now ready to return to the pew. Quickly I stood up to let her by.

Behind her came Aunt Rose, Sister Anne Marie to the other nuns. Her head was bowed, her eyes half-closed. Her fingers were braced together at the tips, forming a slim arrow that pointed upward toward the heavens. In contrast to Aunt Peg's grim-lipped frown, her expression had a soft, unmolded quality. She was talking to her God, I realized. Uncomfortable, I looked away.

The line at the communion rail dwindled, then finally ended. The sisters glided back to their pews. At the altar, the priest mumbled the remaining words of the mass before offering a blessing to the assemblage.

I was turning to retrieve my purse from the bench when the sisters began to sing. Their voices rose, filling the large church with the harmonious cadence of a well-rehearsed choir. I straightened, then paused to listen. The hymn was Latin, its words vaguely familiar. But it was the music itself that reached out to me; the voices joined as one sent a tingle racing up the length of my spine. The sound was pure and sweet and uplifting. For a moment, I could almost believe that the sisters *were,* as I'd been taught years before, in the business of sending souls to heaven.

I waited until the song ended before leaving the pew. Uncle Max, who'd always had a dramatic flair, would have loved the pageantry of it all. As a child, in the years before the family drifted apart, I'd found him fascinating. Everything about Uncle Max was just slightly outsize; he had no use for the ordinary, and little tolerance for anyone who did. He enjoyed beauty and style, and surrounded himself with plenty, like the kennel full of Standard Poodles that he bred and exhibited. The funeral mass, with all its pomp and ceremony, would have suited him just fine.

I rode to the cemetery in the first limousine with Frank and Aunt Peg. Aunt Rose was curiously absent. Perhaps she felt the chauffeur-driven Lincoln was too ostentatious for her station in the world. Or perhaps the impression I'd gotten over the years that she and Aunt Peg didn't get along was true.

Aunt Peg was silent during the drive, and Frank and I followed suit. Somehow I didn't feel I had the right to intrude. The dark brim of a fedora was pulled low over her eyes; the set of her shoulders was stiff. Whatever emotions she was feeling, she kept them to herself.

The graveside ceremony was brief. In keeping with family tradition, there were no histrionics, only a quiet prayer beside the coffin. As we turned to leave, I heard a quiet sigh.

"Goodbye, Max," Aunt Peg whispered. Her lower lip trembled briefly, then stilled.

Walking back toward the line of parked cars, I reached

out impulsively and took her hand in mine. "If there's anything at all I can do . . ."

Little did I know.

❧✿ *Two* ✿❧

The phone call came three days later.

Aunt Peg caught me at a bad moment, but then there are days when my life seems full of them. My duties as a special ed. teacher for the Stamford school system had just ended for the year, but the jubilation I'd expected to feel had been short-lived. That morning, I'd been notified that the summer job I'd counted on—working as a counselor at a camp for handicapped children—had fallen through due to lack of funding.

Then the day's mail had arrived, containing a picture postcard from Bradley, the man I'd been seeing sporadically over the past year. Mailed from Las Vegas, it featured a picture of the Silver Bells Wedding Chapel on the front and a scribbled note on the back, confessing that he'd made use of the chapel the day before with a six-foot chorus girl from Circus, Circus.

To top it off, when I'd tried to drive to the supermarket so that I could drown my sorrows in Heavenly Hash ice cream, I'd discovered that my ancient Volvo was sitting in front of the house with a flat tire. By the time the phone rang, I was in no mood for small talk.

"I'll get it!" yelled four-year-old Davey. He raced into the kitchen, hands outstretched, fingers bright with paint. "Mine! Mine!"

"Oh no you don't." With agility born of experience, I dodged around the counter and snatched up the receiver before he could reach it.

"I need help," Aunt Peg announced without preamble.

"Of course, anything."

"Is Frank there?"

The ripple of resentment was small, but definitely there. Still, I probably shouldn't have been surprised. Aunt Peg was just old-fashioned enough to believe that men were better at getting things done than women; which only went to prove how little she knew about her nephew.

"No, he isn't, Aunt Peg. I haven't seen him since the funeral. Are you all right?"

"Of course I'm not all right. I just told you I needed help. Do those sound like the words of someone who's all right?"

I sighed and took a tighter grip on the receiver. Aunt Peg has always had a way of keeping me just slightly off balance. She'd been married to my father's brother for thirty years, but we'd never really been friends. Now, hearing her distress, I nudged aside the chorus girl from Circus, Circus, who was still dancing at the edge of my thoughts. "Why don't you tell me what's wrong?"

"One of my dogs is missing."

It took a moment for that to register, longer still for my mind to form an appropriate response.

Ever impatient, Aunt Peg simply plunged on without me. "He's been gone since the night Max died, and I think the two things are related."

Abruptly, the chorus girl vanished without a trace. "Aunt Peg, what are you trying to say?"

"I'm not *trying* to say anything. Indeed, I thought I was expressing myself rather well."

"I thought Uncle Max had a heart attack."

"That's certainly what it seemed. But once I realized

Beau was gone, I began to wonder. There must have been someone else in the kennel with him. Perhaps there was a scuffle over the dog."

It sounded pretty far-fetched to me. But then, I work with seven-year-olds; I'm used to humoring people. "Have you spoken to the police?"

"The police," Aunt Peg sniffed, as though discussing a lower, and obviously less intelligent form of life, "weren't impressed by what I had to say. I was told that the fact that an older man with a weak heart had suffered a heart attack did not warrant any investigation on their part. As to the missing dog, the lieutenant had the nerve to suggest that I call the dog warden."

That didn't sound like such a bad idea to me. I wrung out a wet cloth in the sink and began to wipe Davey's hands. "Where does Frank fit in?"

"I want to find out what really happened that night," Aunt Peg said firmly. "And I want my dog back. If the police aren't interested in doing the job, then I'll simply have to see to it myself. I was thinking Frank might help."

"I want to talk to Aunt Peg!" Davey cried suddenly. He jumped up and tried to grab the receiver from my hand.

Turning, I nudged him down and juggled the receiver to my other ear. "Not now. Mommy's busy. Why don't you go play outside?"

"Want to talk," Davey insisted, stamping his foot.

"Melanie, are you there?"

"Yes, Aunt Peg—"

"Can you find Frank for me?"

"Well . . ." I could already imagine what my brother's response was going to be. Poodles, missing or otherwise, had never ranked very high on his list of priorities, and flinty, indomitable Aunt Peg suited nobody's idea of a kindly old lady in need. "You know Frank, he could be anywhere."

The silence between us lengthened. When it had stretched to a full minute, I knew I'd been outwaited. "I do know some of his friends. I guess I could do some calling around."

"Good. Track him down and feed him a good meal. I'll join you after dinner when you've got him softened up a bit. What time should I come?"

Commitment settled around my neck like a noose. "Nine o'clock for coffee and dessert?" I suggested weakly.

"Fine, I'll see you then."

No sooner had I replaced the receiver than Davey began to wail. "I didn't get to talk. I wanted to talk to Aunt Peg!"

"Aunt Peg didn't have time to talk." Without thinking, I wiped away his tears with the same cloth that had cleaned his hands, leaving a long streak of red paint down each cheek. Davey giggled delightedly.

"Come on, sport, let's go wash you off. Then we've got a tire to change."

The house Davey and I live in is small—a square little box on a square plot of land that isn't a whole lot bigger. The realtor who sold it to Bob and me called it a cape, which brought to mind visions of lonely dunes and sandy, windswept beaches. Although the town of Stamford is on the Connecticut shore, there isn't a beach within miles of here. And as for lonely dunes, you can forget those, too. The developer who built Flower Estates packed the houses in like he was paying for land by the foot.

Still, it's a nice neighborhood for Davey to grow up in, and the mortgage has a fixed rate that I tell myself I can afford. As to the house being small, most of the time it doesn't matter. Davey and I don't take up much room. Frank and Aunt Peg, however, are a different matter entirely.

"I still don't see why I had to get mixed up in this," Frank complained later that night. He was sitting at the dining-room table, stirring his coffee slowly while I cleared away the last of the dinner dishes. "It would be one thing if she was upset about Uncle Max, but a *dog?*"

"It's both things together," I told him, not for the first time. "Aunt Peg seems to think the two are related—that the dog was stolen the night Uncle Max died. She needs your help, Frank. The least you can do is listen to what she has to say."

"Do I have a choice?"

"Not that I could tell, so make the best of it."

A moment later a sharp rap on the front door signaled Aunt Peg's arrival. "Brace yourself," I said, as I rose to let her in. "Here we go."

Aunt Peg swept into the front hall like a gale wind and surveyed her surroundings with a look that went straight down her nose. As she stood head and shoulders above me, I had never quite decided whether this mode of assessment was born of necessity or preference. Her hair, now more gray than the rich dark red I remembered from my youth, was combed back into a bun that accentuated her high cheekbones and wide forehead. She carried herself with the assurance of someone who is used to being in charge and immediately took over the house as though it were her own.

"Hello, Melanie dear." She pecked my cheek quickly. "Is Davey still up? Can I say hello?"

I shook my head. "He's been in bed for hours. If I get him up now, he'll never go back."

Aunt Peg shrugged and handed me her sweater to be dealt with. "Next time then. Frank's in the dining room? Don't worry, I'll find my way." She was gone before I even had a chance to reply.

As a child, I'd always been in awe of my dashing aunt and uncle. Their lives seemed glamorous and vaguely mysterious, filled with travel and adventure. Aunt Peg had presence; enough, I'd always thought, to lead armies into battle. I, on the other hand, was the type who was apt to get lost in a crowd of two. Bearing, she told me, had everything to do with it. I myself thought it was height. But beside my aunt's vivid coloring, my own brown hair and hazel eyes had seemed plain and unremarkable. Sometimes the sheer force of her personality left me feeling as though I'd disappeared all together. Looking after her now, I couldn't see that much had changed.

When I joined them in the dining room, Frank was pouring the coffee while Aunt Peg got straight to business. She began with her realization—hours after she'd discovered Uncle Max—that Beau, their valuable stud dog, was missing.

"I don't see why you're assuming the dog was stolen," Frank broke in. "With all the confusion that morning, he probably just wandered away. Dogs do like to roam, you know."

The glare Aunt Peg sent his way held all the warmth of granite in winter. "My dear boy, Poodles do not roam, and Beau did not *wander* away."

I caught Frank's eye and shrugged. He grinned in return, a toothless grimace that questioned the sanity of older relations.

Aunt Peg frowned sternly. "Unfortunately, the authorities were no more excited about Beau's disappearance than you two seem to be. Even the FBI said that they couldn't step in until there was some evidence that the dog had been transported across state lines."

I choked on a sip of coffee. *"The FBI?* Aunt Peg, you didn't really call them, did you?"

"Of course. I've called everybody. And now it appears that I am going to get no more understanding from my own relatives than I did from total strangers."

The line was intended to produce guilt, and it fulfilled

its function admirably. At least I had the good grace to blush. Frank merely settled back in his chair, resigned to hearing her out.

"Suppose you tell us why you think somebody took the dog," he said.

"For starters, the door to his pen was wide open. Beau is smart, but he could hardly have managed *that* by himself."

"Uncle Max was in the kennel," I pointed out. "Maybe he opened it."

"Maybe, but it's highly unlikely. We had three bitches in full season at the time. Nobody in their right mind would stir up that kind of mayhem. Which brings me to my next question—what would Max have been doing out in the kennel in the middle of the night anyway?"

"Sleepwalking?" Frank suggested. I kicked him, hard, under the table.

"Hardly," Aunt Peg said dryly. "He was dressed at the time. Obviously, he'd never been to bed at all."

"Isn't that unusual?" I asked.

"Not for Max." Unexpectedly, Aunt Peg smiled. "He used to stay up to all hours, reading or working in his office. It overlooks the kennel, you know. Still, I'm sure he wouldn't have gone out there unless he had a good reason."

"Granted, there are a few unanswered questions," said Frank. "But do you really think it's possible that someone would have broken into your kennel and fought with Uncle Max, all because of a dog?"

"Anything's possible," Aunt Peg said crisply. "When someone wants something badly enough."

"But why . . . ?"

The look Aunt Peg bounced back and forth between us made it perfectly clear that any relatives of hers should definitely be quicker on the uptake. "Maybe it will be easier to understand if I explain that Beau is not just an ordinary dog. In fact, far from it. He was a knockout as a puppy, and even better as an adult. He finished with four straight majors and had a Best In Show before he was two. This past winter when Max and I retired him to stud, we had more requests than we could possibly handle."

"Even so," said Frank. "He *is* only a dog. What's the most he could be worth?"

Aunt Peg looked pointedly down her nose. "I've had offers in excess of twenty thousand dollars."

"You're kidding!"

"Not at all. Beau commands a stud fee of five hundred dollars. In the last year, he's serviced a dozen bitches and I turned away twice as many as I approved."

I whistled softly under my breath. "I never knew you were making that kind of money from those Poodles."

"You never needed to know. Why should you? But surely you can see that there are people who might be interested in acquiring the dog."

Intrigued by the possibilities, I found myself leaning forward in my chair. Even though I knew the only reason Aunt Peg had come to me was because I'd been able to produce Frank, I still couldn't help being interested. "But purebred dogs have papers, don't they? As long as Beau is still registered in your name, what possible use could he be to someone else?"

"Indeed, they do have papers. And the American Kennel Club keeps track of such things very carefully. But what you need to understand is that a stud dog's value is determined by the quality of the puppies he produces. Who he is, his show record, and even his pedigree become secondary considerations when a dog is producing well. Beau's thief would need only to set him up at stud under some other Poodle's name and wait for the puppies to prove themselves. In time, with his progeny out and winning, breeders would send droves of bitches to the nominal sire, who would become quite famous for producing nicely without anyone ever realizing that it was Beau doing all the work."

"Tell me—" I began, but my brother cut me off.

"I'm sorry your dog is gone, Aunt Peg," he said. "But I'm afraid I don't see what you expect me to do about it."

He wasn't asking for guidance, I realized, but rather stating his intention—not surprisingly—to remain uninvolved. A quick glance at Aunt Peg revealed that she was having none of it.

"Perhaps if you'd have the decency to listen until I've finished speaking, you'd find out."

I winced at her tone. She was going about things all wrong. Frank was temperamental, like a fine racehorse in training. Cajole, and he'd give you anything. Demand, and you lost it all. The moment I saw him stiffen in his seat, I knew which way things had gone.

He began with a patronizing smile and from there, things only got worse. "Look, Aunt Peg, I know you're going through a difficult time right now. You're upset, maybe even a little confused, and certainly in no shape to be getting yourself all worked up. Why don't you just forget about the dog? After all, you've got plenty of others to take his place."

Aunt Peg's expression froze. "My shape, as you call it, is not what's at issue here. I may be in mourning, but I am not incapacitated. Besides, has it ever occurred to you that at this particular point in my life, I might welcome something to be worked up over?"

I tried to get between them, but it was no use. Aunt Peg was on a tear.

"You're right I'm upset. I miss Max terribly. I miss him every minute of every day. But sitting at home on my butt, sipping tea, doesn't help that one bit. My husband's gone, and nothing I can do will bring him back, but I sure as hell can try to find our dog!"

"I didn't mean—"

"Your meaning," Aunt Peg snapped, rising to her feet. "was perfectly clear."

We followed her to the front hall, where she accepted her sweater without another word. Ignoring Frank's attempt to help her on with it, she tossed the cardigan over her shoulders and let herself out. Suddenly the house seemed surprisingly empty.

"Really, Frank," I said reproachfully as we returned to the dining room and cleared the table together. "Don't you think you could have tried a little harder to be understanding?"

"Oh no you don't. You're not going to lay this one on me. All I did was tell Aunt Peg the truth, which is a good deal more than you seemed willing to do."

"What do you mean?"

"Come on, Mel. Don't tell me you actually *believed* all that stuff she said?"

"Of course. Why wouldn't I?"

"A dozen bitches, five hundred dollars a shot? She had to have been exaggerating. If there's one thing Aunt Peg can do, it's tell a good story."

"Well," I admitted, "twenty thousand dollars does sound kind of high for a dog."

"Kind of? Give me a break. She probably pulled that number right out of thin air. Take my word for it; Aunt Peg is feeling lonely right now and she's looking for some attention."

"So? What's the matter with that? Of course Aunt Peg is feeling lonely, and if she wants some attention, I think she ought to have it."

"If you want to humor her, that's your business. Sympathy is one thing, but I don't see any reason why we should let her take us for a ride. Don't forget, she and Uncle Max have had some pretty wild ideas in the past.

As far as I can tell, this stolen dog business is just more of the same. The police didn't buy her story, so she came to us. Don't you think that if there really was something to it, they'd have investigated?"

"I suppose . . ."

"Believe me, that dog will probably wander home all by himself. Maybe he's already there, waiting for her right now."

"Do you really think so?"

"Sure," said Frank. "Anything's possible. Listen, much as I'd like to stay and talk, I've got to be on my way." He bent down and kissed me quickly on the cheek. "How about lending me a little spare cash, do you mind?"

I should have known the request was coming. It almost always did. When our parents were still alive, he'd gone to them. Now that they were gone, he came to me. Twenty-six years old and still my little brother had yet to discover a direction in life. His usual lack of income notwithstanding, he went through money like a Rockefeller.

"I don't have a little spare cash," I said irritably. "I just found out this morning that my summer job fell through. This late, it's going to be impossible to find anything else."

Frank shrugged. "Think of all the money you'll save in child care. And speaking of which, don't try to tell me that the kid's father isn't coughing up a pretty penny for his support. So how bad off can you be?"

Bad enough, as it turned out. Three years earlier at the time of my divorce, I'd been liberated enough to spurn alimony payments, although I had, for Davey's benefit, accepted child support. That was before I'd measured my worth on the open market and discovered that a master's degree in education was barely enough to keep food on the table and a roof over our heads at the same time. It was also before my dear, departed ex had folded his tents

in the middle of the night and moved on, leaving no for-
warding address. None of which, I reflected, was anything
that Frank needed to know.

"Aw, come on, Mel." Frank fixed me with a beguiling
smile. The one I always fell for, dammit. "You can swing
it. Besides, this is only a loan. You know I'll pay you back,
just as soon as my ship comes in."

"Your ship got torpedoed in the South Pacific," I muttered, but already I was digging around in my purse for
my wallet. "Here," I said, handing over a couple of ten
dollar bills. "It's the best I can do."

"Thanks." Money in hand, Frank was gone like a shot.

Typical, I thought. I left the dishes in the sink and went
upstairs to check on Davey. He was sleeping soundly, as
usual, the tattered remnants of his favorite stuffed cat
clutched beneath his chin. I pulled his door shut until only
a crack of light fell across the foot of the bed, then continued on to my own room next door.

Though Bob had been gone from my life for three
years, the bedroom had hardly changed at all since the
day he'd left. At the time, I'd been determined to purge
myself of everything that reminded me of him. It had
come as quite a shock to realize that nothing in the room
would. I wondered now, as I had then, if perhaps when
I'd furnished the room, I'd known subconsciously that his
stay there would be temporary.

The rug was burgundy, the walls cream. The curtains
and the pillows on the brass, queen-sized bed were a
striped combination of the two. There were no ruffles, no
skirted dressing table with an assortment of perfumes. I've
never been a frilly sort of person. Functional is more my
style. Looking around the room, it showed.

On the night table beside the bed was a cut-glass bud
vase, a wedding present from someone whose name I've
long since forgotten. It was filled with a handful of daisies
Davey had found in the backyard earlier that week. They

were drooping now, stems beginning to curl and turn brown. I plucked them out on the way to the bathroom and left them in the trash.

What a way to begin summer vacation.

☙❀ ✤ *Three* ✤ ❀☙

The next morning I overslept, which meant that by the time I got down to the kitchen, Davey had already made his own breakfast. Though the top on the cookie jar had a suspicious tilt, he was sitting innocently at the kitchen table next to a tall box of Cheerios. With a practiced eye, I took in the scene and reached out to rescue the cereal bowl he had turned upside down to use as a drum.

"Look," said Davey, his mouth open wide so that I could see the last spoonful of Cheerios still being chewed.

"Good work. Now swallow, and you can go watch 'Sesame Street.' "

By ten o'clock, I had scrubbed the kitchen floor, balanced my checkbook, and fired off an angry letter to my state representative protesting budget cutbacks in worthwhile programs. Now what? I wondered, sitting down at the kitchen table with a cup of strong black coffee. If every day that summer was going to be as long as this one, I was going to go quietly crazy.

Without even thinking about what I was doing, I pulled the phone across the counter and dialed. Aunt Peg answered on the first ring.

"Hi, it's Melanie. Any news?"

"Nothing," Aunt Peg said flatly. She sounded worlds

away from the hopeful, determined woman who had visited the night before.

"What are you going to do next?"

"Why do you want to know?"

Aunt Peg might be down, but she definitely wasn't beaten. All at once, I knew how I was going to spend my day. "I was just thinking that maybe it might help if I came over and we talked things out."

"Spare me."

"Spare you what?"

"The last thing I need is a condolence call from a pitying relative."

"Good, because that's the last thing you're going to get. I'm going to have to bring Davey." This last was added as a warning. Aunt Peg had been considerably less tolerant of her nephew's visits since the time he'd taken careful aim, then beaned one of her Poodles with a toy truck. On such short notice, however, baby-sitters were impossible to come by and we both knew it.

"I'll manage," Aunt Peg said dryly. With enthusiasm like that, it was no wonder we didn't visit more often.

Twenty minutes later, when we pulled in her driveway, I was still coaching Davey on the rules of acceptable behavior. He was nodding meekly, a sure sign that there was trouble afoot.

The first time I'd seen Aunt Peg's house as a child, I'd found it breathtaking and now, years later, in all the glory of late spring, it was no less so. Huge leafy elms, planted a century before, flanked the long driveway that led, not to the mansion one might have expected from such an approach, but rather to a rambling, ivy-covered farmhouse, once the hub of a working farm. Much of the land had since been sold off, but the house had settled into its surroundings with such charm and dignity that it radiated a sense of rightness that always made me feel immediately at home.

Our arrival was heralded by a chorus of canine voices that grew and swelled in number until a command from inside the house silenced the noise as suddenly as it had begun. Then Aunt Peg opened the door and the Poodles came thundering out like a small herd of buffalo. These were not the dainty little balls of fluff you see in circuses and on greeting cards. Aunt Peg's Poodles were of the Standard variety, which meant they were the kings and queens of the breed. None stood smaller than waist high, with capped heads and plumed tails that added to their stature. Davey was quickly enveloped by the group, but the sound of his delighted giggles assured me he was doing fine.

"Oh for Pete's sake," said Aunt Peg. "Let them get in the door first, would you?"

I thought for a moment that she was talking to Davey and me, but the Poodles knew better. They fell back enough to allow us to move and formed an escort as we came inside. Aunt Peg was carrying an armload of dirty laundry. "Bedding," she said, shutting the door firmly behind us. "I've got a litter of puppies in the guest room."

We followed her down to the basement, retrieving stray towels as they dropped, like leaves, from the bundle. Aunt Peg threw the lot in the washing machine and turned it on. Then she grasped Davey's arms and hoisted him, like another load of laundry, up on top of the dryer. "How's my boy?"

"Fine." Davey sat very still as he pondered the rules I'd imposed on his behavior. Nothing if not smart, he soon came up with a solution. "Can I go outside?"

He smiled with visible relief when permission was granted and he was free to leave. I hopped him down off the machine, and he disappeared out the door.

"Tell me something," I said to Aunt Peg as we went back upstairs. The inevitable honor guard of Poodles was still milling in attendance. "When we came in right now, the dogs made an awful racket. If there was an intruder in your kennel the night Max died, wouldn't they have barked?"

Aunt Peg's eyes narrowed. "I can see you don't believe that Beau was stolen either. Just like that brother of yours, humoring me like I was some sort of a doddering old fool. If that's why you came, you can leave right now. I'll not be anybody's charity case."

Her anger was justified, if misdirected. But I'd been paying the penance for my brother's sins for too many years to take offense now. "If I wanted to humor you, I wouldn't be asking questions, now would I?" I said mildly.

Aunt Peg thought about that for a moment. Apparently I'd passed inspection because when she spoke, she continued on as though nothing at all had happened. "There's no doubt that the dogs must have barked at the thief." She led the way into the living room, where we sat down in the two, thickly cushioned chairs that flanked the fireplace.

"So?"

"So I imagine that's what alerted Max to the fact that there was a problem in the first place. As to myself, when you've owned as many dogs for as long as we have, you don't get up to investigate every little noise they bark at during the night. Instead you stay nice and warm in bed, yell 'shut up!' as loudly as you can, and go right back to sleep. I'm so used to them by now that most nights I can sleep through anything."

"Oh."

"You're curious, aren't you?" The thought seemed to please her.

"Of course I'm curious. You can't just show up, toss around a handful of dreadful ideas, and then expect me to forget all about it. To tell you the truth, I spent a good part of last night thinking about what you'd said."

"And?"

"And . . ." A wry grin slipped out. "It managed to knock Bradley Watermain right out of my mind."

"Best place for him." Their one meeting, at a summer barbecue, had not been a success. "Bradley is a wimp."

"As of two days ago, a married wimp."

"Not to you, I hope."

"A six-foot chorus girl in Las Vegas."

"Bless his heart," Aunt Peg said happily. "Now are you going to help me find this dog or not?"

There are plenty of reasons why people make decisions. In this case, mine ranged from a latent dose of family loyalty to simple curiosity. But what finally tipped the scales in Aunt Peg's favor was a niggling feeling, new in the last few days, that somehow my life was simply slipping away.

In the past ten days, I'd lost an uncle, a job, and a lover. What was worse, I didn't seem to have anything to say about any of the three. That should have shaken me up, and it had. Enough to make me realize that for the last few years—ever since Bob left me really—I'd been coasting along in neutral, going through the motions without really playing the game.

I was thirty years old, a mother, a teacher, and an ex-wife. I'd defined myself in terms of those roles, and for a long time, it had seemed like enough. But now suddenly, there were times late at night when I sat all alone, and the roles slipped away, and I wondered if there was really anyone there at all.

When I was young, I'd thought I could do anything. Brimming with confidence, I'd leapt into teaching, then marriage, then almost immediately, motherhood. It had been a long time now since I'd felt as though I could conquer the world. The realization made me feel old. It also kindled a determination I hadn't felt in years.

"Yes," I said with a slow smile. "I think I am."

In the kitchen, we toasted our new alliance. Aunt Peg poured a steaming cup of tea for herself and, with no apologies, plunked a jar of instant coffee down on the counter for me. I fixed a cup. She filled a plate with scones. Then we sat down to make some plans.

"You'd rather have had Frank, wouldn't you?" I said bluntly. Some things are better gotten out of the way. Lord knew, I'd faced the attitude often enough in my own parents. Eventually, I'd put the hurt behind me. All I wanted now was to know where I stood.

"Frank always seems to have time on his hands," Aunt Peg pointed out. "You don't."

"You must know what he's like . . ." I paused, and saw her nod imperceptibly. "He wouldn't have been much help to you."

Aunt Peg shrugged. "I didn't get to pick my relatives."

My response to that was a half laugh, half snort of indignation. "I could be insulted by the way this conversation is shaping up."

"Could, but won't. You've got too much sense for that." She peered at me closely. "In fact, I'd say you're a lot like me in quite a number of ways."

"Then why haven't we ever been close?"

"I guess we've both just had too much to do—too many commitments and not enough time to sit back and enjoy life. It's about time you took a little time off for yourself, you know."

"Frank could probably give me pointers."

"Probably could." Aunt Peg searched my face and frowned at what she saw. "Forget about him. That boy isn't my problem, and shouldn't be yours either. It wouldn't surprise me at all to find out that we're better off without him. Now then, where do you think we ought to start?"

So much for family, and on to the business at hand. "How about checking out the scene of the crime?"

Aunt Peg looked dubious. "I've been in the kennel dozens of times since that night and I didn't notice anything unusual."

"You keep the kennel locked at night, don't you?"

"Of course."

"Then how do you suppose the thief got in?"

"Through the door, I'd imagine. It was standing wide open the next morning."

"That doesn't mean he went in that way, only that it's probably how he came out. Picture this," I said, thinking aloud. "Somehow the thief gets into the kennel. He nabs the dog and is on his way out when he sees Uncle Max coming out of the house. He scoots back inside and hides in the dark. They scuffle, the thief runs. Of course he doesn't stop to check and see if he's left anything incriminating behind."

"You've got a point," Aunt Peg said thoughtfully. "You know, you're very good at this." Coming from her, that was all sorts of praise.

"I read a lot."

"Nonfiction?"

"Dick Francis."

"He does horses," she said as she rose. She put the dishes in the sink and left them.

I followed her to the back door. "I'll try to scale down."

She stopped at the door and turned. For the first time that I could remember, we shared a smile. "Maybe I did overlook something. Let's go down and see what we can see."

❧❖ *Four* ❖❧

The small kennel building where Beau had been housed stood not more than ten yards from the main residence. It was painted to match—white, with a creamy, yellow trim; and on this bright, sunny morning, it looked like the last place where something terrible might have happened. Somewhat like the witch's gingerbread cottage, I supposed.

A row of long narrow dog runs stretched out from the side wall into the large field beyond. When we left the house they were empty, but as we approached, the swinging doors that connected them to the kennel burst open. Each held a big, black, hairy Poodle, one to a customer, and all barking a frenzied welcome.

I glanced their way, then quickly looked again. Most of the Poodles looked like normal dogs. The two on the end, however, were clipped elaborately. The front halves of their bodies were encased in a huge mane of hair, while the hindquarters and legs were shaved down to the skin, leaving only a profusion of pompons to cover their nakedness.

"Aunt Peg, why exactly are the dogs cut that way?"

"They're in show trim. This is the Continental clip," she said, pausing by the fence of the nearest run. "It's a traditional trim which, according to legend, was developed for practicality's sake by the German hunters who originated the breed."

"German? I thought Poodles came from France."

"Most people do. And the little ones might well have. But the Standard Poodles were first bred in Germany where they were used as retrievers. Because the waters there were so cold, they needed the long thick coats for warmth, but then they got bogged down trying to swim in them. To help out, the hunters clipped away all the hair that wasn't essential.

"The mane," Aunt Peg said, pointing to the big ruff of hair on the front, "serves as protection for the heart and lungs. The bracelets on the legs warm the joints. The hip rosettes cover the kidneys. And the pompon on the tail stood up to mark the dog's spot when he dove underwater after a bird."

"I never knew any of that," I said, joining her beside the run. I threaded my fingers through the fence to pat a closely clipped, inquisitive muzzle. It felt surprisingly like my ex-husband with a case of five o'clock shadow. Dark intelligent eyes regarded me calmly as, with utmost dignity, the Poodle began to lick my fingers.

"Now you do," Aunt Peg said briskly. "Poodles aren't just any dogs, you know. They're very special."

"Of course," I murmured, and kept the rest of my thoughts to myself. Every mother thinks her own child is the best.

Davey came racing around the front of the building as Peg opened the door. He glanced inside, then kept on going. Just as well. No doubt he would get up to less trouble outside the kennel than in.

The room we entered seemed to be part sitting room and part grooming area. A rubber-matted grooming table was parked in the middle of the floor, and I stepped around it to inspect the well-stocked shelves that filled one side wall. The quantity of equipment she had lined up and ready for use was nothing short of amazing.

Of course there were brushes and combs, each in several different varieties. But I also saw clippers and nail grinders, three kinds of shampoo with matching conditioners, colored rubber bands, special wrapping papers, and a leather case filled with scissors. And those were only the things I recognized. Obviously the time and effort it took to keep Aunt Peg's Poodles in top shape had to have been staggering.

That her efforts had paid off handsomely, however, was apparent from the condition of her trophy cabinet, which overflowed with an assortment of gleaming silverware. It was an impressive display, and I said so.

Aunt Peg shrugged off the compliment and passed by the hardware without so much as a glance. She stopped at a collection of framed pictures, all eight-by-ten shots, all taken at dog shows. Each one featured Aunt Peg holding one Poodle or another while the judge awarded them a prize.

"Champion Cedar Crest Salute," she said, tapping her finger against several of the frames in turn. "My first Best in Show winner, and Beau's great-grandfather."

We moved a bit farther down the wall, and the pictures shifted from black-and-white to color as they became more recent. "These two here are Beau," Aunt Peg said proudly.

I leaned over and peered closely at the pictures. Like all the others, they showed Aunt Peg, a judge, and a big black Poodle. How she managed to tell the dogs apart, I had no idea.

"He's very pretty," I said politely.

Aunt Peg smiled but didn't comment. I hadn't fooled her for a minute.

When we reached the end of the row, she led the way through an arched doorway, and we entered another large rectangular room. This one was lined on both sides with wire pens, most of them taken. As we walked down the aisle, Aunt Peg stopped to greet each dog by name.

"This is the inside half of the runs you just saw." She gestured toward an empty pen at the end of the row, then quickly looked away. "That's where I found Max."

I nodded, eyes down, and headed that way. The back wall, with two windows and a door had definite potential, and I bent down to inspect the area. There was nothing unusual about the first window, and its latch was still securely fastened. Aunt Peg leaned down over my shoulder to have a look, too.

"What are you doing?" asked Davey, sneaking up behind us as we hovered solicitously over the sill.

Aunt Peg and I both jumped, and I could tell from the look on her face that she felt every bit as foolish as I did. "We're looking for clues," she said, mustering a considerable show of dignity. "You can help if you want."

"Okay," Davey agreed, disappearing again.

Aunt Peg and I went back to our examination, but the second window was no more promising than the first. An inspection of the back door showed that it was bolted as, Aunt Peg maintained, it had been all along.

"Maybe the windows in the other room?" she suggested, and we went back to look. They yielded nothing of interest either.

Frustrated, I stood in the archway between the two rooms. We'd checked every entrance to the kennel, and they all looked as though they'd never been disturbed.

"Mommy! Aunt Peg!" Davey called out. "I'm hiding. Come find me."

It was bound to happen sooner or later. Davey has two passions in life: cars and playing hide-and-seek. At any given moment, he's either involved with one of those two pursuits or plotting how to get that way. Now I knew from experience that he was probably wedged into some impossibly small spot that was the last place I'd think to look. Unfortunately, he wouldn't leave either one of us alone until he'd been found.

Aunt Peg and I checked all the obvious places first. None of them panned out. But since I could hear him giggling, he had to be in the kennel. Suddenly I realized that the door to the empty pen at the end, which had been open, was now shut.

"Aha!" I cried, pouncing on the gate and opening it wide. To my chagrin, the pen was empty. Then I noticed the large dog door that led to the outside run. Aunt Peg had the same idea at the same time. We left through the human door and went around the side of the building.

Davey was sitting in the outer pen, enclosed in wire mesh fencing, and playing happily in the gravel. "You found me," he said with a pout, clearly disappointed in the outcome of the game.

"We sure did. But how do we get you out of there?"

"Easy enough," said Aunt Peg. "There's a gate at the end of each run for getting in to clean up. As you can see, I couldn't fit through the dog door."

"You might," I said slowly. "If you wanted to badly enough."

Aunt Peg looked up. "You know, I might at that. At any rate, it's not impossible. The gates are locked so that the neighborhood kids can't come over and let the dogs out, but I suppose it would be easy enough to climb the fence." She went inside to get the key, and within moments, Davey had been freed.

"Were any of the runs empty that night?" I asked as she clanged the gate shut.

"That one there." Aunt Peg pointed to the third from the end. "It's been empty for several weeks. I only put Lulu in there yesterday."

Lulu was forty pounds of shaggy, playful puppy, and I saw right away that her exuberance had probably destroyed any clues we might have found. All the same, it was worth a look. Aunt Peg went back around into the building again. I heard her call, and Lulu disappeared, whisked inside through the dog door to be moved to another run.

We covered every inch of the inside pen, then moved to the run outdoors. To be honest, I didn't know what exactly what we were looking for, or what we'd have done with it if we'd found something. Still, it was hard not to be disappointed when nothing turned up.

I was just about ready to give up when Davey, who was back in the dirt by the dog door, began to laugh gleefully. "I'm rich!" he cried, tossing a handful of pebbles and small shiny objects into the air.

"What have you got there, Davey?" I scrambled to my feet. If he'd found marbles, I would have to move fast. For some reason he persisted in thinking that, like olives, they were meant to be eaten.

"Buried treasure!"

I went to look and discovered that he had indeed found money, a small pile of coins mixed in with the gravel near the door. I scooped the money into my hand and counted it. Two quarters, three dimes, and a nickel, including three Canadian coins. Hardly a fortune, even by my standards. "You don't suppose this is the clue we've been looking for, do you?"

"I hope not," said Aunt Peg. "Because if it is, it's a damn poor one. All it tells us is that maybe I was robbed by someone who carries change in his pockets. And that includes just about everyone. On the other hand, it could just as easily have been dropped by the workmen who fixed that fence for me last month."

I juggled the change in my hand. "Do people show Poodles in Canada, too?"

"Of course, their system is quite similar to ours. Why?"

I showed her the Canadian coins. "Do you suppose

there's a chance that someone came down from Canada and took him?"

"A small one, if that. Good as Beau is, he's had almost no exposure outside this country. I just can't imagine that anyone up there could have wanted him that badly. Besides, what's the big deal about a few Canadian dimes? You can get those from any supermarket. It happens to me all the time."

"Want my money back," said Davey, tugging at my leg from the ground.

I handed it over, then stood him up and dusted him off. "So much for easy solutions."

Aunt Peg gave me a look. "I don't know what ever made you think this was going to be easy. If it was easy to find Beau, I'd have done it myself a week ago."

As usual, she had a point.

↜✸ *Five* ✸↝

Back in the kitchen, I leaned Davey over the sink and lathered his hands and arms with soap. The house Poodles vied among themselves for the best vantage points, then sat down and watched every move. I'd never seen dogs that were so intensely curious about everything that went on around them. Next I'd be expecting them to form an opinion.

Aunt Peg came upstairs from putting the towels in the dryer and stepped around the lounging black animals with practiced ease. "He keeps you busy, doesn't he?" she asked.

Davey grabbed for the soap, narrowly avoiding knocking over a bowl of soaking kibble. I settled for answering with a nod.

"I guess that's what children are all about."

She was stalling, I realized, and I wondered why. I used the sprayer to rinse Davey off, then dried him with a paper towel. "In another couple weeks, things will get better when he starts summer camp. I can't wait."

"Nine to five?"

I smiled at her naiveté as I hopped Davey down and steered him into the den toward the TV. "Mornings only. When they're four, you take what you can get, and thank God for it."

Thanks to the wonders of syndication, "Father Knows Best" was on. I'd grown up with Marcus Welby. Leaving Davey with Robert Young was like leaving him with a member of the family. A peanut butter and jelly sandwich completed the picture, then Aunt Peg and I were free to go in the living room and talk. The Poodles, seeing the possibility of a handout, elected to remain behind.

"So," said Aunt Peg. "You're the one who reads mysteries. After we've checked out the scene of the crime, what are we supposed to do next?"

"That's easy. Compile a list of suspects."

"I tried that. I'm afraid I didn't get very far."

"Short list?"

"Very."

"Let's hear it."

"You're not going to like it."

Aunt Peg waffling? Now I knew there had to be something wrong. "What's the matter?" I joked, trying to lighten things up. "Am I on it?"

"No . . . but Rose is."

"Rose—as in Aunt Rose?" My voice ascended an octave. "Sister Anne Marie?"

Aunt Peg shoved her hands in her pockets and strode across the room. "I told you you weren't going to like it."

"True, but you didn't tell me I wasn't going to believe it."

"How well do you know your Aunt Rose?"

I held the pause long enough to make my point. "About as well as I know you, give or take the first five years of my life."

"You were educated by the nuns, weren't you?"

"I only admit that to people who are liable not to hold it against me."

"It sounds to me as if you hold it against yourself."

"Only on bad days. On good days I tell myself I'm strong enough to overcome it."

Aunt Peg walked over and took a seat. "You're very flip about the subject. I wonder why."

"Trust me, twelve years of convent schooling is enough to drive anyone to flippancy."

"Considering your attitude, perhaps you won't be surprised by what I'm about to say."

"That depends," I said carefully.

Aunt Peg patted the chair beside her. "Come sit down. We'll talk about Rose."

"The chief suspect."

Aunt Peg didn't even crack a smile which was, as I saw it, a bad sign. Obediently, I came and sat.

"As you may or may not know, Rose was very young when she entered the convent."

"Seventeen, right?" Where I'd picked up that information I wasn't quite sure. It had happened before I was born.

"Right. That was the way things were done in those days. If you felt you had the calling, you entered the novitiate right out of high school. I didn't know Rose then, of course. I didn't even meet Max until several years later. But as I understand it, Rose had led quite a sheltered life up until that point. She was not only the youngest, but also the only daughter in the family. She'd been educated by the nuns as well, so that sort of life was really all she'd ever known."

"So far, it sounds more to me as though you're trying to make a case for Aunt Rose not having been involved."

"Maybe I should skip on ahead."

I nodded, and she continued.

"Rose came to see your Uncle Max last month. I'd like to say that she came to see us both, but it wasn't true. She specifically requested privacy for their meeting, and I was happy to give it to them." A sly grin slipped out. "I knew Max would tell me everything after she left.

"Anyway, the reason for the visit was that Rose had

some rather incredible news. She's planning to leave the convent and get married."

That landed with a jolt. "She . . . *What?*"

"I know, it came as a shock to us, too. Less so for me, I suppose, but Max was rather dumbfounded. It almost seemed as though he had a hard time grasping the idea that such a possibility could even exist. You know Max. He was just so very . . . Catholic."

"Just like the rest of the family," I said, then brightened. This was the juiciest gossip I'd heard in years. "Tell me all about it. Who is Aunt Rose going to marry?"

"He's a priest from the local parish."

"A priest!"

Aunt Peg gazed calmly down her nose. "Think about it, Melanie dear. Living in a convent, how many other men would she be likely to meet?"

"I guess. It's just that it all seems so . . ."

"Incredible, I know, that's exactly the way Max and I felt. Once Max got his bearings back, he even tried to talk her out of it. Big brother to little sister, if you know what I mean. But of course she's been out from under Max's wing for years, and I gather his advice didn't go over very well."

"Is that why Rose came then, she wanted to ask Uncle Max's opinion?"

"No, actually that wasn't it at all. She'd already made the decision, and as far as I know, she has every intention of going ahead with it."

"So?"

"So, you know how it is with nuns and priests and all those rules about worldly goods. Apparently she and the good father haven't got a sou between them. What Rose wanted from Max was enough money to enable the two of them to get started."

"Wait a minute. Do you mean to tell me that she presented Uncle Max with a proposal she knew he wasn't going to like—one that was already more or less a *fait accompli*—then expected him to underwrite the whole idea?"

"Well, yes, although Rose didn't look at it that way. You see, according to what Max told me, she seemed to think that he owed her the money."

"I don't get it," I said flatly.

"How old were you when Nana died?"

Nana was my father's mother. Spry and energetic, she'd been the much-beloved lynchpin around which our family had revolved. She'd outlived her husband by a half-dozen years, then died during my senior year of college. "Twenty-one, I guess. Why?"

"Do you know anything about her will?"

"A little," I said, hedging. "I know it contained a trust fund for Frank's and my education."

"You know more than that," Aunt Peg guessed. "But in case you don't, I'll tell you. The bulk of the estate went to Max."

I did know that, although I hadn't thought about it in years. There'd been a lot of silent, telling looks passed back and forth between my parents after Nana's will was read.

"Your father, who, I believe, was doing rather well as a stockbroker at the time, received a lesser amount. And Rose, who, of course, had no need for money, received almost nothing at all."

"And now," I said slowly, "all these years later, she wants back what she considers to be her share of Nana's estate."

"Exactly." Aunt Peg nodded.

"What did Uncle Max say to that?"

"Well, as you know, I wasn't there, but I'm sure he wasn't pleased. The money itself wasn't necessarily the issue. It's just that he seemed to think that the whole idea was so rash and ill-considered. He asked to meet the man in question, and Rose became furious. She declared that she was fifty-two years old and she didn't need anybody's permission to do anything."

"She had a point."

"Not really. The thing is, I'm sure he'd have given her the money in the end. But Rose didn't know that, and when she left that day, she was absolutely livid."

"I didn't think nuns were allowed to show that much emotion," I commented mildly.

"Obviously Rose isn't your common garden-variety nun. She stormed out of here in a real huff, and although I'd missed their earlier conversation, I did hear her parting words. You might say they were delivered at a rather loud pitch. She said 'You can try, but you'll never keep me away from the man I love. I want my money, Max, and one way or another, you're going to give it to me.'"

I pulled in a deep breath, then slowly let it out. Coming hard on the heels of Aunt Peg's other revelations, it was all a bit much to take. "You really think Aunt Rose is a dognapper?"

"Why not? Her motive was as strong as anybody's. I'd imagine the plan was to take the dog and simply keep him stashed somewhere until Max came up with the money she needed."

"But if she does have Beau, wouldn't you think she'd have gotten in touch with you by now?"

"After the way things turned out? I doubt it. Catholics may preach forgiveness, but that doesn't mean they expect it or even offer it to themselves. For all we know Rose may be feeling stuck in a situation that's gotten way out of hand."

"So you haven't spoken with her at all?"

"No, I just said—"

"What you just said," I interrupted calmly, "is that Aunt Rose hasn't contacted you. What you didn't explain is why you haven't called her."

There was a moment of silence, just long enough to be uncomfortable. I sat back in my chair and waited her out.

"Rose and I have never gotten along," Aunt Peg said finally. "It's old stuff that goes back years. To tell the truth, I think she was jealous when I married Max— thought I was taking over her place in the family or some nonsense like that. Suffice it to say that she and I have never been friends, and as things stand now, I doubt that's about to change."

I had no idea what to say to that, so it was almost a relief when the doorbell rang. Immediately the herd of Poodles came charging out of the den, barking wildly.

"I wonder who that is," Aunt Peg said with some annoyance. "I hate people who drop by without warning."

I pondered the irony of that remark as I waited in the living room while she went to answer the door. Peering out the side window offered me an excellent view of the proceedings, though unfortunately for my budding career as a snoop, I wasn't able to hear a thing.

Aunt Peg's visitor was a man of medium build, with a compact body that ran to thickness through the middle. Not quite as tall as Aunt Peg, he had dark brown hair liberally shot through with gray, and a bushy moustache that was holding its color better. He spoke with great animation, his hands gesturing in the air for emphasis.

It was clear from Aunt Peg's reaction that they were at least acquaintances, perhaps even friends, but she didn't invite him inside and he didn't seem perturbed by the omission. Their conversation was brief. At its end, the man leaned over and brushed a quick kiss on Aunt Peg's cheek that left her looking severely taken aback.

I wondered what that was all about and didn't have long to wait. As soon as he had gone, Aunt Peg came back into the living room, her arrival preceded by the swarm of Poodles. She still looked somewhat bemused, as if she had no more idea what the unexpected visit was about than I did.

"Who was that?" I asked as she sat back down.

"His name is Tony Wasserman. He and his wife Doris are our next door neighbors."

Considering the size of Aunt Peg's property and the fact that no other houses were visible, I'd never given her neighbors any thought. "Where?"

Aunt Peg waved a hand vaguely in the direction of the kennel. "To the north. Because of the way the land dips, you can't see their house from here, but it really isn't that far away. When Tony and Doris first moved in five years ago, we actually became rather good friends."

"Then why did you look so surprised to see him?"

"Did I?" Aunt Peg frowned. "I thought I'd covered it rather well. Unfortunately our relationship has been considerably less cordial in the last year. I'd like to say that it was the Wassermans' fault, but I suppose Max and I were equally to blame. For some reason Tony got the idea that our dogs were making entirely too much noise. They *do* bark sometimes, of course, but he and Doris had never seemed to mind before. Anyway, Tony came marching over here one night really quite angry, and told Max to shut the goddamned dogs up."

"And did he?"

"Hardly. You know Max, he didn't take criticism lightly. For a moment I almost thought the two of them were going to come to blows. They didn't, of course, and things cooled off. But once he'd gotten started, Tony kept right on complaining."

"Is that why he came over today?"

"Oh no, quite the opposite. He was checking to see if there was anything he and Doris could do for me. Rather nice of him actually, even if he did take me by surprise."

"What about Doris?"

"What about her?"

"I would think the wife would be more likely to make a call like that—you know, woman to woman?"

Aunt Peg dismissed the idea with a sniff. "Doris is a twit. I'm sorry about it, but there it is. Always was, and probably always will be. Now then, where were we before Tony arrived?"

So much for the neighbors. Doris was a twit, end of discussion. I decided it was probably that innocent peck on the cheek that had put Aunt Peg off, and didn't press it.

"We were talking about Aunt Rose." From the direction of the den came the familiar strains of a T.V. theme song. "Father Knows Best" was ending, which meant that any minute now Davey would come tooling back out to see what I'd arranged next for his entertainment. I had to work fast, so I got straight to the point. "I suppose I could go see her."

"I suppose you could," Aunt Peg agreed. "Rose isn't the only one who can issue an ultimatum. You tell her that whatever else happens, I intend to get that dog back."

⌒❋ *Six* ❋⌒

The Convent of Divine Mercy was situated on twenty acres of prime land in back Greenwich. The elegant Georgian mansion that housed both the convent itself and the girls' school that accompanied it had been donated to the order at the turn of the century. Their benefactor was a robber baron who'd found God late in life and been persuaded accordingly to give up his weekend home to atone for the past sins that had accompanied sixty years of high living. In the mid-nineteen eighties, the soaring cost of Greenwich real estate had elevated the value of the holding to truly heavenly heights. Now, their vow of poverty notwithstanding, the thirty sisters in residence lived in genteel splendor on an estate whose worth measured in the millions.

Since school had just finished for the summer, the convent was entering its yearly three months of rest and renewal. When I'd called, Aunt Rose had insisted her schedule was clear and sounded positively delighted by the prospect of a visit.

My early recollections of Aunt Rose are hazy at best. She was a name more than a presence, the one relative who'd always been left out of impromptu family gatherings and summer backyard barbecues. Before she'd been posted back to Greenwich the year after my graduation, her visits had been infrequent, yet terribly exciting when they came. As a child, I'd been fascinated by the thought of someone giving her life to God. Even when I was older and wiser, the impression had remained. Wrapped in the protective mantle of the church, she'd still seemed a woman of principle and power.

Was she actually capable of engineering the plot that had resulted in Uncle Max's death? I wondered, as Davey and I drove to the convent at the allotted time. My first impulse, already demonstrated to Aunt Peg, was to deny the idea out of hand. And yet, I couldn't help but imagine how I'd feel in her place. Twelve years of that sheltered existence had been more than enough to nurture my own rebellion. I could only wonder at the shock and desperation that would have accompanied the realization that, after thirty-five years, what the church had to offer wasn't enough . . .

From force of habit, I bypassed the massive grillwork gates that guarded the main entrance and continued on to the back driveway that led directly to the student's parking lot. From there, we walked around the front of the building, where I clutched Davey's hand and we ascended the wide steps together. Tall Ionic columns supported an ornate portico that rose majestically above us. Davey leaned back for a better look, his head tilting at an angle only a four-year-old could manage as I pushed the doorbell and the deep tones of the chimes echoed through the halls.

The door was opened by a smiling young woman in a plain gray dress. A novice, I guessed, one of the new order who didn't feel that a long black habit was needed as a sign of her vocation. She led us to a small study off the front hall and went in search of Aunt Rose.

As soon as she had gone, Davey began to explore. He climbed onto the seat of a large mahogany chair, his eyes intent on a gleaming crystal ashtray atop the table beside it. I was in the process of swinging him down to the relative safety of the floor when the door opened and Aunt Rose appeared.

She looked different, and the change came as something of a shock. Like the young sister who'd admitted us, Aunt Rose was dressed in street clothes. The severe black habit and immaculate white wimple were gone, replaced by a simple navy blue suit and a pair of low-heeled pumps. For the first time in my life, I was seeing her as a woman rather than as an emissary of God.

Her hair, now revealed, was the same medium shade of brown as my own. Though short, it was fashionably cut. Her face, with its direct gray eyes, slim nose, and stern jaw, was bare of makeup, as it had been for years. Her only jewelry was an inexpensive watch on a plain black strap.

"You . . ." I began, then stopped, uncertain whether the wisest course was to comment on the change or simply ignore it.

"Have hair, yes." Aunt Rose turned toward Davey, who was looking at her shyly, and her features softened into a smile. "I see you're still the explorer of the family. Think you're brave enough to come over here and give me a hug?" After a moment's hesitation, Davey allowed himself to be gathered into her arms.

"I was going to say you look very nice."

"Do I?" The smile turned my way. It was eager and more than a little pleased. "We don't have mirrors in our rooms, you know. And after so many years in a habit, I'm a little rusty with anything else."

She wasn't the only one who was having trouble adjusting, I realized with a start. In my mind, the trappings of her calling—the flowing habit, crisp headband, raised wimple—were indelibly intertwined with the image I'd carried of Aunt Rose. Today, she seemed a different woman altogether than the one I'd known: smaller, softer, and more approachable. As I digested the change that had taken place, I found myself wondering which had made the bigger difference—renouncing the habit or falling in love?

Davey stepped back out of Aunt Rose's grasp and tugged on the side of my denim skirt. "Wanna go outside!" he announced. "There's nothing to do in here."

"We'll walk in the garden," Aunt Rose decided. "The tulips are lovely this time of year."

A door at the other end of the hall deposited us on a gravel path that meandered in a leisurely fashion through a large, well-tended garden. As Davey ran on ahead, I pondered how to politely broach the reason for my visit. Before we'd gone more than a few feet, the problem was taken out of my hands by Aunt Rose.

"I take it this isn't a social call?"

I glanced over at her, surprised. "What makes you say that?"

"Give me some credit, Melanie. In all the years since you graduated from Divine Mercy, this is the first time you've ever been back. I'm assuming there must be a reason."

I looked at the tulips, the path, the sky—anywhere but at Aunt Rose—and tried to tell myself I didn't feel guilty. It didn't work. "You're right, there is a reason. I need to talk to you about something important. It has to do with Uncle Max's death."

"Go on." Coming from Aunt Peg, it would have been an order. Rose, to her credit, simply sounded interested.

"Aunt Peg seems to think that someone was in the kennel with Uncle Max the night he died, someone whose presence may have contributed to his death."

We'd been strolling amiably, but now Rose stopped mid-stride. Her face was pale with shock. "Are you saying Max was murdered?"

I watched for a moment until Aunt Rose had her emotions firmly back under control. Like all the Turnbull women of her generation, she was made of stern stuff. "I'm saying that he wasn't alone when he died, that his heart attack may well have been provoked. Aunt Peg asked me to come and talk to you about it."

"Why?"

"As I understand it, you were very angry the last time you saw Uncle Max."

Rose's features hardened. "Of course I was angry at Max. He was acting like an old fool."

"It seems he thought the same of you."

Instead of answering, Rose spun around and continued on down the path. The sudden movement took me by surprise, and I jogged several steps to catch up. For a moment, we walked side by side in silence.

Finally Aunt Rose spoke. "Have you ever been in love?"

Definitely a loaded question considering my situation in life and the church's views on divorce. "I guess so," I said slowly. "At any rate, I thought so once, when I was young."

"When I was young, I entered the convent. I thought I knew what love was, too. Not the physical love that most adolescents seem to experience these days, but something on a higher plane—a spiritual love, if you will."

Aunt Rose looked over to see if I was following what she'd said. When I nodded, she continued. Her tone was low, almost confiding. It was the voice one used for telling secrets—or making a good confession.

"Looking back now, I realize that the calling I had for the church was tied up with many things, among them, duty and devotion, and the need to do what was expected of me. Of course at the time, I thought I knew what I was doing. I had no idea that I was simply too young and inexperienced to make such a momentous decision."

"Are you sorry?" I asked. Once again, I found myself

wondering what it would feel like to devote the majority of your life to a belief, an ideal, only to find out later that you'd come up short. It was something I never wanted to find out firsthand.

Aunt Rose, however, seemed surprised by the question. "Sorry? No, of course not. I've had a very full and rewarding life. It's just that now, after meeting Peter, I realize that my vocation no longer lies within the convent walls. I've been content here all these years. When you don't know what true happiness is, contentment's quite a comfortable feeling. But now, for the first time in my life, someone's taught me how to dream. Deep in my soul, I feel quite sure God wouldn't ask me to turn and walk away."

"I see," I said, and I did, perhaps even more than she knew. Perhaps I wasn't the only one who'd been coasting along in neutral. Whatever opposition Aunt Rose might face from the rest of the family, she had my blessing all the way.

"Mommy, Aunt Rose, look what I have!" Davey dashed around a corner in the path, his feet skidding on the loose gravel. His face was all smiles as he offered his gift. Clutched in a grubby, outstretched hand was a beautiful bouquet of fresh-picked tulips.

"Oh no, Davey, you didn't—" I stopped as I saw his face fall. "Honey, they're beautiful, but you weren't supposed to pick them. They belong here, in the garden."

"I suspect Sister Hibernia will not be pleased," Aunt Rose said sternly. I looked up just in time to see her slip Davey a wink. Sly as a fox, my four-year-old son winked back.

"Here." Loyalties transferred in an instant, he snatched the flowers from beneath my nose and gave them instead to Rose. "They're for you."

"Thank you, Davey." Aunt Rose accepted the bouquet with suitable dignity. "I'm sure even Sister Hibernia would agree they'll make a lovely decoration for the chapel. Is that all right with you?"

Davey gave his assent and we went back inside. It wasn't until Aunt Rose had arranged the tulips in a tall vase, then set the bouquet at the feet of a statue of the Blessed Virgin that I realized how deftly she'd managed to avoid the topic of Uncle Max's demise. No sooner had I brought the subject up than I'd been very neatly sidetracked into a discussion of chances taken and chances lost. The only thing I'd learned was that, by Rose's own admission, Uncle Max had tried to come between her and her dreams. I couldn't help but wonder how far she'd have been willing to go to stop him.

"How do you feel about dogs, Aunt Rose?" I asked as the three of us walked outside to the car.

Rose smiled faintly. "I can't say as I ever give them much thought one way or another. Why?"

"One of Max's Poodles was stolen on the night that he died. Whoever was in the kennel with Max took the dog with him with he left."

"You're quite sure, then, that there was someone else there?"

I nodded. "There has to have been. According to Aunt Peg, a very valuable dog is missing—"

"Beau?"

I stopped and stared. "What do you know about Beau?"

"Only what Max told me," Rose said with a shrug. "He was always going on about that dog, never cared a whit whether anyone was interested or not. And to turn down a blank check for him, well . . . ! I never heard of such idiocy in my life."

"Blank check?" I repeated, my thoughts spinning away in several directions at once. "Aunt Rose, what are you talking about?"

Rose gave me a serene look, the one I'm convinced all

nuns spend the first year of their novitiate perfecting. "You mean Peg didn't mention Sam Driver?" she asked, satisfaction coating the smooth tones. "Isn't that just like her, telling you just what she wanted you to know and no more."

"Is there more?" I tried not to sound too eager, even as I cursed inwardly at Aunt Peg and her judicious omissions.

Aunt Rose took her time about answering, waiting until I'd settled Davey into the passenger's seat and closed the door. "There's always more," she said then. "You may find that your poking around is the quickest way to turn up things that are much better left buried where they are."

I was being warned, that much was clear. But about what?

"I don't understand."

"Perhaps that is God's will." Aunt Rose walked me around the car to the driver's side.

"Perhaps that's a lot of bullshit."

Aunt Rose's brow lifted ever so faintly, and all at once I felt like a fifteen-year-old who'd been brought before Mother Superior for a reprimand. "I don't know why Peg sent you over here today, and to tell the truth I don't really much care. I suspect she's just trying to make trouble for me; she's done it often enough in the past—"

"Aunt Peg isn't trying to make trouble for anyone," I snapped. As far as I was concerned, that business about God's will was a cheap shot. "All she wants is to get Uncle Max's dog back: safe, unharmed, no questions asked."

"And she actually had the audacity to suggest that *I* might know something about it? That's rich. I may be leaving the convent; it doesn't mean I've taken leave of my senses. Stealing goes against the commandments, as I'm sure you well know. It's a mortal sin."

For the first time in a long time, my years of convent

schooling stood me in good stead. "So is coveting thy neighbor's goods," I said as I climbed into the car. "Think about it."

⌦✻ *Seven* ✻⌫

On the way home, Davey and I stopped at McDonald's for Chicken McNuggets, chocolate milkshakes, and a large order of fries, which we shared. He was filled with animation, reliving in detail the highlights of his day. I ate my food in silence and let him hold the stage. One of the first things motherhood had taught me was to conserve energy whenever possible. By now, I was a master at it.

Half an hour later, when the Volvo chugged into the driveway and stalled in the garage with what sounded like a sigh of relief, Davey's internal clock had wound down as well. He was fast asleep in the back seat and never even stirred when I carried him upstairs and put him to bed.

That done, I turned on the coffee maker, then went directly to the telephone. As far as I could see, my visit with Aunt Rose had accomplished little, other than to raise more questions. I could only hope that Aunt Peg was going to have the answers.

"How'd it go? Did Rose tell you anything about the dog?" she asked immediately. Obviously it had never occurred to her that she was the one who had some explaining to do.

"As a matter of fact, she did."

"She knows where he is then?"

"No—at least not that she's telling." The light on the

coffee maker began to glow. I poured myself a cup, added a dollop of milk from the refrigerator, then sat down at the table. "Aunt Rose claims she knows nothing at all about Beau's disappearance, although I should mention that she guessed right away that he was the dog who'd been stolen. So apparently she knew enough about Max's affairs to know where he was most vulnerable."

"That doesn't surprise me one bit. Did you ask her where she was the night of the twenty-eighth?"

"No." I paused for another sip of coffee. "Somehow I just can't picture Aunt Rose climbing over that fence to get inside the kennel. Besides, as far as I know, nuns aren't allowed to come and go as they please—especially in the middle of the night."

"She could have gotten that priest to do it," Aunt Peg argued. Clearly she was still enamored with her first suspect's chances.

"True, but then she wouldn't need an alibi, would she?"

Aunt Peg knew when she'd been bested. For a long moment she didn't say anything at all. I gave silent thanks that it was a local call and used the time to drink more coffee.

"So you think Rose was telling you the truth?"

"Well, yes . . . I guess so."

"That's hardly a glowing recommendation."

"It wasn't meant to be. To tell the truth, I'm not sure what I think. It's hard to judge someone you've known for years, especially when she's a member of your own family. Besides, you know perfectly well that I was brought up to believe that the clergy were the next best thing to God. I may not like the attitude, but it's ingrained pretty deep. I just don't see how Aunt Rose could be involved and nothing she said changed my mind."

"Well." Aunt Peg's voice was huffy. "Then I guess I'll just have to be satisfied with that."

"There was one other thing . . ."

"Yes?"

"Aunt Rose mentioned a man named Sam Driver. She seemed to think you would have told me about him."

"Oh." The single syllable spoke volumes.

"Well?"

"Actually, it's a little embarrassing."

"I'd be embarrassed, too, after an oversight like that. Did he really offer Max a blank check?"

"Well, yes . . . but that's not the embarrassing part."

"Oh no?" After the awkward position Aunt Peg had put me in that afternoon, a gleeful chuckle would have suited my mood perfectly. I settled for a silent smirk instead. "What else did he do?"

"Maybe I should come over and we'll talk about it in person."

"Now? Tonight?"

"Melanie, dear, it's only eight-thirty. The night is young, as they say."

"Only for people who don't have four-year-olds."

Aunt Peg ignored the comment as I'd known she would. She made good time in her souped-up station wagon. Even allowing for the stop she'd obviously made, it was only just after nine when she arrived.

"Doughnuts," she announced, thrusting the bright pink box into my hand. "I'll require a pot of tea and a napkin, and then you may ask me anything."

As she stepped into the hall, I realized she wasn't alone. A black Standard Poodle bitch stood at her heel, eying with polite interest the box I now held. This one wasn't in show trim, which meant that she had a short blanket of dense curly hair covering her entire body. But beyond recognizing that, she might have been any one of the Poodles I'd met earlier.

"Simba," Aunt Peg said, following the direction of my gaze. The Poodle looked up happily at the mention of her name. "Don't worry, she won't be a bother. You don't have any cats, do you?"

I shook my head. As children, Frank and I had always wanted a pet, but my mother's wishes had prevailed. She said that cats were never home and dogs peed in the house. The discussion had ended there. Aside from telling Davey that he couldn't have a dinosaur, I hadn't thought about getting a pet in years.

I reached down a tentative hand. The Poodle sniffed my fingertips, then leaned into an ear scratching. "Doesn't she like cats?"

"Simba likes them fine. I'm the one who worries. This time of year, houses with cats often have fleas. With all the dogs I have in hair, I have to be very careful."

"Oh." I wondered if my housekeeping was being insulted and decided it probably was. Since Simba was still watching the box, I lifted the edge of the lid to peer inside. No dog treats as I'd half-suspected, only the promised doughnuts. A full dozen, at least. Judging from the amount of food Aunt Peg seemed to pack into her svelte, size-eight body, people who were just shy of six feet didn't have to worry about their weight. Unfortunately the same couldn't be said for me. The more time we spent together, the tighter my clothes seemed destined to feel.

"Jelly and glazed," said Aunt Peg. Her hand positioned itself between my shoulder blades and aimed me toward the kitchen. "Let's get on with it, shall we?"

I took her at her word and provided tea and a napkin. Plates would only have to be washed later anyway. "Tell me about Sam Driver," I said when we'd gotten settled at the table, with Simba lying underneath. "Who is he, and what does he have to do with Beau?"

Aunt Peg flipped open the box and took her time selecting a doughnut. Like Poodles, they all looked alike to me. I reached in and grabbed the first one that came to hand. No doubt something basic about our different approaches to life had been revealed. As an unemployed, divorced, single parent on the trail of a dog I'd never even seen, I didn't dare think about what.

"Quite simply put," said Peg, "he's a man who's shown an inordinate amount of interest in acquiring the dog."

"The other night you said you'd been offered twenty thousand dollars—and Rose said something about a blank check . . . ?"

"That was Sam on both counts. Over the last couple of months, he tried to buy the dog from us several times."

I took a large bite and chewed slowly. The cake was light and spongy, the jelly cloyingly sweet. I was in heaven. "Why didn't you tell me about him before?"

"Before what? Before I set you after your saintly Aunt Rose, or before she had a chance to mention it first?"

"Both." I swallowed and immediately went back for more. Talking with my mouth full was getting to be a habit. "You have to admit, it's a bit odd. Most people, faced with two possible suspects, would tend to think the worst of the stranger first."

"Most people," Peg stated imperturbably, "don't know Rose."

It was easy to see that line of questioning wasn't going to get me anywhere. "All right, the method may have been roundabout, but at last we've arrived at the mysterious Mr. Driver. Would you please explain how the man could possibly be a source of embarrassment?"

Aunt Peg sighed. "Perhaps chagrin is a better word. You see, if Sam Driver is the man behind this mess, then I'm afraid I may have only myself to blame."

"Keep going." I was happy to let her do all the talking. It made eating easier.

"I've met Sam, of course, but I wouldn't say that I know him well. Apparently he's been breeding and showing Poodles in Michigan for the last five years. He came east in February for the Westminster Dog Show. That's when he saw Beau, and that's when he made his first offer. He's a very polite man, and rather well-spoken. Looks a bit like Mel Gibson, to tell you the truth—"

I choked on an unexpected laugh. "Aunt Peg, what would you know about Mel Gibson?"

"My dear girl, I may be old but I am not dead."

It was amazing how neatly both feet could fit into a mouth that was already full. I busied myself with slipping Simba a bite of my doughnut.

"You'll teach her to beg if you do that," Aunt Peg said, but she didn't sound entirely displeased. "Anyway, after Max turned Sam down at Westminster, we both just assumed that would be the end of it. Then, a few weeks later, the letters began arriving. He told us all about his breeding operation, his plans for the future, and what a good home he could offer Beau. When that didn't work, the phone calls started."

Aunt Peg frowned. "He seemed to have targeted me, you see. After all, it wasn't hard to see that Max was rather a fanatic where that dog was concerned. I'm sure Sam figured out that if someone was going to listen to him, it had to be me. Toward the end, we spoke rather frequently."

"When did he offer Max a blank check?"

The frown deepened. "Less than a week before he died. I'd told Sam already that it was no use, but he wouldn't listen . . ."

Interesting, I thought, how chummy they seemed to have been. "And he was still in Michigan at the time?"

"Oh no, I was just getting to that. You see, a few days earlier he'd shown up on our doorstep in person. It seems he'd quit his job out there and moved to Connecticut, bringing his kennel with him."

I didn't like the sound of that at all.

"I'm afraid there's more," Aunt Peg admitted. "Max

was away at the time—out of town for a day or two, and I was feeling rather at loose ends. Of course, by then I had spoken to Sam enough so that I felt as though I knew him. Once he'd arrived, I invited him in and we spent quite a pleasant afternoon, drinking tea and talking dogs. I even introduced him to Beau and gave him a tour of the kennel."

"Aunt Peg, you didn't!"

"Well, of course I did. Why wouldn't I? He seemed genuinely interested."

"I'll bet." I could see how it had gone—a tall, blue-eyed hunk of a man pulling out all the stops to make a good impression on Aunt Peg. Not that she was gullible certainly, just that she tended to see virtue, warranted or not, in people who felt the same way about dogs as she did. Her next admission only added to my suspicion that she'd been had.

"The reason I didn't mention Sam right off is that he doesn't seem at all like the type of person who would do something like this. He's really a very nice young man."

"That's probably just what he was hoping you'd think, Aunt Peg. He wanted you to let down your guard."

"Believe me," Aunt Peg said slyly, "with a man like that around, my guard was never up."

"Shame on you!" I teased. "What would Uncle Max have said?" As soon as the words were out of my mouth, I wanted to pull them back.

To my relief, however, Aunt Peg began to smile. "He'd have said that being married meant you couldn't touch. But looking with appreciation, that's something else entirely."

"Uncle Max was a nice man, wasn't he?" I said quietly.

"One of the best." The smile faded, then returned. "I was lucky, you know, damn lucky to have had Max all the years I did. I'm not the type to go all weepy and maudlin about things. I never have been, and I refuse to start now. So don't go getting all embarrassed every time you mention his name. Talking about Max isn't half the tragedy that forgetting him would be."

"You're right."

"Now then," Peg said briskly. "Where were we?"

Equilibrium restored, we forged ahead. "With Mel Gibson's alter ego, I believe."

"Ah yes, Sam. You'll have to talk to him."

"I suppose so."

Aunt Peg looked up from the wedge of lemon she was squeezing into her second cup of tea. "What's the matter?"

"Nothing, really. It's just that asking questions of people I already know is one thing. Strangers are another matter all together."

The corners of Aunt Peg's mouth twitched. "Surely you didn't think we were going to find the dog by hopping from one family member to another?"

"No, of course not, but . . . To tell the truth, I guess I didn't think about it."

"Then do it now. Because from now until we figure out where Beau is, that's just about all it's going to be—pigeonholing people you don't know and asking them questions they'd probably just as soon not answer."

"You make it sound like I'll be out there on my own."

"You will be."

That came as a surprise.

"Think about it," said Peg.

When I did, of course it made perfect sense. "I take it that's why you haven't contacted Driver already?"

Aunt Peg nodded. "If he has got Beau, I'm obviously the last person he's going to talk to."

"Which puts me second to last."

"Not if he doesn't know who you are."

"Don't tell me, let me guess. You have a plan."

"Of course," Aunt Peg said blithely. "Somebody has to."

I should have known.

❧❀ *Eight* ❀❧

"It's really quite simple," said Aunt Peg. "Let's begin with the assumption that whoever has Beau is planning to use him at stud. Otherwise, what's the point? He's probably got some bitches of his own to breed Beau to, but sooner or later he's going to have to offer him to the public, or he'll never make any real profit."

"And all this will be done under another dog's name," I said, recalling the explanation she'd given to Frank and me earlier.

"Precisely. The easiest way for the thief to attract outside bitches is to show off some top-quality puppies the dog has sired. So as far as he's concerned, the most important thing right now is for Beau to be bred, and bred well. What we're going to do is offer around a bitch so perfect for Beau that the thief will jump at the chance to make the breeding."

As plans went, it didn't sound so brilliant to me. "I don't get it. Didn't you just tell me that he probably has bitches of his own? Why would one more make any difference?"

"It makes all the difference in the world!" One look at the baffled expression on my face was all it took to have Aunt Peg launching into an explanation. "What you have to understand is that every breeder is always hoping to produce the perfect dog—even though they know perfectly well that it doesn't exist. Each dog, no matter how good, is going to have some faults.

"The whole idea behind sound breeding is to perpetuate a dog's good points while compensating for his bad ones. This is done by breeding to a bitch who excels in those areas where your dog is weak. Of course, you're never going to get everything right, but you can see how some breedings would nick better than others, can't you?"

Why not? I thought, nodding.

"What the thief desperately needs now is access to bitches who would match with Beau, both physically and genetically in such a way as to have the potential capability of producing superior puppies. And you're going to have one of those."

I looked at her warily. "Do I have to go out and buy a Poodle?"

"Don't be silly. You don't actually have to have a bitch, you just have to say you do. Once I work up a description and a pedigree, you'll be all set."

"So what you want me to do is dangle this mythical bitch under a few noses and see who jumps at the bait?"

"Precisely." Aunt Peg nodded. "There are plenty of shows coming up, more than enough to hope that you'll run into the thief somewhere along the way. And when you do, I'll just bet he won't be able to resist telling you about the super new stud dog he has at home."

The following Saturday was the first of the month, which meant that Frank would be by early in the morning to pick Davey up for what my son gleefully referred to as "boys' day out." Whatever irritating habits my little brother may have had, they were more than compensated for by the way he'd behaved with Davey since my divorce. Unasked, he'd stepped in to provide my son with the male influence and companionship Davey so desperately needed. What had started as a series of casual visits had gradually evolved into a monthly routine that only the most dire of emergencies was allowed to disrupt.

I was never consulted on their plans in advance and often not even privy to what happened during their meetings. Davey's outings with Frank were a special time, and a vacation from his mother's supervision. Once he'd brought home a new catcher's mitt; another time, a skateboard I was certain he was much too young to use safely. He was often disheveled and always tired. As I tucked him into bed, he would murmur about all the "man things" he had seen and done, then fall contentedly asleep. If I hadn't loved Frank already, this alone would have been reason enough.

Early Saturday morning, I delivered Davey to his uncle's care and set out. For once the Volvo was running like the marvel of Swedish technology it was supposed to be. I arrived at the showground in late morning, leaving myself several hours to look around before the start of the Poodle judging at two.

Eyes wide, like a kid at her first circus, I took in the sights. The large field had been broken up into rings of various sizes, all at least partially covered by brightly striped tents. The dogs came in all shapes and sizes as well. Some, like the Golden Retrievers and Collies, I recognized right away. Others didn't look even the slightest bit familiar. Still others were hardly recognizable as dogs at all.

Slowly I browsed from ring to ring, watching the breeds that were being shown. Aunt Peg had explained the judging procedure to me in great detail, but even so it took a while before I was able to sort things out. According to what I'd been told, the whole purpose of the exercise was to win enough points to make one's dog a champion. This was done within each breed by first entering a class: say, Puppy, or Bred-By-Exhibitor, or Open. The classes were divided by sex, and after they'd been judged, the class winners returned to vie for the points and the title of Winners Dog and Winners Bitch. The number of dogs in competition on the day determined the number of points awarded.

These two competed against the finished champions for either Best of Breed; or in the case of breeds like Poodles, Dachshunds, and Fox Terriers, that had more than one variety, Best of Variety. The breed winners went on to fight it out in the groups. Ultimately by day's end the narrowing down process was complete, and one dog was awarded the coveted title of Best in Show.

At the end of the field was the grooming tent, where exhibitors gathered to put the last-minute touches on their entries. As Poodles require a great deal of preparation before being shown, I knew this was where I'd find the breeders and professional handlers I needed to speak to. Still, once I'd slipped beneath the striped expanse, I found myself dawdling once more, fascinated by the nature and scope of the grooming that was going on.

People were working on their dogs in ways that I never would have dreamt of, let alone considered doing. I spent five minutes watching a woman work a whole cookie tin full of white powder into the coat of a little terrier. She kept shaking it in and brushing it out, and the dog got whiter and whiter with each application. A majestic sable Collie stood patiently on top of its crate while the handler dampened its coat then back-brushed it, smoothing the hair in the opposite direction from which it lay naturally. There were two English setters wearing wet towels draped over their backs, and an Afghan with a snood wrapped tightly around its neck. A tiny Yorkshire Terrier appeared to be completely done up in hair curlers, but when I asked, they turned out to be plastic wraps, put in to keep the long silky coat from dragging on the ground.

The Poodles, when I finally reached them, weren't faring much better. Some—the lucky ones, I quickly decided—were merely being brushed. Others were having the long hair in their topknots doused with hair spray, then combed into an upright position with the same sort of ardor that produced beehive hairdos in the fifties. Still others were being shaped—handlers hovering over them with scissors, nicking off the tiniest bits of hair in an attempt to make the pompons that already appeared impossibly round even rounder.

If I'd have been doing such things to a dog, I don't think I'd have been able to keep a straight face. But not only were these people not laughing, they looked deadly serious about the whole affair. One or two were talking as they worked, but for the most part, there was silence, punctuated only by the loud, annoying whine of a generator which powered a blow dryer that stood almost as tall as my shoulders.

Aunt Peg had set up her table off to one side. She glanced up at my arrival, then pointedly looked away. During the week, she'd worked up a pedigree and description for my mythical Poodle bitch and presented both to me with a flourish. She'd done all she could, her look seemed to say. Now it was up to me.

Maybe it was sexist on my part, but somehow I'd just assumed that it was a man who had fought with Uncle Max and left with his dog. Now, however, looking around the tent, I was surprised to see that with the exception of the large setups belonging to the professional handlers and manned by their armies of assistants, the majority of the Poodle exhibitors seemed to be women.

In front of me, a tiny woman was completely engrossed in her preparations of a large white male. She had to stand on tiptoe to reach his head as he stood atop his grooming table, but it didn't seem to cramp her style any. She fussed over her entry like a second grader's mother at the school play. The Poodle, for his part, suffered her attentions nobly. I passed her by for the moment as her dog was white, but made a mental note to ask Aunt Peg later whether all breeders had only one color, as she did, or whether there were some who kept a mixture.

Several tables down, a black bitch reclined gracefully, her grooming obviously finished. A rather large woman with carefully coiffed blond hair was leaning back against the edge of the table, munching on a sugar-coated pastry. Her shelf of a bosom collected crumbs as she ate, a habitual occurrence, I decided when she reached up and flicked them away without so much as a glance.

Between bites, I made my approach. "Excuse me. Do you have a minute?"

"Just about," she said. "I haven't picked up my number yet. What can I do for you?"

I watched as she broke the last bit of pastry in two pieces, ate one herself and fed the other to the Poodle. Carefully she cupped her hands under the dog's chin so that no sugar would spill into the gorgeous mane of hair.

"I'm looking for some advice actually. I have a Standard Poodle bitch that I'd like to breed, and I'm looking for a stud dog for her."

The woman leaned down and rummaged through a well-stocked cooler, coming up seconds later with a cold can of soda. "I'm afraid I can't help you there. I don't keep a stud dog. I've got five bitches, you know what I mean? You might want to try Louise." She pointed toward the little woman with the big white dog.

"I was hoping to find a black. That's what color my bitch is."

"Then you're looking for Margaret Turnbull," the woman said firmly. "She's got the best blacks in the area.

That's her there, the tall lady. Give her a try. I'll bet she's got a dog for you."

My first dead end. "Thanks," I said, ambling away. "I'll ask her."

The next person I spoke with asked about my bitch's pedigree. Dutifully I recited as many ancestors as I could remember. It was, I thought, a stellar performance, and the woman seemed suitably impressed. The bubble burst a moment later, however, when once again I was directed to Aunt Peg.

Suddenly things weren't looking as simple as I'd thought they'd be. Finally, two tries later, my luck began to change. A slim man, sporting a black goatee as beautifully groomed as the coat of his Poodle, glanced up from his scissoring and said, "Why don't you talk to Crawford Langley? I hear he's got a new stud he's been raving about."

"Who's Crawford Langley?"

The man stared as though he couldn't believe I wouldn't know, but I let the question stand and finally he explained, "Langley's a handler. Just about the best in Poodles. He's got a stud dog for everybody."

That sounded promising. What could be easier than to add one more stud dog to a kennel that was already full of them? "Where would I find Mr. Langley?"

"You won't be able to talk to him now. He's much too busy. Those are his assistants down there." He pointed toward one of the large setups I'd noticed earlier where two young men with a row of Poodles and tables spread out between them seemed to have taken the assembly line approach to grooming. "They stay here and do all the work, then Langley takes the dogs into the ring. Come back when the judging is over. I'm sure he'll be around then."

I was debating where to try next when I felt the unmistakable tug of somebody's gaze upon me. Aunt Peg, I guessed, probably monitoring my progress and far from satisfied with the way things were going.

I spun around, fully intending to give her the glare she deserved, only to find myself looking into a pair of the bluest eyes I'd ever seen. I had to blink twice before the rest of the picture came into focus, but it was well worth the wait. Along with the eyes came rugged features, sandy blond hair, and a body that belonged on a Hollywood billboard. My stomach didn't exactly plummet, but I have to admit it did drop a notch or two.

Sam Driver. It had to be.

Perhaps because Aunt Peg had described him in movie star terms, I'd pictured him that way—pretty, but two-dimensional, like a slick magazine cover with a story that could be flipped through at will. In my mind, I'd relegated him to the ranks of the bit players, someone who'd be no problem at all to get around.

But while the looks were certainly there, she'd somehow completely neglected to mention the piercing quality of those slate blue eyes. In the space of a single glance, I felt as though I'd been weighed, measured, and dispensed with accordingly. It was not a comfortable feeling.

Pasting a smile on my face, I started in Driver's direction. I thought he'd go back to his grooming while I approached, but he didn't. Instead, he simply stood there, waiting. Under other circumstances, I'd have been flattered. Now, I couldn't help but wonder at his interest.

So this was the man who'd wanted Beau badly enough to offer a blank check. The man Aunt Peg had given a tour of her kennel to. The man she seemed so sure that we could trust.

Oh boy.

Nine

"I couldn't help but overhear," he said as I drew near.
"You're looking to breed a bitch?"

I nodded. "She's black, from the Bel Flor line. I'd like
to find a dog that's compatible."

"Why?"

A sports jacket was hanging on the tent pole behind
him. I watched as he slipped it off the hanger and pulled it
on, then filled the pockets with a metal comb, a stuffed
rat, and a handful of dried liver. "Why what?" I asked.

"Why do you want to breed a litter of puppies?"

Of all the questions Aunt Peg had prepared me for,
that one hadn't been on the list. "Why not?" I asked
brightly.

My answer made him frown. "Because there's a tre-
mendous pet overpopulation problem. The pounds are
filled with unwanted puppies, many of them bred by people just like yourself who thought it might be fun to have a
litter. Every bitch that's bred without good reason only
adds to the problem. That's why not."

"I see." I pretended to ponder what he'd told me. No
use in trying to justify the breeding of a nonexistent Poodle. "Then I guess you wouldn't have a stud dog for me."

Driver stood up the tall rangy Poodle on his grooming
table and fluffed out her bracelets. "As it happens, I don't

have any dogs at all, only bitches. Are you aware of the genetic testing that should be done before your bitch can be bred—hips, eyes, SA?"

I hadn't the slightest idea what he was talking about, but his superior attitude was beginning to get on my nerves. "Of course," I said. "I'm planning to have all that done."

"When?"

I raised my nose a notch. "I'm working on it now."

"Is that so?" With great care he hopped the bitch down from her perch, then waited while she shook out. "Any responsible breeder will make you prove that. If you're determined to find a stud dog, I guess you may as well talk to Peg Turnbull. She's the tall woman—"

"I know who she is."

"And?"

"I'm not interested in her dogs."

A further proof of my stupidity, if the look he gave me was anything to go by. "Well, you should be. Peg has bred some of the finest Poodles on the East Coast, and the dog she has now, Beau, is probably the best she's ever had."

"Really? What can you tell me about him?"

"There's no point in my telling you anything. Talk to Peg. She's the one whose approval you'll need."

With that, he turned his back and left. I figured he was just being rude, but when I looked around, I saw that most of the other exhibitors were heading up to the ring as well. Checking my watch, I was surprised to discover that it was almost two o'clock.

I followed the heavy woman with the little black bitch over to the next tent, fascinated by the contortions she went through to push, wave, and bump everyone out of the way so that throughout the course of the journey, no one came within three feet of her immaculately coiffed entry.

At the gate, a steward was handing out numbered armbands and calling the first class's entrants into the ring. I found an empty chair and sat down to watch.

In breed competition, the judge assesses the correctness of each dog's conformation and movement, using both his hands and eyes as a guide. Although a certain standard of training and behavior is expected, the dogs are not required to perform anything even approaching the intricate maneuvers seen in the obedience classes. For the most part, they are examined singly, first standing still, then trotting a predescribed pattern. The judge then weighs his choices and makes his selection.

Although the process itself was not rife with excitement, now that I knew some of the players in the game I found out how easy it was to become involved. I hadn't stopped to buy a catalogue at the gate, but the woman sitting beside me had. The classes for the males went first, and as they came and went, I read over her shoulder, smiling at the Poodles' elaborate names and skimming through their parentage in search of a familiar line.

As all of the people I'd spoken to were showing bitches, my attention wasn't entirely on the ring. Still, I couldn't help but notice a tall, flamboyantly dressed man who appeared again and again. There was definitely something about him that drew the eye. It might have been that he was dressed in lime green slacks, a pink jacket, and a madras tie; or maybe it was because he used the outsized gestures of a Broadway star playing to the balcony. Either way, he was hard to miss. Judging by the fact that he won almost every class he entered, it seemed to be a successful system.

"Excuse me," I said to the woman with the catalogue. "Could you tell me who that man is?"

She didn't even have to consult the book to find out. "That's Crawford Langley. Everybody knows him."

"He certainly shows a lot of dogs."

The woman nodded. "He's a professional handler.

People who don't have the time or the talent to show their own Poodles pay him a fee to do it for them. He's got a big string now, and a waiting list after that. He's the best there is."

That was the second time I'd heard that accolade. Curious, I turned back to the ring to study the man. He was tall, tan, and whippet-thin; also reasonably good-looking in a studied sort of way, his brown hair carefully styled and blown dry, his fingernails manicured and buffed to a high gloss. He controlled the ring with authority, exuding an air of aggressive confidence that left little doubt but that he knew that he was good at what he did.

When the bitch classes began, Langley's dominance continued. He piloted a pretty cream to the head of the line in the Puppy class, then won the American-Bred as well, beating the big blond woman, who looked none too pleased. Finally the Open class filed into the ring. Aunt Peg took her place in line, as did Sam Driver, Crawford Langley, and seven others, most of them—according to the talkative woman sitting beside me—professional handlers as well.

The judge went through his individual examinations, then pulled out four bitches to receive further attention. Aunt Peg was pulled, as were Langley and Driver. The fourth bitch singled out was a blue with a beautiful head and melting, dark brown eyes. I looked her up in the catalogue and saw that her handler was listed as Randall Tarnower, Agent. Another pro.

"Watch this," the woman beside me whispered.

The conventions of good handling can be pretty subtle, so it took me a minute to catch on, but when I did I realized I was witnessing a real battle between two experts as each of the professional handlers pulled out all the stops to showcase his bitch's good points for the judge. While Tarnower pushed the blue's pretty head, Langley was all over his Poodle's correct hindquarter, both of them working with a seriousness and sense of purpose that seemed more suited to weightier decisions.

Finally the judge made his selection. He went with the blue bitch and placed Langley's black in second. Aunt Peg was third, Sam Driver, fourth. I joined in the applause as the previous class winners were brought back into the ring to contest the Open bitch for Winners Bitch. Langley, in with the puppy, gave it his all; but once again Tarnower's blue prevailed. The scowl on Langley's face as he accepted the striped ribbon for Reserve left no doubt as to his feelings on the matter.

The woman chuckled with satisfaction as she snapped her catalogue shut. "There'll be hell to pay for that. Crawford and Randy are the worst sort of rivals. Even though they're both immensely talented, neither is willing to give the other even an ounce of credit. That's the first time Randy's beaten Crawford with that bitch. Next we'll hear the rumors starting: the judge was paid off, he's in Randy's pocket, etc."

I stared at her in surprise. "Do things like that really happen?"

"The rumormongering or the paying off?"

"Both."

"Sure, they do. And more often than most people would like to admit."

After the battle that had gone on in bitches, Best of Variety seemed almost anticlimactic. There was only one champion entered, shown by yet another of the pros. The judge awarded it the prize almost summarily.

The judging over, I followed the exhibitors back to the grooming tent. After the hours they'd spent preparing their Poodles to go into the ring, yet another hour would now have to be devoted to taking everything apart. Langley's huge setup was down at the end. In a regrettable bit of placement, I saw that Tarnower's crates were only one row over. All concerned were ignoring each other determinedly.

The assistants, who never seemed to take a break, were busy brushing out and rewrapping. Langley stood back and surveyed the scene, his face a study in boredom. Obviously he was not so bored, however, that he would stoop to helping out with the chores, so I leapt in to fill the gap.

Catching his eye, I strode purposefully over and introduced myself. In the manner of all those who make their living by charming total strangers, Crawford Langley was very pleased to meet me. "I'm sure I can help you," he said when I'd finished outlining my quest. "I currently have several stud dogs, including a new one that I'm very high on. He's here with me today, back in my motor home, if you'd like to see him."

This was too good to be true. "I'd love to. Do you have time now?"

"Sure." He removed his sports coat and flung it over his shoulder, then barked out a command to the two flunkies, and we were off.

As we reached the edge of the field, a shout went up from under the grooming tent behind us. We both turned just in time to see Tarnower's blue Poodle come racing out from beneath the tent, running free. Beautiful as she was, I still felt my breath catch. What if she ran out to the road? How would they ever catch her? Luckily, when Tarnower appeared only seconds later and called the bitch to him, she gamboled happily into his arms, and the crisis was averted.

If he hadn't chuckled, I probably wouldn't even have looked Langley's way, but when I did, I saw that his expression was tinged with satisfaction. Then he glanced over and caught me staring. "Kid got lucky," he said.

Kid? Did he mean Tarnower? I supposed there was a gap in their ages. Was that why the rivalry was so intense?

The old guard being pushed aside by the new young buck?

"How do you suppose she got loose?" I wondered aloud.

"Who knows?" Langley shrugged, but he sounded more than a little pleased. "Poor management, probably."

After that, we walked in silence for a few minutes, past the first parking lot and on to the next, where the overnight vehicles were parked—a dazzling display of vans, trucks, and motor homes that fanned out in all directions.

"Who do all these belong to?" I asked.

"Handlers mostly. We need something this size just to carry all the dogs we bring to each show. The rest belong to regular exhibitors who use them to save on hotel bills. This one's mine here."

We'd arrived at a sleek white number, and he hopped up the three steps into the coach. "Be back in a minute. I'm sure the dog will be just what you're looking for."

A moment later he reappeared in the doorway, his hand cupped around the muzzle of a black Standard Poodle. Hoisting him up and out, he dropped the dog into a chrome exercise pen beside the door.

I gasped audibly with disappointment. Langley's Poodle was in full show coat. Beau, who had retired from the show ring months ago, had had his coat cut down. There was no way this Poodle could have been Aunt Peg's missing stud dog; he simply had too much hair.

Crawford Langley, however, mistook my gasp for one of pleasure. "He's a beauty, isn't he?" he asked, a rhetorical question if I'd ever heard one. Langley, the salesman, pressed on. "He's producing gorgeous puppies, too. He's terrific with heads and hindquarters."

His spiel sounded like the come-on on the back of a cereal box. Idly I wondered if there was a free prize offered with every mating.

"What do you think?"

"I'm afraid he isn't the right dog for me," I said. The disappointment in my voice was genuine.

"Maybe you'd like to see him move." Obviously Langley was not about to let a potential client slip away without a fight. "It's hard to tell too much before you've seen the dog come and go."

Without waiting for my reply, he threw open the gate to the pen, fished a leash from his pocket, and looped the collar around the Poodle's neck. "Watch," he called back over his shoulder as they trotted away.

There didn't seem to be much else I could do under the circumstances, so I watched. Next he'd have the dog jumping through hoops.

"Well?" Langley asked as he and the Poodle slid to a stop.

"He's very nice. But I'm afraid he's just not what I'm looking for."

"Well, think about it. You may change your mind." His hand slid in his pocket once more and came out with a card. I reached for it, but he didn't let go right away, so for a moment our hands locked. "In this business, you've got to be careful whom you deal with." His eyes flickered off in the direction of the grooming tent. "Not everyone's on the up and up. You know what I mean?"

He released the card and I pocketed it, reasonably sure that I did.

☞❧ ✻ *Ten* ✻ ☞❧

When I got home, I found I'd beaten Frank and Davey back. I was checking around in the refrigerator to see what was there that might make dinner when the telephone rang. Before I even picked up, I knew it would be Aunt Peg. Actually, I was surprised she'd managed to control her curiosity that long.

"What did you find out?" she demanded.

"For starters, Crawford Langley's new stud dog isn't Beau."

"Of course not. Why on earth would you think he might be? That dog's in full show coat."

"So I discovered. You might say it was the first thing I noticed."

"I saw you managed to talk to Sam Driver. Tell me what he had to say."

Of course she would bring him up first. "Nothing useful at all. In fact, for the most part all he wanted to do was lecture me."

"Lecture you?"

"Mmm-hmm." I dragged a stool over to the counter and sat down. "He went on and on about unwanted puppies and genetic testing. He asked if my bitch had had her hips and eyes done, and something else—something with initials."

"SA?"

"That's it. I hadn't a clue what to tell him, so I bluffed my way through. What was he talking about?"

"Hereditary problems," said Aunt Peg. "All breeds have them. Poodles perhaps more than most. There are so many things to look out for, you wouldn't believe it. Anyone who knows what they're doing tests all their stock before they allow it to be used. Hip x-rays for hip dysplasia, eye exams for cataracts and PRA, and then punchskin biopsies for sebaceous adenitis—otherwise known as SA. Those are the three most Standard Poodle breeders start with."

Hip dysplasia seemed pretty much self-explanatory, so I moved on to the next. "What's PRA?"

"Progressive retinal atrophy. It's a degenerative eye disease, more common in Minis and Toys, although we're beginning to see a few isolated cases in Standards. Unfortunately in Poodles, we're dealing with the late onset variety, which means that it usually can't be diagnosed by your local ophthalmologist until the dog is well into adulthood. Dogs that are affected will eventually go blind."

"Sounds delightful," I muttered. "What about SA?"

"Another hereditary disease that can't be diagnosed until it's in the clinical stages. That one attacks the dog's sebaceous glands. The skin becomes rough and scaly, and if the dog isn't managed right, most of his hair will eventually fall out."

"Better than going blind," I said, thinking aloud.

"No, it's not! It's a terrible disease, absolutely devastating."

I wondered at her vehemence. "Do you test?"

"Of course. Anyone who calls herself a responsible breeder has to. Any Poodle that comes up positive on any score is eliminated from the breeding program. It's as simple as that. Now then," she said impatiently. "Get back to Sam. What else did he tell you?"

"Nothing. To tell the truth, he was very abrupt."

"Well, you did catch him at a busy time."

"Aunt Peg, why are you making excuses for him?"

"Because I like him. He seems like a genuinely nice man. Just because he wanted to buy Beau, it doesn't follow that he'd stoop to stealing him."

I wasn't nearly as convinced. "He did mention Beau by name. Driver said he was the best dog you'd ever produced."

It was a moment before Aunt Peg replied. When she did, I could tell she was pleased. "You see? I told you he was a man who knew what he was talking about. I take it he referred you to me?"

"He did. Along with just about everyone else I spoke to." While she was thinking about that, I changed the subject. "Now I have a question for you."

"Shoot."

"Were you under the grooming tent when Randall Tarnower's Poodle got loose?"

"I suppose I was. Why?"

"How did it happen?"

"I haven't any idea. By the time I heard the commotion and looked up, she was already out in the field."

"Do you suppose somebody might have turned her loose on purpose?"

The question brought another pause. "I guess it's a possibility," she said finally. "The animal rights groups have been very active in this area recently. Do you know anything about that?"

"Not a thing." I'd wanted to see if she might implicate Langley or maybe one of his assistants. Instead, we seemed to be heading off in a different direction entirely.

"There are two groups that are big at the moment. PAR—People for Animal Rights, and WOAF—Welfare Of Animals First. They're the ones who organized all the resistance to wearing fur and who periodically blow up the research labs that do animal testing."

"Fanatics, in other words."

"I'd agree with you," said Aunt Peg. "But amazingly, a lot of people support them. Recently their goals have become even more outrageous. They're promoting the idea that animals should have the same rights as humans and that keeping them as pets amounts to slavery. They believe we should neither own dogs nor, heaven forbid, breed them. In protest, the activists have been showing up at some of the events in the area. They picket for a while, then sneak under the tent and open all the crates so that the dogs can run loose and return to the wild."

I thought back on the dogs I'd seen that day, with their snoods and special pillows and bottled water. They hadn't looked to me like they were itching to get back to the wild. I couldn't imagine why anyone would think they might be. "They're not serious, are they?"

"Deadly serious. That's why whenever there's a threat that they might appear, all the exhibitors pass the word and stay on the look-out. I have to say, however, I saw no evidence of PAR or WOAF today."

"Then how did the bitch get loose?"

"I haven't a clue. Probably somebody got careless, that's all. Poodles are trained to stay on their grooming tables, you know. They're never tied like the other breeds. Maybe she simply fell off her table and decided to have a romp."

Carelessness. That's what Langley had said, too. "So I guess I'm back to square one."

"There's another show next weekend."

I never doubted it for a moment.

"You know what they say. Perseverance is its own reward."

"That's virtue, Aunt Peg."

"Whatever gets the job done, Melanie dear."

Monday morning, Davey started summer camp. During the winter, Emily Grace presided over Graceland Nursery School where he'd been a student for the last two years. Summers, she used the same facilities to operate Graceland Camp. It was the first year Davey was old enough to qualify for the summer program, and I thought he'd be excited. I know I was.

Opening day at camp was like the first day of school—a zoo. Everybody was present and accounted for, but nobody seemed to know exactly where they were supposed to be. The kids solved that problem by going everywhere—running, screaming, finding their friends—while mothers tracked down lockers to deliver lunchboxes and bathing suits, then pigeon-holed counselors to discuss things like bee stings, poison ivy, and extra coatings of sunblock.

I delivered Davey to the Sunfish group and left him, along with a dozen other four- and five-year-olds, under the watchful supervision of three teen-aged counselors. A quick trip to his locker completed my duties for the day. On the way back to my car, I ran into Emily Grace. She was sitting on the edge of a portable podium—a little command center set up among the trees—checking off names against a list she held on her clipboard.

"You're in for a busy summer," I said.

Emily looked up and smiled. She was a pretty woman in her mid-thirties with long blond hair fastened back in a French braid, and warm, brown eyes. We'd met two years earlier when I'd signed Davey up for nursery school, and we had liked each other on sight. We spoke frequently, mostly mornings and afternoons when I was dropping Davey off or picking him up, and only the demands of two busy and varied schedules had kept us from becoming better friends.

"You don't know the half of it. People look around at all this . . ." She waved vaguely toward the chaos ensuing behind us in the large field. ". . . and think that it's controlling some eighty-odd kids that's the problem."

"Isn't it?"

"Hell no. The campers are a breeze. Try coordinating the schedules of twenty-five teenage counselors, many of whom have never held a real job before and think that if something interesting comes up—like their boyfriend asks them out that day—it's no problem to call in sick."

"Don't you have backups for emergencies?"

"I thought I did." Emily sighed. "I had two girls, sisters, all lined up. Then I got a call yesterday saying that they'd taken an au pair job up on Martha's Vineyard, and that was that."

As she spoke, the wheels were turning in my brain. "You mean you're looking for extra help?"

"I would be, if I thought I had a prayer of finding any. But this late, all the good kids are already booked."

"How about a good adult?"

"Here? You've got to be kidding."

"I'm not."

She looked up with sudden interest. "You mean you have someone in mind?"

"Someone loyal, thrifty, trustworthy, and brave."

"An adult boy scout?"

"Even better."

"Sounds promising. Who is this paragon?"

"You're looking at her."

Emily's face fell. Mine went with it.

"Oh," she said. "I thought you were serious."

"I am."

"But Melanie, you're a teacher."

"Think of me as qualified."

"*Too* highly qualified."

I tried another approach. "Think of me as unemployed."

"I thought you had something lined up."

"So did I, but the project lost its funding, and I lost my job."

Emily thought for a moment. "I might be calling you as often as a couple times a week."

"I'm available."

"And I can't afford to pay you very much—certainly not what you're worth."

Obviously she had no idea how bad my finances looked. If Davey's camp fees hadn't already been paid in early spring, we wouldn't have been there at all. "How much is not much?"

Emily considered. "Thirty dollars a day? A morning, really. Of course you know the hours are nine to one. I wish it could be more, but the budget is pretty tight . . ."

"It's fine," I said, and it was. "I'll take it."

"Super!" Emily looked as pleased with the arrangement as I felt.

It took us a few minutes to work out the details, then Emily was off to lead the older campers on a scavenger hunt while I headed back home. As I reached the car, I paused, turning back for one last look at Davey. He was over in the playground, much too happily involved with the rest of the Sunfishes to take any notice of my departure.

At times like this, I couldn't help but wonder if he missed the siblings he seemed destined to do without. I wasn't getting any younger, after all, and men didn't seem to be lining up on the doorstep. Not that I'd done anything to encourage them. One failed marriage was enough, thank you.

I'd always felt that Bob and I should have tried harder before giving up. But as things turned out, when the end came, I wasn't even consulted. One Saturday I'd come home from the supermarket, ten-month-old Davey strapped in the snugli across my chest, and found Bob's things gone and a rather inadequate note left in their place. He took the car and the stereo and left his son behind. I thought that illustrated his priorities perfectly.

My mother was the type who would have said, "I told you so." She'll never know how much I longed to hear her say the words. She was also the type who would have said to put the whole thing behind me and get on with the rest of my life. Easier said than done, of course, but then my mother had never cared a bit about practicality when she was handing out advice.

My eyes drifted heavenward, and I found myself smiling. I'd never doubted for a moment that she and Dad were up there somewhere, probably playing honeymoon bridge. They'd always made me proud, I thought. I was damned if I wouldn't do the same for them.

Eleven

I picked up two days of work at Davey's camp the following week. The money wasn't great, but it felt good to be back among the ranks of the semi-employed. With a little luck and a lot of teenage irresponsibility, Davey and I might even make it to the end of the summer in a somewhat solvent state.

On Thursday morning I dropped Davey at camp and swung by Aunt Peg's. I found her clipping the faces and feet of a litter of puppies in her guest room.

"I was thinking I might go pay the Wassermans a visit," I said.

"Tony and Doris? Why?"

"The other day when Tony was here you said that their house was to the north, which should place it out somewhere behind the kennel. I know it's a long shot, but maybe one of them saw or heard something the night Beau disappeared."

Aunt Peg was skeptical, but she agreed that it couldn't hurt. I thought I'd simply walk over, but once she explained about the fence and the stream, it proved easier to climb in the car and drive next door than trek there over hill and dale. Like Aunt Peg's, the Wassermans' house was set back from the road. Theirs, however, was of a more recent vintage—a contemporary whose glass and cedar design was so pure as to be timeless.

Only one car was parked in the driveway: a silver Taurus sedan. I climbed the front steps and pushed the doorbell. From inside, I heard not the chimes I'd expected, but rather a tinny rendition of the first four bars of "Somewhere My Love." I was still smiling when the door opened.

Doris Wasserman was short and plump with long umber-colored hair drawn back into a bun at the nape of her neck. A smear of flour highlighted one high, Slavic cheekbone. Another decorated the front of her skirt. She held her hands, also flour-coated, up in front of her like a surgeon who'd been sterilized and wanted to avoid contamination.

"If you're selling something, I'm not interested." Her eyes were wary and she leaned one elbow against the door, ready to slam it shut.

"I'm not. My name is Melanie Travis. I'm Margaret Turnbull's niece." Without thinking, I held out my hand. Doris ignored it, for which I could hardly blame her. "I was hoping I might be able to talk to you and your husband about the night Max Turnbull died."

"What about it?"

"If you don't mind, I just have a few questions . . ." I let my voice trail away and looked past her into the house, hoping she'd take the hint.

She did. "I guess it's all right. Tony isn't here and I'm baking, so it'll have to be in the kitchen."

"No problem."

Inside, the house was every bit as impressive as it had looked from without. There were high cathedral ceilings, skylights, and an abundance of light and space. I'd have thought the furnishings would have a similar feel, but they didn't. Most of the pieces were dark and solid. Many were covered with cheap knick-knacks. It looked as though the

Wassermans had compromised: one had chosen the house and the other, the decor.

I looked at the heavy, somber furniture, then back at Doris and decided they belonged to together, which meant that Tony was the one in the family with taste.

When we reached the kitchen, Doris went straight to a mound of dough that was sitting on the counter. I perched against a stool that had been pushed to one side of the room and breathed in deeply. When it came to baking bread, Doris was obviously a pro. The air in there alone had to be worth a whole day's ration of calories.

"This is a beautiful house," I said.

"Nice to look at, lots of work to keep up." Doris dug her fingers deep into the dough and went to work. "Tony says sometimes he wishes we'd never bought it at all."

"Is he at work?"

Doris glanced up. It was only a fleeting impression, but for a moment she looked distinctly uneasy. "Of course he's at work. Where else would he be?"

I could feel the climate in the room cooling and made another stab at putting Doris at ease. "What does he do?"

"He sells insurance." One fist pounded into the dough with a sharp slap. Then it was lifted, flung over, and pummeled anew from the other side. "He has his own agency downtown. Not the biggest, but he does okay."

"I guess he must, if he has his own agency."

"Tony works hard for what he gets. Long hours, weekends, too. Nobody ever gave him anything for free." Doris threw the dough into a big bowl and covered it with a piece of cloth. "You said you wanted to talk about the Turnbulls. What about them?"

So much for chitchat. I hiked myself up onto the stool and got down to business. "The night Max Turnbull died, did you or your husband see or hear anything unusual?"

"No." Doris didn't even stop to think before answering. At this rate, she'd have me back out the door in no time. "Why should we?"

"I don't know if you're aware of this, but Max was in the kennel when he died. It's just over that rise, maybe not visible, but certainly within earshot. Peg and I have reason to believe that Max wasn't out there alone. Someone was in the kennel with him, someone who may have caused his death, or contributed to it significantly."

I'd thought perhaps she might be shocked, but Doris Wasserman surprised me. If anything she looked almost pleased. Like someone who'd opened the *Encyclopedia Britannica* and found a copy of the *National Enquirer* nestled within.

"How about a cup of coffee?" she offered.

"No thanks, I'm fine. What would help, though, is if you could try and remember—maybe reconstruct what you and Mr. Wasserman were doing that night? It was a Tuesday, May twenty-eighth."

"I don't know . . ." Doris shook her head. "That was a couple of weeks ago."

"It was an unusually warm day for May."

Her head was still shaking.

"It was just after Memorial Day, does that help?"

"No . . ."

" 'Roseanne' was on T.V. that night. It was the last new show of the season—"

"Oh yeah sure." Doris began to smile. "I remember that. She's some broad, that Roseanne. I never miss her if I can help it. And I'll tell you, her mother, she's great, too. That show where they opened the loose meat place—"

If I didn't jump in now, it could be hours before I got another chance. "Mrs. Wasserman, did you hear anything out of the ordinary while you were watching T.V.?"

"Oh no, I wouldn't have. I keep the set turned up pretty loud. I don't want to miss a thing."

"How about later, maybe around two A.M.?"

"I'd have been asleep then."

"And Mr. Wasserman, he'd have been asleep, too?"

"I guess so." Doris drew her lips into a thin line. "I mean, when I'm not watching him, how the hell do I know what he's up to?"

"But he was here?"

"Yeah, sure, but . . ." She stopped, frowning. "Wait a minute. I remember that night. It must have been that night. Those Poodles were barking like crazy. It went on and on, and Tony was just about going nuts."

"I don't suppose he went to investigate?"

"Nah, he wouldn't have done that. But later I heard a car drive by, going real fast. We don't get much traffic here late at night. When we do, it's usually kids looking to vandalize mailboxes, so I went to the window and had a look. It was a dark colored station wagon. That's all I saw."

"Which way was it heading?"

Doris gestured away from Aunt Peg's. "East."

"Then what happened?"

"That's it. The car drove by and was gone. Look, I've got to get back to my baking, okay?"

"Okay." I slide down off my stool. A dark station wagon. That probably narrowed the field of suspects down by at least a million or two. If indeed the person I was looking for had been driving the car. "Thanks for your time."

"Don't mention it." Doris walked me to the door. "Just as well you caught me rather than Tony, seeing as it's the Turnbulls you wanted to discuss. I'll tell you, he's been complaining something awful about those dogs."

I paused on the front step and listened. I couldn't hear a thing. "Do they really bark that much?"

Doris shrugged. "It doesn't bother me. White noise— you know what that is? Mostly I don't even hear them. But Tony, well, you never know when something's going to get on his nerves. When it does, I don't try to understand, I just stay out of the way."

I smiled at that, feeling an unexpected link with Doris Wasserman. There'd been times during my marriage when I'd felt exactly the same way about Bob. Poor Aunt Rose, with no experience to draw on, and all of this still ahead of her.

I started down the steps. "If either you or Mr. Wasserman thinks of anything, no matter how small, would you let me know?"

"Why not? Although if you don't mind my saying so, dead is dead. What does it matter now?"

I turned and looked back up at her, still standing in the doorway. "Whoever was in the kennel with Max that night stole one of the dogs. My aunt would like to get him back."

"Someone really took one of those big Poodles? Imagine that." Once again Doris sounded pleased. No doubt I was providing fresh information for the neighborhood gossip mill. I'd started toward my car, so I almost missed her last words, muttered under her breath as she closed the door.

"I hope it was one of the barkers," she said.

Saturday morning I awoke to the beat of steady rain and a weather forecast that promised thunderstorms all day. I called Aunt Peg when I got out of bed, catching her just before she left.

"Are we still on?" I asked, drawing back the curtain to stare at the driving sheets of rain that swept across the yard.

"Of course. They never call these things off. Dress warmly, dear!"

She hung up before there was even time to comment, and I knew I was committed. I didn't even want to think about what the show would be like with Davey in tow, dragging him along as he stomped from puddle to puddle, so my second phone call was to the neighborhood baby-sitter.

Joanie is everything a mother could wish for. A girl of rather solid proportions, she is fourteen going on forty-five—mature, dependable, and loving. She adores children of all shapes and sizes, and plans to marry her boyfriend and start a family of her own just as soon as she graduates from high school.

In the meantime most of the neighborhood children serve as her surrogate family, an arrangement that pleases all of us enormously. Davey is crazy about her, an affection fostered by Joanie's endless enthusiasm for the games he delights in. They spend hours playing Daytona 500 and hide-and-seek and I think it's a tossup as to who's actually having more fun. She's a gem as my mother would have said, and I'm lucky to have her.

That arrangement made, I pulled on my oldest pair of blue jeans and a faded red tee shirt. Donna Karan would have cried just looking at me. A rummage through the hall closet turned up a crumpled yellow slicker and a pair of rubber duck shoes. I slipped it all on. In no time at all, I'd been transformed into the Ancient Mariner.

The trip, which should have taken an hour, took two instead as my aging, senile Volvo registered its protest of the weather. In the prime of its youth, the car had been a paragon. Now at the advanced age of twelve, it was merely less than the sum of its parts, a crippled old warhorse with perhaps only one or two good charges left. The Volvo usually obliged me by performing in good weather; only sheer effrontery on my part compelled it to do the same in bad.

When I finally reached the show ground, the dog show was in progress, business as usual. The grooming tent and rings were full, as was the exhibitors' parking. Only the spectators seemed to have stayed away in droves. There were limits, apparently, to what the paying public would put up with.

Regretfully I left the dry haven of my car and slogged through the mud to the grooming tent. There Aunt Peg was holding court, describing an argument she'd had with the superintendent at Westminster that February over her benching assignment. She'd decided to say nothing for the time being about Beau's disappearance in the hope that the matter might be brought to a quick and quiet resolution. She'd muttered something about the American Kennel Club and proof of parentage, and since I didn't have the slightest idea what she was talking about, there was nothing I could do but agree. According to Aunt Peg, the dog-show grapevine operated with an efficiency the Pentagon might have envied, but for now her secret seemed safe.

I skirted around her audience and introduced myself to a woman who was brushing out a bushy black Standard Poodle puppy.

"Mildred Davis," she said, holding out one hand while the other continued to brush, uninterrupted. She was a short, stocky woman who looked like she'd brook no nonsense from dogs or people. Her brown hair was sprinkled with gray, and her skin had the tough, weathered look of too many summers spent in the sun.

I got right to it and delivered my pitch.

"I might be able to help you," she said at the end. "I have this puppy's sire at home. His name is Champion Blackwatch Pendragon. He's young and just beginning his stud career, but I have very high hopes for him."

That sounded promising. Beau was just beginning *his* stud career, too, somewhere. I tried to remember all the questions Aunt Peg had coached me to ask.

"I'm looking for a dog with a good front. And one that's sound, coming and going."

"That's Dragon all right. Here let me give you my card." Mildred dug down into her overflowing tack box and came up with a slightly soiled scrap of paper. "Give me a call. I'm sure you won't be disappointed."

"I'll definitely be in touch," I said, tucking the card safely away. Rain and mud forgotten, I found myself grinning as I continued down the aisle. Finally someone had actually nibbled at the bait.

I spent several minutes talking to a man with a Mini who said he had some Standards at home, until I discovered that he, like many of the others, kept only bitches. A woman grooming a small bitch was very interested until I told her I was looking for a large dog with a good coat, then she shrugged her shoulders and I drifted away.

Aunt Peg, I saw, now had her Poodle up on her feet. She was scissoring the bitch's bracelets and talking to a dapper-looking gray-haired man. He was dressed in an elegant tweed suit, crisp cotton shirt, and a silk rep tie. His only concessions to the storm that raged around him were the rubber boots on his feet and the Burberry raincoat he'd draped casually over his arm.

A patch of color caught my eye, and I realized there was a small green ribbon affixed to his lapel, identifying him as a judge.

A judge? Under the exhibitors' tent?

I wasn't the only one who was staring. Crawford Langley was frowning; Randall Tarnower, shaking his head. The heavyset woman I'd met the week before looked openly envious.

What was that all about? I wondered. Now I had two things to discuss with Aunt Peg later.

ᔐ❀ *Twelve* ❀ᔐ

When judging time came, I wove a circuitous route through the grooming tables and crates to the edge of the tent nearest the rings. They were partially covered by a tent of their own, so braving the elements was only a matter of dashing across the forty-foot expanse in between.

I flipped up my hood and was steeling myself for the drenching bath to follow when someone came up beside me. "Excuse me, if you're on your way to the other tent, do you think you could give me a hand?"

The voice rang a bell. When I turned to look, the startlingly blue eyes completed the picture. I lifted my head and the hood fell back.

"Oh," he said. "It's you."

No beating around the bush with this man. Sam Driver looked past me and around the tent. It didn't take a genius to figure out that he was looking for someone else—anyone else—from whom to solicit aid. Finally his gaze returned to me.

"I need to get her over to the ring dry," he said.

"Why?"

"Why what?"

It wasn't me, I decided. It was them. These dog people were crazy. Anyone could see that on a day like this, the chances of keeping a dog dry were slim and none. Especially since as soon as the judging started, the Poodles would be sent out from under the tent to gait around the ring in the rain. What was the difference whether they got wet now or later?

"Look," said Sam, sounding a trifle desperate. "I know she'll get soaked eventually, but at least I can make a good first impression. Every other Poodle in the Open Bitch class is going to walk into that ring dry, and I'm damned if Casey will be the only one who looks like a drowned rat. I forgot my umbrella, or I could probably manage on my own. Now do you think you can help me or not?"

"I guess so," I said, grinning. Somehow the sight of a man in distress always cheers me up. "What do you want me to do?"

Quickly Driver shed his slicker. "If you take one side while I get the other, we should be able to hold it over her while we run across. Okay?"

Wordless, I nodded. Under the coat he was wearing a tight polo shirt that stretched smoothly across a well-muscled chest. It was tucked into a pair of khakis that hugged his trim hips and defined the contours of a molded bottom. Even an objective observer had to admit that when it came to admirable attributes, Sam Driver wasn't entirely lacking.

He shoved the edge of the coat into my hands. "Ready?"

"All set."

Casey was a compact black Poodle who greeted this new game the humans had thought up with a devilish expression and a wagging tail. She waited patiently while I positioned myself on Sam's right side. At his signal, the three of us dashed together across the expanse of muddy field and scooted under the flap of the other tent.

Too late I realized that I'd forgotten to flip my hood back up. My hair hung in limp strands around my head; rivulets of water gathered at the tips to flow down the front of my jacket and onto my pants. As Sam bent down to check Casey's condition, I devoted myself to making amends. I wiped the water off my face and ran my fingers through my hair. It all did about as much good as solar energy in an Alaskan winter.

Sam finished with the Poodle and looked up at me. I must have flunked the inspection because he fished Casey's metal comb out of his pocket and handed it over. As I ran it through my hair, he shook out his slicker and put it back on.

"Thanks for the help." Sam's grip tightened on Casey's lead as he led her away into the crowd.

I stood there staring after him for a long moment. It wasn't until the next set of exhibitors making the tent-to-tent run jostled me aside that I realized I still had his comb. He would need it in the ring, I knew. Especially on a day like this, the primping never stopped, even while the dog was being judged.

I pushed through the crowds that had gathered in the dry center aisle until I found the ring where the Poodle judging was already in progress. Sam was standing by the in-gate, adjusting his armband as the steward called out his number to enter the ring.

"Wait!" I called.

He turned to look, and I tossed the comb to him. Sam snatched it out of the air, flashed a smile, then hurried Casey into the lineup. They won the Open Class handily, and also went on to take the points. Idly, I hung around and watched as the photographer was called for and the win pictures taken.

"See what I mean?" asked Aunt Peg, materializing at my side. Her bitch, who had gone Reserve, danced around us, a felt squeaky toy clutched between her teeth.

"What?" Nobody seemed to be paying the slightest bit of attention to us, so I figured it was safe to talk.

"The man is a dreamboat. Now if I were twenty years younger . . ."

"If you were twenty years younger, you'd still be married to Max."

"Spoilsport."

I knew full well what Aunt Peg was doing. She wasn't wishing for herself; she was trying to tempt me. But though Sam Driver might be the sort of man that dreams were made of, it wasn't going to work. I'd put my dreams away when my marriage ended. I had no intention of resurrecting them now.

When I looked around again, Aunt Peg was gone. I probably should have left as well, but the thought of sloshing back through the rain and mud held little appeal. When the man whose Poodle had won Winners Dog went marching angrily over to the steward's table in the corner of the ring, I was just as pleased to wait and see what would happen next.

I missed the first thing he said to the steward and took that as a clear indication that I needed to move closer. As I inched in along the rail, the judge finished with her pictures and headed back toward the table. Obviously she was experienced with inclement weather, for she was encased in clear plastic from head to toe. The steward intercepted her as she drew near. He whispered something, and she nodded. She gathered together her judge's book and her other belongings, then turned to face the irate exhibitor.

"This dog needs only a major to finish," he said.

"So you told me. In the ring."

From the tone of her voice, I gathered that was something that wasn't done.

"The major was in bitches."

"I can count as well as you can, sir."

"If you could," the man said rudely. "You would have put him Best Of Winners."

Sharing the points, it was called. I knew all about it thanks to Aunt Peg's explanations. While both Winners Dog and Winners Bitch were awarded points, the number varied according to how many dogs of their sex each defeated. It was possible, and often happened, that one sex had only enough entrants for one point while the other might provide two or three. During the course of the Best Of Variety judging, either the Winners Dog or the Winners Bitch was chosen as Best Of Winners. That dog then received the higher number of points awarded on the day, whether they came from his sex or not.

Further complicating the issue was the fact that in the course of compiling fifteen points to secure a championship, each dog had to win at least two "majors." Major wins were those consisting of at least three points, which meant that a sizable amount of competition had to be present. Majors were often hard to find and always hard to win. According to today's catalogue, there'd been two Standard Poodle dogs entered, and thirteen bitches. I gathered this exhibitor thought today's major in bitches should have been his as well.

The man leaned over the knee-high railing. Clearly his posture was meant to be intimidating. "This dog," he snapped, "was Winners Dog at a specialty last week. *That* judge knew what he was doing."

"That judge," the woman said calmly, "perhaps saw something deserving in your dog that I did not. The bitch beat him on merit—"

"The bitch already had the major!"

"I can't help that." The judge picked up her things, shouldered past the man, out of the ring, and kept right on going. Good for her, I thought.

"Shit."

The man was still standing there, staring after her. I scanned his armband and looked up the number in the catalogue. Will Perkins, it said. He hadn't been entered at the show I'd gone to the weekend before, or at least I hadn't seen him. As to his Poodles, he obviously kept males; there was one on the end of his leash now.

"Got a minute?" I asked.

Perkins's laugh held no humor at all. "Sure," he said. "What's one more minute? All I have to do is take Bravo back to the setup, break down his coat, wrap his ears, load my car, and drive the hundred miles home. How long could that possibly take? Especially if you don't count the fact that with all the rain that got in his coat today, I'll pretty much have to bathe him the minute I get home. Then blowing dry, that's another three hours or so, even if I don't put him back in oil. But hey, what's another minute?"

I talked fast, whether for his sake or my own, I wasn't sure. In no time at all I managed to ascertain that Perkins owned several other stud dogs besides the Poodle he'd brought to the show. He tore the back page out of my catalogue and wrote in a looping scrawl his name, address, phone number, and the names of his other dogs.

As he handed it back, he asked, "When do you expect your bitch to come in?"

"Come in what?"

Perkins snorted. "In season. When do you think she might be ready to breed?"

That was a new question. How the hell was I supposed to know when a nonexistent bitch might be ready for breeding? First the Poodle needed a pedigree. Now it seemed she needed a due date. Hoping bitches ran true to female form, I said, "I'm not really sure. She's not terribly regular. It should be sometime soon, though."

"Well, let me know when the time comes. Or before, if you want to see the dogs."

From there I walked over to the food stand where I bought a tepid hot dog on a soggy bun. The grooming tent was emptying fast as breed after breed finished for the day and the rain continued to pour down. I looked around for Aunt Peg, but she had already packed up and left. Cold, wet, and tired, I decided to follow suit.

As I slogged back across the field to my car, I remembered the crumpled card in my pocket. The sliver of paper was damp and somewhat the worse for wear, but still legible nonetheless. Finally I had two real leads to follow up. Aunt Peg would have to be pleased by that.

Figuring it was just as easy to be warm and dry at her house as at mine, I drove straight there from the show. Aunt Peg answered the door wrapped in a thick terry cloth robe, having just emerged from a hot shower.

She looked cozy and comfortable and restored, which was everything I was not. I sighed as she directed me to the middle of the kitchen floor so that I could drip on the linoleum rather than her rugs. With some show of heart, she heated up a pot of tea. Not quite the black coffee I'd been hoping for, but it was warming, which was something.

"I have great news," I announced, wrapping my frigid fingers around the mug.

Aunt Peg cocked a brow and calmly took a sip from her steaming cup.

"I met a woman named Mildred Davis. She has a young stud dog named Champion Blackwatch Pendragon and—"

"He won't do," Aunt Peg said with infuriating certainty. "What else have you got?"

"What do you mean he won't do? I haven't even told you anything about him yet. The dog's new at stud and she seemed very anxious to get him bred. How can you possibly say he won't do?"

This time Aunt Peg let me finish, but she stood there shaking her head throughout. "Didn't she tell you that the dog is white?"

"White?" I stared at her stupidly. "He can't be. I saw

one of his puppies at the show and it was black. And his name is Blackwatch . . ."

Aunt Peg was still shaking her head. "I've seen the dog, last year when he was being shown. He most definitely is a white dog. Blackwatch is the name of the kennel, like Cedar Crest is mine. It has nothing at all to do with the dog's color."

"Even with a black puppy?" I protested weakly.

"Sorry, but that doesn't mean a thing. White dogs sire black puppies all the time. I don't mix between the colors, but many breeders do. Do you know anything about genetics?"

"I majored in English."

"Dominant and recessive genes?"

"Like Mendel?"

"Good for you." Aunt Peg nodded. "This is going to be an oversimplified view, but color breeding is all a matter of dominant and recessive genes. Black is the dominant color in Poodles, so that any dog who carries the black gene shows it. That is to say, he's black.

"But a black Poodle might carry any number of recessive color genes—cream, blue, brown, or even the rarer colors, silver and apricot. All of those colors can be produced by a black Poodle providing he carries the appropriate gene and is bred to a bitch who does also. So you see, the breeding of a white dog and a black bitch could very easily have produced the puppy you saw today."

"I guess so." It wasn't that I wasn't convinced, only that it was disheartening to realize that once again I'd come up empty.

"What about the man who went Winners Dog? I saw you talking to him. Will Perkins, wasn't it?"

"Do you know him?"

Aunt Peg waved a hand. "Poodle breeders and exhibitors are actually a pretty small family. I don't know everybody, but I know who most people are. Will's from up-state New York, I believe."

"Chatham." I pulled out the crumpled page I'd torn from the back of my catalogue.

"I don't know another thing about him except that he's shown some rather nice Poodles. What else did he tell you?"

"He's got a bunch of stud dogs, and I've been invited to go have a look."

"What's their breeding?"

"Dover and Regency lines," I read from the paper.

Aunt Peg looked thoughtful, "Those are both compatible with Beau's breeding. I don't see any reason why Beau couldn't be passed off as a Regency dog. It seems Will Perkins might definitely merit a closer look."

"Really?" I'd been brushed off so many times it took a moment to digest the fact that I'd actually found something of value.

"Why not? You didn't think we were going to keep running around in circles forever, did you?"

I didn't dare tell her that was exactly what I was beginning to think, so instead I changed the subject. "Who was that man I saw you talking to?" I asked. "The one wearing the judge's badge."

"Oh that was Carl Holden." Aunt Peg smiled. "He sent me a note when Max died, but he wanted to come by and offer his condolences in person."

"Everybody was staring at the two of you. Is the judge allowed to come and talk to the exhibitors like that?"

"If he's judging their breed on that day, certainly not. Most judges won't come under the tent at all. Carl had the Sporting Group today, but the Poodle people still know who he is. He's judged the breed for years."

"Were he and Uncle Max friends?"

"Friends *and* rivals. Carl started out in Irish Setters about the same time we began with Poodles. But while

Max and I stayed with our first breed, Carl branched out in several directions. In the late seventies, he even had a Standard Poodle—one of ours, I'm happy to say. She had several group wins, as I recall."

"Then he's a breeder, too."

"Oh no." Aunt Peg shook her head. "Not any more. He applied and got his judge's license more than twenty years ago. It was much easier then. Not that Carl wasn't qualified, but it just was. Now he judges a number of different breeds and his services are in great demand. Every single weekend of the year, he's flying off to one cluster or another.

"Carl thrives on the travel, and the competition and the politics. Even after these years, he still finds it tremendously exciting. It works for him, certainly. But I'm glad Max and I chose another route."

"Where does he live?"

"Texas is his home base. But as I said, he travels all over North America for assignments. This week, obviously, it was Connecticut. He's a very nice man, actually. Courtly, in a rather old-fashioned way. I was pleased to have the opportunity to see him."

I walked over and put my mug in the sink. It was time to get home to Davey. "So what's next?" I asked.

"A visit to Will Perkins when you get a chance. And then Farmington, week after next."

"More shows."

"Of course, more shows. Every exhibitor doesn't go every week. Trust me, it'll be a while yet before you run out of new faces."

"So I just keep doing what I'm doing."

"Again and again," said Aunt Peg. "Until it works."

❧❀ *Thirteen* ❀❧

Davey was in high spirits when I got home. He and Joanie and his best friend, Joey Brickman, had spent the afternoon frog hunting.

"In the rain?" I asked, although the answer was evident. His clothing was soaked through. I peeled it off and ran a hot bath. "What did Joanie have to say about that idea?"

"She liked it."

"I'll bet."

His overalls were in a heap on the floor. Davey stared at them in fascination. Just for the hell of it, I had a look, too. It wasn't my imagination. They were moving.

I didn't really want to know, but I felt I had to ask. "Davey, what's inside your pocket?"

Naked, my son bounded down off the bed. "That's Harry. He can take a bath with me."

"Oh no, he can't." I rescued the hapless frog as Davey fished it from his pocket and cupped it, none too gently, in his hands. "Harry belongs outside."

"But he's my new pet!"

"He is?"

"Yup. Joey took his frog home, too. We even found one for Joanie."

Ah yes, Joanie. The baby-sitter *extraordinaire*. I could see that she and I were going to have a little chat.

"Honey, we don't have any place to keep a frog."

"Sure we do. In the bathtub. We can dig up worms for him to eat."

Right. "Davey, Harry is a wild frog. I don't think he could survive in captivity. We have to let him go."

"But I just caught him."

"And you did a great job, too." I pulled his bathrobe down from its hook on the back of the bathroom door. For now, the bath could wait. "But I'm sure Harry has a family outside that's waiting for him to come home. We wouldn't want them to be worried about him, would we?"

"I guess not." Reluctantly, Davey followed me down the stairs, the long flannel bathrobe trailing around his ankles. When we reached the back door, he spoke again. "Our daddy doesn't come home. We don't worry about him."

I felt my heart constrict, the same way it always did when he talked about Bob. I'd explained to Davey that his father was a fine man who loved him very much but who wasn't able to live with us right now. When he'd been smaller, it had been easy. Now that he was in preschool he was beginning to realize that the other children had two parents while he only had one. The questions were coming more frequently.

"That's different."

"How?"

"Well for one thing, your daddy didn't just disappear." I crossed my fingers behind my back over that one. Then I gave Bob a thorough silent cursing for making these explanations necessary. "We don't worry about your daddy because we know he's okay."

"How do we know?"

"We just do. Your daddy and I got a divorce which

means that even though we both love you very much, we just can't all live together. Okay?"

Davey considered that. "Maybe Harry has a divorce, too," he said finally.

I opened my fingers and had a look. The frog had hunkered down in my palm. Its eyes were closed, but I could feel the slight motion that indicated it was still breathing. Davey reached out and stroked the smooth green back. The frog blinked one large eye. All things considered, he didn't look too unhappy.

"He can't live in the bathtub," I said. "And I'm not going out in the rain to dig up any worms."

"Yeah!" Davey jumped up in the air, tripped over the belt to his robe, and just missed cracking his head on the cabinet.

That's how we got a pet.

I spent the better part of the week playing telephone tag with Will Perkins. The nearest shows the following weekend were on Cape Cod. Aunt Peg wasn't planning to drive that far, and neither was I. I'd hoped to set up something for Saturday with Will, so when the phone rang first thing in the morning, I ran to get it.

It was Aunt Peg. "Rose is coming over," she said. "She wants to discuss money. I was thinking you might want to be here."

"Do you want me to be?"

There was a long pause on the line, Aunt Peg deciding whether or not to admit she needed moral support. "That's up to you," she said finally. "Rose will be here in an hour."

That gave me just enough time to arrange a play date for Davey, make myself presentable, and drive down to Greenwich. As I pulled up to the house, I saw a plain blue

Ford sedan parked by the side of the driveway. It looked like the kind of car a nun would have access to.

Aunt Peg opened the front door before I even had time to knock. For once the chorus of Poodles was silent. They didn't come tumbling out the door or leap down the steps to overwhelm me in the hall. I took it as a sign of how seriously Aunt Peg was treating this meeting that she'd locked them away in their crates.

"What took you so long?" she hissed under her breath as she grasped my shoulder and pulled me inside. Before I could answer, I saw Aunt Rose standing in the living-room doorway.

"Melanie?" Rose's smile was tentative. "I didn't expect to see you here."

I crossed the hall and gave her a quick kiss. "Aunt Peg thought perhaps I might like to join you. Have you been here long?"

"Only a minute or two. We haven't even had a chance to sit down." She looked pointedly at Peg. "You *were* planning to offer me a seat, weren't you?"

Antagonism shimmered in the air between them. "Of course she was," I said brightly. Ignoring the undercurrents, I positioned myself between them, took each aunt by the arm, and led them into the living room.

It came as no surprise when the women chose to sit in the two high-backed wing chairs that faced each other in front of the fireplace. Briefly I considered moving all breakables from within arm's reach.

"How about some coffee?" I asked.

"No," Peg and Rose answered in unison. It was nice to see them agree on something.

"Do sit down, Melanie." Aunt Peg waved vaguely toward the couch.

"Yes, sit on her side," said Aunt Rose. "That is why you're here, isn't it?"

"No, it isn't." I remained standing. It was the only way

I'd ever get a height advantage on these two, so I figured I might as well hang onto it. "I'm not on anybody's side. You two obviously need to talk to each other. I'm only here to listen."

"Well?" Aunt Peg demanded.

"Well what?" Rose's tone was equally strident. I looked around for the nearest escape route in case I should need it in a hurry.

"You wanted to talk." Peg folded her hands in her lap. "Go ahead."

Peg would have bristled at being given such an order. Rose looked like she wanted to do the same. But years of convent training prevailed. She stifled her temper and began. "You know, obviously, that I met with Max the week before he died. I'll assume that he told you what we discussed?"

Aunt Peg's nod was stiff and short.

"Then you know why I'm here. I needed money then. I still need it now. I'm not asking for charity. I know there was a sizable amount in Nana's estate. Max has had the benefit of it all these years. Now I'd like my share."

"Nana left you nothing in her will. That was her choice."

"She had no choice! I had taken a vow of poverty."

"And now that you plan to renounce your vows, you feel you should be rewarded?"

I winced at that. Resentment had simmered between these women for more than thirty years, but even so, that was pretty harsh. I said nothing and waited for the next blow to fall.

"I can see why you and Max got on so well all these years," said Rose. "You're both alike, stubborn and selfish. When Max died, I was sorry I hadn't had the chance to set things right between us. But now I wonder if things could ever have been made right. Dear Lord, the two of you have been wrapped up in those dogs of yours for so long, you can't remember how to deal with real people."

"The Poodles have nothing to do with this," Aunt Peg said firmly. "Unless there's something I don't know that you'd like to tell me about?"

Aunt Rose frowned. "So you haven't found the dog yet. I'd wondered. Max was quite attached to him."

"Yes, he was." For the first time, Aunt Peg's tone softened. She waited a long moment before continuing, and Rose didn't push her. "You know, Max was very upset with you after you came to see him. You took him so much by surprise, I'm sure he didn't know what to think. Eventually he would have calmed down. Eventually I imagine he'd have given you the money."

Rose nodded. Evidently she'd come to the same conclusion. "Now it's up to you," she said. "Will you give it to me?"

"I can't."

"You just said—"

"What Max might have done and what can now be done are, unfortunately, two different things. Max's will has gone into probate. The money isn't available."

Just like that, the brief moment of rapprochement was gone.

"Probate, my foot!" cried Rose. "You're stalling, just like Max did. He hoped I'd change my mind."

"Actually," Peg interjected mildly, "he hoped you'd come to your senses."

"My senses are perfectly in order. You're the one who's behaving like a jackass!"

Coming from anyone else, the insult would have sounded mild. But from a nun, somehow, it seemed to carry extra weight. The two of them were getting nowhere. I sighed and entered the fray.

"Aunt Rose, maybe you should think about what Aunt Peg said. If the money isn't available—"

"I knew you were here to stand up for her," Rose said angrily. "The only reason you're on her side is because you only know half the story. If you had any idea of the truth . . ."

"What truth?"

Aunt Peg stood. "I think we've said all there is to say. Rose, you'd better go."

"What truth?" I repeated.

"There are things you don't know," said Rose. "Things Peg would just as soon you never found out—"

"Rose, don't!" Aunt Peg said sharply.

I looked at the two of them: both strong women, both family, each determined to have her own way at any cost. Despite what Rose said, I hadn't chosen sides, but my precarious neutrality was becoming harder and harder to maintain. Maybe I needed more facts.

"What are you talking about?" I asked.

Aunt Rose looked angry; Aunt Peg, torn. Finally, it was she who spoke. "Melanie, dear, are you sure you don't want to sit down?"

I shook my head, crossed my arms over my chest, and waited.

Rose looked at Peg. "So now you have nothing to say," she snapped. "I imagine I wouldn't either if my husband was responsible for his brother's death."

Pandemonium broke loose then. Even the Poodles, crated in another part of the house, began to bark.

"That's preposterous!" cried Aunt Peg. "How dare you say such a thing? How dare you even think it!"

"I think it because it's the truth."

"The truth only a warped mind would see!"

This time I did physically step between them. Since I seemed to be the only sane person in the room, I had to do something. "Will one of you please tell me what's going on?"

"I will," Rose declared. "You're a grown woman now,

Melanie. It's time you heard what really happened. When Nana died, the bulk of her estate went to Max, her youngest son. I received a few momentos, your own father, even less."

"Yes, I know." None of that was news. "My father didn't need the money."

Rose shook her head. "That might have been what you were told, but it wasn't why. Michael had already received his share of his estate—and lost it."

"I don't understand."

"You know what your father did for a living?"

"Of course, he was a stockbroker. A very good one."

Aunt Peg's eyes narrowed, but she said nothing.

"Your father was very charming," said Rose. "But he had no head for business. He was wonderful at attracting customers. Less so at keeping them. Because of that, he changed jobs with some frequency."

I remembered my childhood as a time bathed in golden light: happy, secure, and filled with laughter. There hadn't been any upheavals or moves. If my parents had been worried, I wasn't aware of it.

"He worked for Merrill Lynch," I said.

"Among others," Rose confirmed. "There are a number of brokerage houses in New York. At one time or another, Michael tried almost all of them."

"Your father worked very hard," Aunt Peg said gently. "He just wasn't very good at what he did. Your parents went to great pains to conceal that from you and Frank."

"Well, they succeeded." I hadn't realized I'd been retreating until I felt the couch nudge the backs of my knees. There was more coming. I sat.

"After you went off to college," Rose continued, "your father was let go once again. He turned to Nana for help. She didn't give him any money outright, but she contacted some old friends, and soon your father had a job again. Included in the package was her own, rather sizable account, which your father was to manage for his new firm."

I swallowed heavily. "The money he lost."

Rose nodded. "Oh, it took several years, but in the end it was gone. When Nana died, she was considerably poorer. That was how her will came to be set up the way it was. Max reaped the benefits, and Michael never recovered. He began to drink quite heavily after that."

"No." I shook my head. "I would have known."

"You were away," Peg said softly. "At college, then graduate school. You couldn't have known. You parents made sure you didn't know. They didn't want you and Frank involved."

How could we not be involved? I wondered. We were a family. Why hadn't they let me help? I could have come home and gotten a job. If only I'd known. If only I hadn't been too wrapped up in myself and my new life to see what was going on.

I drew in a deep breath and slowly let it out. "Is there more?"

"No," said Aunt Peg.

"Yes," said Rose.

I looked back and forth between them. "Since I'm finally hearing the truth, you may as well tell me all of it."

"The rest isn't truth," Aunt Peg said quickly. "It's nothing more than harmful conjecture."

"Tell me," I said. "And I'll decide."

"The night your parents died . . ."

I remembered it well. Bob and I had been married for less than a year. We'd gone out to dinner and then to a party. I was slipping off my dress at three A.M. as I played back the message on the machine and heard . . .

"Your father was here that afternoon," said Peg. "Michael had been laid off once again, and he asked us to bail him out."

"Which Max refused to do," said Rose.

Peg shot her a glare. "He didn't refuse," she said firmly. "But Max insisted that Michael get control of his drinking first."

"Max and Peg didn't help," said Rose. "And they were the last people to have the chance. Later that evening, your parents' car plunged off an embankment, carrying them to their deaths. Michael's blood alcohol level was quite high at the time. It was never made public, but the possibility of suicide was raised."

Pain, thick and numbing, began in the center of my stomach and radiated outward. I'd told them I was old enough to know what had really happened, but now I realized I wasn't. I'd never be old enough to accept what Rose was saying, that everything I thought I knew about my parents—their lives, their marriage, even their deaths—had been a lie.

"No," I whispered. "That isn't true. It couldn't be."

"We don't know," said Aunt Peg. "Maybe it truly was an accident. Or maybe your mother was trying to stop him, and they lost control of the car." She crossed the room and wrapped an arm around my shoulder. "We'll never know for sure."

I shrugged away the comfort she wanted to offer. Anger welled up inside me now. It was better than the hurt and the sense of betrayal. I thought of the alliance I'd formed with Aunt Peg, the feeling of family I'd thought we shared. Maybe that was all just a facade, too.

"I have to go," I said.

"Melanie, wait!"

I turned back for one last look at the two of them. Neither looked happy. Each had goaded the other, and in the end, neither had gotten what she wanted. Did Rose actually blame Max and Peg for my parents' death? I wondered. Or had she only said that to drive a wedge between Peg and me? Rose might have spent the last thirty years in a convent, but clearly she hadn't lost her touch for playing hard ball.

What a pair. They were half the relatives I had in the world, and at the moment I didn't care much for either of them. But if I walked out now, with the way things were, Rose would think she'd won. I was enough of a Turnbull myself not to want to give her that satisfaction.

"Farmington," I said to Peg. "Next weekend. I'll see you there."

She didn't move except to wink. I didn't return the gesture.

⮑❊ *Fourteen* ❊⮐

Aunt Peg and I didn't talk at all during the next week, which probably suited both of us.

I had plenty of thinking to do, at least that's how it seemed at first. But with four days subbing at Davey's camp, and excursions to the beach, the park, and the Discovery Museum in the afternoons, I somehow ended up with no time to think at all. And in its own way, that was fine, too.

I had a new set of facts about the past to absorb and deal with. But I also had a life to live in the present. In reality nothing had changed. I still had to shop and cook and clean. I still had Davey to hold and hug.

And when I watched my son take Harry for a swim in the bathtub, I thought about a frog with a divorce and realized Aunt Peg wasn't the only one capable of glossing over a few facts when she thought the situation warranted it. Maybe we all did what we felt we needed to do.

I thought I might tell her that at the dog show, but as it turned out, I didn't see her there either. Aunt Peg hadn't liked the judge and hadn't entered her bitch. Since I was on my own, I decided to take Davey with me. We'd spent the last several Saturdays apart; it was time for a little togetherness.

"We're going to a dog show," I told him cheerfully

early Saturday morning as I laced up his favorite red sneakers.

As usual, Davey was full of energy. He sat on the edge of the bed, pumping his legs up and down in a way that made my job next to impossible. "Yeah! Are you going to buy me a dog?"

"Dog shows aren't for buying dogs, honey. They're for looking at them. We're going to have a great time."

Davey slowed his feet while he considered, and I quickly double knotted the last bow. "I had a great time last Saturday," he said, sliding down off the bed. "Frank and I went to the tennis courts. I got to drink beer with the guys."

I stopped, dead still. "Frank gave you beer?"

"Yup," Davey said proudly. "Just like the grownups."

I marched out of Davey's bedroom and into my own, where I picked up the phone. Frank's croak, when he answered on the fourth ring, confirmed that he'd still been asleep.

"Is the house on fire?" he asked.

"No."

"Then call back later."

"Frank!" My voice rose to combat the inevitable click. A long moment passed. "Yes?"

"I want to talk to you *now*. Davey tells me he's acquired a taste for beer."

"Oh yeah?"

I could see the smirk on his face just as plainly as if he were sitting in the room with me. "Is that all you can say? What was my son doing drinking beer in the first place?"

Frank's voice slipped down an octave into its most persuasive tone. "Come on, Mel, what's the big deal? He only had a tiny glassful when some of the guys came back to my place after we played tennis. I didn't want him to feel left out."

It sounded reasonable, but I wasn't sure I was ready to forgive him that easily. "How big a tiny glassful?"

"One of those jelly glasses. And it was less than a quarter full to begin with. Besides, he didn't even like the stuff. He took one sip and then left the rest in the bottom."

"Oh," I said, feeling rather foolish. After speaking with the aunts the week before, I'd thought about calling Frank. Then I'd told myself that if he was as innocent as I had been, I should leave him with his illusions. But now that we were speaking, I knew I had to ask.

"Do you have a minute?"

"Mel, I'm in bed."

A sudden thought hit me. "Alone?"

He laughed, which I took as a good sign. "Yes, alone."

"I saw Aunt Rose last week."

"Yeah? How's she doing?"

"Fine. You knew she was planning to leave the convent?"

"I heard. Pretty wild, eh? After all these years . . ."

"We were talking about when Dad and Mom died."

"Oh?"

Was it my imagination, or had his voice turned wary? "I was away at school all those years, but you were home. What was going on?"

"What do you mean what was going on? It was normal, just like always."

"Was Dad drinking?"

The silence on the other end of the line said it all.

"Why didn't you tell me?"

"Hell, what could you have done? Mom and I were right there, and we couldn't do a damn thing about it."

"The night they died . . ."

"The car went off the road, Mel. It was an accident, that's it. Like Father O'Malley said at the service—it was just their time."

I'd never thought of Frank as being particularly religious. Interesting that something the pastor had said should stick in his mind after all these years. Still, I had the answers I'd sought; there was no use in pressing him any further.

I let my brother go back to sleep, collected Davey, and headed off to the dog show. The weather was clear and warm. It agreed with the Volvo, and the car purred all the way to the polo grounds in Farmington. The show, laid out over the spacious green expanse, looked like a picture postcard.

By now, I had the routine down. We parked, then headed straight for the grooming tent. Together, Davey and I made our way through the crates and tables to the Poodle section of the tent. Sam Driver was there, working on a bitch I presumed to be Casey. He glanced up as we approached. I smiled and kept on going.

My first conversation of the day took place with a smug, cigar-smoking Poodle owner who said that he couldn't possibly make a decision concerning the use of his dogs without first consulting his handler, Barry Turk. I followed the line of his pointing finger to a jumbled assortment of battered equipment that had been arranged into a setup on the other side of the aisle. The handler himself was nowhere in sight, but two harried assistants were holding down the fort. I was able to find out from them that Barry Turk did indeed have access to many stud dogs, several of which might be right for my bitch.

"Give us a call at home," said a petite blond girl who seemed to be in charge of the chaos. She plucked a card from the tall hardwood tack box and shoved it into my hand, then hurried away with a white Toy Poodle tucked neatly beneath each arm.

I'd slipped the card into my pocket and was looking around for another prospect when Davey grabbed my hand and pulled me across the tent. An Old English Sheepdog was standing on top of a large metal crate while a woman in a red plaid smock made last minute adjustments to its coat.

"Look at that." His awe of the enormous, shaggy gray and white animal was clear in his voice. Davey reached up a tentative hand to pat the dog's paw. "I want one like this. Can I, Mommy?"

Not in my lifetime. The Sheepdog was the size of a small bear. "I don't think so, honey. A dog like that would be too big for our house." A dog like that would be too big for the whole neighborhood.

"Do you mind if he touches?" I asked.

"Not at all." The woman smiled and stepped back, wiping her hands on her smock. "Sergeant loves children."

The dog turned several times on the crate—no mean feat on a surface that was barely larger than he was—then heaved his bulk into a prostrate position. Davey patted the dog's nose, which was now within reach, and had his fingers cleaned in return.

Over his head, I glanced back at the Poodles. There were more familiar faces than not. From the look of things, I'd already spoken to almost everyone in attendance.

The woman followed my gaze. "Is that your breed? The Poodles?"

I nodded. "I'm trying to find a stud dog for my bitch, but I don't seem to be having much luck, and I've already spoken to just about everyone here."

"Have you tried out back in the exhibitors' lot?"

"The parking lot?"

"You know, where the motor homes are. A lot of the regulars don't bother to unload and groom under the tent. They just set up an awning next to their van and do it there. Why don't you go take a look around? I'm sure you'll find some more Poodles."

I hadn't thought of that. But it was true, when I'd been

back in the lot with Crawford Langley, I'd seen quite a few grooming tables sitting out among the exercise pens. It was certainly worth a try.

Davey's protest at leaving the Sheepdog behind was quickly cut short when I explained where we were going. Then he began to run. I wouldn't have thought that legs the length of a four-year-old's could move that fast, but thanks to my son, I'm constantly learning new things.

The exhibitors' lot was on the far side of the rings, but it was worth the walk for both of us. Davey got to see the big rigs and gleaming motor homes up close, and I discovered that there were almost as many people grooming beside their vans as there were under the tent. When we came to a sleek blue and white motor home whose matching awning shaded a grooming table holding a black Standard Poodle, we were both pleased to stop for a closer look. There was no one in sight, so I ventured a knock on the trailer door.

"Just a minute!" A moment later, a head emerged from within. "Can I help you?"

"I've been admiring your Poodle, and I was wondering if you had any others at home."

"Sure. Be right out." I saw through the door that he was just finishing getting dressed. He knotted his foulard tie, pulled it up into place beneath the collar, then shouldered the door aside and hopped the three steps down to the ground.

He was tall, at least six foot two, but he moved with grace and confidence. His dark hair was short, neat, and graying at the temples; his clothing, well cut and obviously expensive. Hardly the sort of man who looked as though he needed to make an easy buck.

"I'm Melanie Travis."

"Jack Berglund." He held out his hand and we shook on it. "What can I do for you?"

I told him, and he nodded thoughtfully throughout.

"I might have just the thing," he said at the end. "I have a gorgeous new dog at home. I bred him myself three years ago, but sold him as a puppy to a family in Texas. Unfortunately they switched hobbies—went from Poodles to parasailing overnight—and the dog never made it into the ring. I'm just happy to have him back."

"My bitch could use a better head," I said. "And she could stand some improvement in front."

"They could all stand some improvement in front. That's one of the problems with this trim. But I think when you get your hands on Ranger, you'll be pleased."

His mention of the trim reminded me of my last mistake with a dog in hair. "You said he'd never been shown. Does that mean you're going to be bringing him out yourself?"

Jack shook his head. "I'd love to, but the dog came back to me zipped down with a seven blade. It'd be eighteen months at least before he could even begin to be ready, and I don't have that kind of time. It's a real shame. He's a beauty, and I'd have loved to finish him."

"Why would such a good dog be sold in the first place?"

"It was my mistake. You can't always tell at eight weeks how they're going to turn out, but you can't afford to keep every one either. You make your picks and hope for the best. When I did this litter, I was wrong, that's all. Kept the chaff, and sold the wheat. Nobody's right all the time. I was just lucky to get the chance to buy him back."

"Kept the chaff and sold the wheat," Davey chanted at my side, a sure sign that he was growing restless.

"Don't let the fact that he's not a champion bother you. That was just bad luck. The dog's bred to produce. I'm sure he's going to do fine." Jack scribbled his phone number on the back of my catalogue. "Come on by and have a look. You'll see what I mean."

It was now only minutes until the start of judging, and I

hurried Davey over to the Poodle ring. There, quite by accident, I got my third tip of the day. We settled down to watch beside a tiny older woman. Her gray hair was pulled back into a chignon, and she was wearing an elegant, if slightly wrinkled, linen suit.

Clearly she was knowledgeable about the breed. Not only did she mark down the numbers of the winners and losers, but the margins of her catalogue were filled with cryptic notes about their quality. I discovered all this by reading over her shoulder shamelessly and was delighted to learn that the brown Poodle I didn't like had a straight shoulder while the white I favored was a sound mover.

Unfortunately it didn't take long for her to catch on to what I was doing. When she did, she snapped her catalogue shut. "Do you have a Poodle entered?" she inquired archly.

"No." I pulled back quickly, but of course it was too late. "Actually I'm here looking for one. I'm sorry, I didn't mean to read your notes. It's just that I have a lot to learn, and they were fascinating."

"That's all right." Her tone softened. "I was concerned I'd just written something scathing about your dog." The woman reopened the catalogue and went back to scrutinizing the Poodles in the ring.

"Do you have a dog here today?" I asked.

"Yes, this one." She pointed down the page to her entry. I peered over and read that her name was Mrs. Anna Barnes, her Poodle was a champion entered for Best Of Variety, and the agent listed was Crawford Langley. "Sammy will be along in a minute, as soon as Randy goes Winners Bitch with that blue. I just hope she doesn't beat him in the specials class."

I looked up. The Open Bitch class was in progress and Randall Tarnower was indeed showing the blue bitch I'd seen a few weeks earlier. But she hadn't even won her class yet. I wondered how Anna Barnes could be so sure she was going to take the points.

When I asked, she seemed to think the answer was perfectly obvious. "This judge should adore that bitch. He's a silver nut and always has been. You don't see many silver Standard Poodles, and even fewer blues. Not only that, but she's a good one besides. Randy told me earlier she's been undefeated since he got her."

As we watched, the blue did indeed take the points. Anna Barnes nodded with satisfaction. "Now just don't beat Sammy," she muttered under her breath as the champions filed in.

"Sammy's your dog?"

Anna nodded again. She pointed toward the front of the line, where Crawford Langley was easy to pick out. As always, he looked to be in total command of the ring. She watched with great care as her own dog was examined by the judge, then continued our conversation.

"You said that you were here to look for a dog. Did you mean a puppy?"

"No, a stud dog. I have a bitch I'd like to breed and I'm looking for a suitable mate."

Her eyes never leaving the ring, Anna said, "Tell me something about the bitch."

Dutifully I recited all the facts Aunt Peg had drilled into me. With each retelling, the bitch was beginning to seem more real. I could almost believe there was a black Standard Poodle at home, waiting for me to get back and let her out.

"Actually, I have a dog at home you might be interested in." The judge was now taking another look at the blue bitch. Anna fidgeted in her chair. "His name is Champion Troughbridge Beauty. He's a homebred of mine, but don't think I'm just spouting off when I say there's a lot to like about him, because there is. He's got size, substance, brains, and he can move."

"I'd love to see him." I flipped to the Poodle page of my catalogue and circled her name and address. "Is this where you can be reached?"

Anna nodded. "Try me in the early morning. That's the best time to find me at home."

The judge sent the Poodles around the ring one last time. Anna's champion was still in front and when the judge pointed, he won the variety. Randall's blue bitch was Best Of Opposite Sex.

"Thank you Lord," Anna muttered.

Because of Anna, I'd been caught up in the drama in the ring. Belatedly I realized I hadn't heard anything from Davey in a long time. A quick turn to the left revealed the reason why. The chair beside me was empty. Davey was nowhere in sight.

⌬❋ *Fifteen* ❋⌬

A lesser woman might have panicked, but I knew my son too well for that. All right, so my stomach did tumble a notch. Then I told myself how much Davey loved to play hide-and-seek. It was probably a game. Please God, I prayed. Let it be a game.

"Davey?" I called as loudly as I dared. "Davey, honey, where are you?"

He didn't answer, but I knew that was part of the game, too. I stood up to get a better view of the surroundings.

"Have you lost something?" asked Anna.

"I've lost someone. My son." I continued to scan the area. "He was sitting right there just a minute ago, but he seems to have left while we were talking."

Anna Barnes was smiling. It seemed like an unusual response to me. Maybe she wasn't a mother.

"Is he wearing red sneakers and blue shorts?"

"Yes. Do you see him?"

She pointed across the ring. "I can see him right now. He's in there."

When I looked where she was pointing, I saw him immediately. Somehow he had managed to crawl through the slats and into the ring. Now he was ensconced in what I'm sure he thought was the perfect hiding place—underneath the steward's table.

When I was standing up, he was invisible. Sitting down, he was hard to miss. Laughter eddied around the gallery as Davey waved to the ringside, enjoying the sensation he was creating.

Mortified, I hurried around to the spot where the long table abutted the side of the ring. I knelt down and poked my head underneath. "Davey!" I whispered. "You come out of there this instant!"

"You found me." Clearly he was disappointed. "I was playing hide-and-seek."

"Well the game's over. Come on out."

"Don't want to come out. I like it here."

I couldn't reach him from where I was, and he knew it. Nor, according to ring etiquette, was I allowed to go in after him. Momentarily stymied, I rocked back on my heels and found myself looking up into the face of the curious steward who obviously thought she was watching me talk to her table.

"Can I help you?" she asked.

"Er . . . my son seems to be under your table."

One eyebrow ascended. The woman leaned over and peered under her end of the table. "So he is. Please remove him at once."

"I'd love to. But he doesn't want to come and I can't reach him."

The steward gave me the sort of scathing look that dog people, whose pets are perfectly trained, reserve for parents whose children are less so. She reached under the table, grasped Davey firmly by the arm, and pulled him to his feet. "Out of my ring, young man," she ordered. "We are judging dogs here, not children."

Davey took one look at her stern expression and scampered for the exit. I jumped to my feet and did the same. Knocking no more than one or two people aside, I managed to reach the gate the same time he did, and grabbed him as he shot through.

Ignoring the laughter around us, I took his arm and marched him away. We were out of the tent and past the rings before I even paused. "David Edward John Travis, I have never been so embarrassed. What did you think you were doing?"

"Playing hide-and-seek," Davey said with perfect four-year-old logic. "Pretty good place, huh?"

We might have debated the merits of that if a shrill cry hadn't stopped us where we stood. A line of protesters had massed in front of the grooming tent. They were carrying signs and chanting something about freeing all dogs from slavery. The cry seemed to have come from an irate woman who'd crossed their path. She cradled a tiny white Maltese protectively next to her chest.

If it hadn't been for Davey, I would have moved in closer. Instead I remained where I was and tried to hear what was being said as the woman with the Maltese confronted one of the protesters and received an angry reply.

Since the Poodles had just finished being judged and were on their way back to the exhibitors' tent, inevitably they got caught up in the fray. One look and the protesters began to circle. No doubt the carefully coifed, exquisitely groomed Standard Poodles embodied everything they were against.

So far the march had been peaceful, but as soon as the protesters targeted Randy Tarnower, I sensed there was going to be trouble. Rather than backing him up, the other Poodle handlers scattered. It took only a moment for Randy and the blue bitch to be surrounded by the chanting group. When someone reached down to touch the Poodle, Randy exploded.

From where I was standing, I couldn't see exactly what happened. Randy might have thrown a punch, or maybe it was just a shove. In any case, the protester went down, his sign breaking beneath him as he fell. Randy took the opportunity to cut and run. By the time the protester had regained his feet, the handler had disappeared under the tent. The marchers regrouped and continued their demonstration.

"Ashes, ashes," Davey sang happily. "All fall down."

We'd seen enough for one day and I took my son home.

That evening Davey went straight to bed, and by morning, he'd come down with a forty-eight-hour flu that managed to last twice that long. When he was finished with it, I had a turn. In the meantime Aunt Peg had gone off on something called the New England Circuit, which I gathered was a midsummer opportunity to hold shows for an entire week straight.

I wasn't expecting her back until after the weekend, but she showed up Sunday morning. Davey was settled down in front of the T.V. with Big Bird for company, and I was just sitting down to my second cup of coffee when she appeared at the back door.

"You look awful," she said. "Whatever's the matter with you, I hope it's not contagious."

"Flu, and I'm recuperating, so you can stop holding your breath." I got up to heat some water for tea. "Where were you when I needed a nurse?"

"Off at the shows, and happy to be there."

Par for the course. I waited at the stove as the kettle steamed, then whistled. "How did you do?"

"I finally finished that little bitch I've been showing. It's about time."

"Is that why you came home early?"

Aunt Peg accepted her cup, frowned at the tea bag, and reached for the sugar. "Oh no, I wasn't planning on staying until the end anyway. I wasn't even entered today. For Harvey Winesap? I wouldn't dream of showing to him."

"Why not?"

"The man is a Bulldog specialist and he's got no eye at all for a Poodle. There's no use in taking your dog to a show if you don't respect the judge's opinion."

I came over and joined her at the table. "What does their opinion have to do with anything? I thought the judges were supposed to be comparing each dog to a standard of perfection for the breed."

"They are." Aunt Peg paused to stir her tea. "But each judge interprets the standard in his or her own way. Not only that, but each feels that different things are important. Some judges demand sound movement. Others go crazy for style."

"I was told that the judge at Farmington loved silvers."

Aunt Peg nodded. "On top of everything else, personal preference plays a part. Judges are supposed to be color blind, but of course they aren't. There are a dozen different angles you have to think of in deciding whether or not a particular judge might like your dog. And then there are those judges who just don't have any idea what they're doing. Like Harvey Winesap. The man hasn't a clue about Poodles."

"Does that happen a lot?"

"More often than it should. Unfortunately the system is heavily weighted in favor of judges who are approved to do lots of breeds. So even though judges always start with a breed they're an expert in, very soon most are looking to branch out.

"Poodles are very popular because although the three varieties work from a single standard, they are judged in two different groups. Standard and Miniature Poodles are in the Non-Sporting group, while the Toy Poodles are part of the Toy group. For the judges it's kind of a two-for-one deal."

"But they must know something," I argued. "Otherwise what happens when they get an assignment and it's time to judge the dogs?"

Aunt Peg chuckled. "There are lots of different ways to cope with that problem. Sometimes they go with the most famous handler or the one with the biggest string. They hope that will make them look like they know what they're doing. The ringside is usually fooled, and the handlers are grateful. But the breeders and the owner-exhibitors see what's happening. Then they make sure not to enter under that judge again."

I sipped my coffee and thought about what she had said. "A few weeks ago, I sat next to a woman who was talking about politics at dog shows and judges being paid off. Does that stuff really go on?"

"Sometimes," Aunt Peg allowed, "although not nearly so much as some people would have you believe. Dog shows are just like any other sport. Some people are there for the fun of it, and others are there only to win. There will always be those who try to give themselves an extra edge, legal or not.

"Now enough of that depressing subject. Get on with it and tell me who you saw in Farmington."

Aunt Peg leaned forward on the edge of her seat. I thought that meant I had her undivided attention, but it turned out she was reaching for a bagel from the basket on the counter. I set her up with a plate, a knife, and some cream cheese, and we were finally ready to begin.

"Do you know a man named Jack Berglund?"

Aunt Peg looked up. "I most certainly do."

"Apparently he has a new stud dog he's just crazy about. He seemed to think he'd be perfect for my bitch . . ." One look at the expression on her face and my voice trailed away. "What?"

"Perhaps I should have prepared you. Especially after last week."

"Prepared me for what?"

"Jack Berglund isn't just a Poodle breeder. He was also a business associate of your father's."

I pictured the charming, sophisticated man I'd met the week before. That image jibed perfectly with the memories I had of my father. I could well imagine the two of them doing business together, regardless of what Rose had said.

Aunt Peg must have followed the direction of my thoughts, for she began to shake her head. "That shouldn't make you less wary of Jack Berglund, but rather more so. I never dabbled much in the money end of things, but I know Max didn't trust him. Something to do with junk bonds, I believe, and perhaps a hint of a suspicion that he'd led your father down the garden path—"

I'd heard quite enough about my father's shortcomings already. As far as I was concerned, the subject didn't need reopening now. "Tell me about Jack's Poodles," I broke in.

My lack of manners was enough to bring her up short. Aunt Peg stopped and considered for a moment, then evidently decided to humor me.

"Jack's kennel name is Shalimar, and he's been breeding for years. I believe he has a pretty large operation up in northwestern Connecticut. There's no reason to think his new stud dog might not be worth a look."

"Good." I filed that information away for future reference and deliberately changed the subject. "I also met a woman named Anna Barnes. She recommended a dog of hers named Champion Troughbridge Beauty. Like half the other people who've described their Poodles to me, he sounded almost too good to be true. Do you know the dog?"

"Yes, I know Beauty." Aunt Peg smiled. "And I don't think we have to worry about him or dear Anna. The dog is every bit as good as she says he is. All of her Poodles are. Anna's getting older now and doesn't show nearly as much as she used to. That's probably why you didn't run into her sooner. Nevertheless, she has no need for Beau.

Beauty is every bit as good as Poodle, and he's already proven his worth as a stud.

"If anything," Aunt Peg concluded, "I ought to be stealing from Anna, not the other way around."

Shot down again. By now I should have been getting used to it. "How about a handler named Barry Turk? What do you know about him?"

Aunt Peg thought for a moment. "I've been looking at this in terms of a breeder wanting Beau," she said finally. "To tell you the truth, I haven't given the professional handlers much thought. Although of course, they do often act as agents for their clients' dogs."

"From what I could see, Barry Turk's operation didn't look anything like Crawford Langley's, or even Randy Tarnower's. Where does he fit in?"

"Somewhere lower down the scale, I'd say. Crawford's been doing it for years and has all the right connections. Randy's made his name on raw talent. Either of those two, even with a bad dog on the end of a lead, is a threat. And when they actually have something really good to show, all you can do is try and stay out of the way."

"And Barry Turk?"

"He's nowhere near their league. Sometimes I think Barry's lucky to win even when he has a good one, which in itself is rare. I can't for the life of me imagine anyone being so foolish as to send a dog to him."

"Why do people do it then?"

"Oh, he's a little cheaper, I guess. And I doubt he has a waiting list like some of the others do. Besides, the clients he gets are usually newcomers who don't know any better."

"Too new to recognize an illicit stud dog?" I asked.

"Most certainly."

"I wonder if Beau might have looked to Barry Turk like a ticket up in the world."

"Maybe in more ways than one. Handlers work on

something of a reward system, you know. No matter whether a dog wins or loses, they still get their fee. But some wins are worth a bonus on top of that."

"So Barry Turk would stand to gain not only the commissions on the breedings he handled, but also the possibility of better dogs to show in the future. That could raise his earnings potential considerably."

Barry Turk was suddenly looking very interesting indeed. "I think I'll go look at some stud dogs," I decided.

The phone was on the counter with Turk's card beneath it. I dialed the number listed in the corner. One of his assistants answered, and we made an appointment for Tuesday morning.

Davey went to camp on Monday, then home with a friend. I spent most of the day with Aunt Peg going over a collection of photographs which chronicled Beau's development from baby puppy to majestic show dog. The last shots, taken in the early spring, showed the dog as he was now, clipped down but still displaying the elegance and carriage that were the hallmark of the Cedar Crest line.

Aunt Peg worked with me until she was sure I understood that how a Poodle was trimmed could do a great deal to fool the eye. Since Beau had now been missing for six weeks, it was possible that at least superficially, he could look entirely different. She outlined his virtues and his faults, and drilled me until she was comfortable with my knowledge of both.

We were almost done by late afternoon. Aunt Peg had Simba, who was Beau's half sister, in the living room, and we were going over her one last time when the doorbell rang.

"Probably a delivery," Aunt Peg said as the Poodles ran from all corners of the house to mass in the front hall. I followed her out to see.

It wasn't a delivery. It was Sam Driver. Aunt Peg

grinned. I gulped. The Poodles like all visitors; they went wild.

You know how sometimes the hair stands up on the back of your neck and you just know something's going to go wrong? That's how I felt. Unfortunately there wasn't a damn thing I could do about it.

❧❋ *Sixteen* ❋❧

If Sam was surprised to find me at Margaret Turnbull's house, his expression didn't betray it. Then again, he was pretty busy as Aunt Peg opened the door and the inevitable onslaught of Poodles all but knocked him over. He handled the barrage with aplomb, however, greeting each of the big dogs with a pat on the head or a tweak beneath the chin.

As the Poodles danced happily around his legs, Sam looked up at me. "I see you took my advice."

It took me a minute to figure out what he was talking about. Then I remembered that he'd been one of several people who'd directed me to Aunt Peg. Obviously he thought I was there in my guise as a stud-dog shopper.

Before I could reply, he was already turning to Peg. "I apologize for barging in like this. I wanted to talk to you about something, and I took a chance that you might be free. Obviously it's better if I come back another time."

"Not at all. I'm delighted to see you." Aunt Peg was at her gracious best. She counted noses as the Poodles ushered Sam inside, then shut the door behind them. "Now then, what advice did you give to Melanie?"

"Sam was one of the people who recommended that I speak with you about a stud dog," I said quickly.

"How nice." Aunt Peg patted his arm. "You have very good taste."

"You have very good Poodles."

Just what I needed—a mutual admiration society. Aunt Peg and I were just about through, but it wasn't only curiosity that kept me from leaving. I knew how she felt about Sam Driver. The minute I was gone, she'd probably spill the beans about everything.

"Of course that wasn't really necessary—"

"Aunt Peg!"

"You see Melanie is actually my niece."

So much for my good influence. I guessed that meant now I could go.

"Your niece?" Now Sam looked surprised. To his credit, he recovered quickly. "Then I guess that must mean that Beau *is* missing. I heard a rumor down in New Jersey this past weekend. That's actually what I wanted to talk to you about."

"Well good, I'm glad you're here. Come on into the living room and get comfortable."

Sam walked in and sat down. Gracie, who, until the doorbell rang, had been lying at my feet, crossed the room and climbed up into his lap. That traitor.

Aunt Peg watched with approval as the Poodle turned a precarious circle over his legs, then settled down to drape across his knees. Obviously neither one of them saw anything unusual about having an animal the size of a small pony set up housekeeping in someone's lap.

"Who was talking about Beau?" I asked.

Driver thought for a moment. "I'm pretty sure it was Mildred Davis. She and Crawford were standing ringside, and I overheard them discussing it."

"Interesting," Peg said. "I've been trying to keep the whole thing quiet, but you know how small the dog world is. Word was bound to get out sooner or later. Beau isn't just missing, Sam. I'm quite certain he was stolen. He disappeared from our kennel the night my husband Max died."

That silenced him for a bit. "So the dog Melanie is shopping for is Beau," he said finally. "I guess that makes sense in a roundabout sort of way. Have you come up with any leads?"

"We have several," I said firmly. It was one thing for me to wonder if our methods were working. It was quite another for Sam Driver to question their efficiency. "Not that I'm sure it's any of your business."

"Perhaps not. But I'd like to help."

Aunt Peg grinned enthusiastically. "How?"

"The scheme you're working isn't perfect, but it's not all bad either. It seems to me that things would go a lot faster if there were two of us out there asking questions."

Aunt Peg and I exchanged a glance.

"Think about it," said Sam. "I'm a new face on the East Coast. Most of the Poodle people here don't know any more about me than they do about Melanie. There's no reason why they shouldn't accept my queries at face value."

Aunt Peg was nodding as he spoke.

I wasn't that easy to convince. "So far we've done just fine on our own."

"Have you? It's been what . . . ? At least six weeks. And you still don't seem to have any idea where Beau is. I'd say you can use all the help you can get. Two people can cover a lot more ground than one."

"Which probably means that much of the same work will get done twice."

"I don't see that as a problem," Sam told me. "In that case, there's less chance that we'll miss something important."

His argument made sense, but that didn't mean I was buying it. The harder Sam pushed, the more I wanted to shove him right back. It wasn't the first time he'd had that effect on me, and the whole thing left me feeling distinctly uncomfortable.

Aunt Peg had listened to both sides. I could see she was wavering. "It's very kind of you to offer—"

"Believe me," Sam broke in, "there is nothing kind about my offer at all. I want Beau. I have for a long time. I still haven't given up on the idea that you might agree to sell him to me, but barring that, at the very least, I plan to breed to him. So you see I have a stake in getting the dog back, just as you do."

He sounded sincere, I had to give him that. So why did it all seem so smooth, and maybe just a little too easy?

He and Aunt Peg were smiling at each other like old friends. Thick as thieves, I thought. The aptness of the phrase brought me to my feet.

"Aunt Peg, could I see you in the kitchen for a minute?"

"Now?" Her tone clearly questioned the quality of my upbringing.

I nodded.

"If you'll excuse us, Sam?"

"Of course." Gracie tilted back her head and licked his chin. He was scratching behind her ears when we left the room.

I waited until the kitchen door had swung shut behind us. Aunt Peg had no such inhibitions. "Now what?" she demanded.

If she'd been any louder, we might as well have stayed in the living room and spoken in front of him. Deliberately I lowered my own voice. "I think we need to move a little more slowly here. Has it occurred to you that despite what he says, Sam Driver may be the one who has the dog? He admitted himself that he was desperate to get him. Maybe he only came over here today to see how much we've learned."

Aunt Peg's lips twitched at that. "Then we've certainly

disappointed him, haven't we? Melanie dear, what he said was true. It's been six weeks and we're no closer to finding Beau than we were at the beginning. We have to widen our search. And if Sam can help us do that, so much the better."

I knew that I was fighting a losing battle. The problem was, half of me agreed with Aunt Peg. Unfortunately, the other half wanted to run like hell. So I dug in my heels and kept arguing.

"Once we agree to work with Sam, he's going to know every move we make."

"Yes, and while he's watching us, we can be watching him. Quite frankly, if he isn't on the up and up, I can't think of a better way to keep an eye on him."

As usual, she had a point.

"I'm beginning to get the impression you're not going to let me talk you out of this."

"It's about time," said Aunt Peg. "Now that we've got that settled, do you suppose he should go with you to visit Barry Turk tomorrow?"

For all I knew, seeing the handler might provide the discovery we'd been waiting for all along. No way was I going to have Sam Driver horning in on my big moment.

"Definitely not. This is my lead. I'm going to follow it up."

"As you wish." Having won the war, Aunt Peg conceded the last battle. "Now let's go back out and see to our guest."

Sam was sitting in the chair where we'd left him. He started to rise when we entered, then glanced down at Gracie and thought better of it. "Is everything all right?"

"Just fine," Aunt Peg said happily.

We spent the next few minutes discussing which of the upcoming shows Sam and Aunt Peg had entered, and who among the circle of local exhibitors I'd already spoken to. Counting on Aunt Peg's discretion is a little like hoping for clouds during drought season, but for once she followed my lead and never even mentioned Barry Turk's name. By the time she and I walked Sam to the door, the plan was a go.

Outside, Sam paused on the step. "You know I haven't had a chance to meet many people in Connecticut yet. All I've done since I got here is work and go to dog shows. I was thinking maybe we could get together sometime and you could show me some of the local sights."

I have to admit, the invitation caught me by surprise. But immediately the cynic in me had an answer ready. Sam knew he'd won over Aunt Peg. Now, no doubt, he wanted my compliance, too. If so, I wasn't going to make it easy for him.

"Connecticut's actually a pretty dull state," I said. "There isn't much to see."

"Really?" Sam grinned. "I guess you don't work for the Chamber of Commerce."

"I'm a teacher," I said shortly, not that he'd really asked. Then I threw out the clincher, the one that separates the men from the boys. "And a mother. I have a four-year-old son, Davey."

"You're married then?"

"Divorced. So I like to make sure I spend as much time with Davey as I can."

Over his shoulder, Aunt Peg was watching the exchange with amusement. I felt like a ninth grader coming home from a date to find her parents waiting on the porch.

"Bring him with you," said Sam.

If it was a bluff, he was pretty damn convincing. But when I shook my head, Sam didn't push it. Of course then I had to tell myself that I wasn't disappointed he hadn't tried harder.

"Shame on you," Aunt Peg said we watched him stride

down the walk and get into his car. "Letting a man like that get away."

I didn't need her to tell me what I was already telling myself. Instead I snapped back, "If you're so interested, why didn't you take him up on his offer?"

"I wasn't the one who was asked."

"This is the nineties, Aunt Peg. A liberated woman doesn't have to wait to be asked."

She snorted under her breath. "A lot of us were liberated in my day, too. We just didn't feel obliged to hit people over the head with it."

Peg shut the door, and we watched through the glass as Sam's car disappeared down the driveway. We both turned away when it was gone.

"How long are you going to keep using that child as a buffer against things you don't want to face?" Aunt Peg asked abruptly.

"As long as I want to."

For once, that shut her up.

Now I had two problems to contend with—Aunt Peg's missing Poodle and a partner I didn't want. It was a tossup as to which one worried me more.

≈❖ *Seventeen* ❖≈

Davey had camp on Tuesday morning, so I was covered there. Unfortunately when I dropped him off, Emily Grace came running over to the car. She apologized for the short notice and asked if I could sub.

I hated turning her down, for her sake and mine, too. I could have used the money. But I'd made a commitment to Aunt Peg and especially now, with Sam in the picture, I didn't want to slacken my efforts. The sooner I located Beau, the sooner life could return to normal.

The trip to Barry Turk's kennel in Poughkeepsie took just about an hour. To my surprise, the directions led me into the midst of a heavily populated, residential area. Somehow Turk had managed to squeeze a kennel housing forty dogs onto less than half an acre of land. The sound of their barking hit me like a shock wave when I stepped out of my car. I couldn't imagine how the neighbors let him get away with it.

Barry Turk's house was a dilapidated, shingled ranch. At one point it must have been white, but now it had faded to a weathered shade of gray. The kennel building, visible beyond, was in similar condition. Its roof sagged in one corner; and the short, narrow runs that fanned out on either side to cover every available inch of space looked as though they were held together with bailing twine. Dogs, many of them Poodles, raced up and down within, eyeing me with manic fascination.

I was standing there watching them when the front door to the house opened and Barry Turk emerged. "You must be Mrs. Travis," he said, holding out his hand. "Beth told me to expect you."

He was short but powerfully built. His hair was too long, and he was at least two days past his last shave. I took his hand but held it for as short a time as possible.

"She said you had some stud dogs I might be interested in."

"Could be." Turk ran his fingers through his hair, pushing it back out of his face. "I'm not going to hand you a line like some people do, saying their dogs are perfect. They may be what you want, maybe not. You'll just have to see for yourself."

"Fair enough."

He set off at a brisk pace. With little conviction and even less enthusiasm, I followed. An overgrown path led back to the kennel, which looked worse and worse the closer we came. The idea that Beau might be housed in such a place was thoroughly depressing.

"That was a Standard you were looking for, right?" Turk asked as he held open the screen door.

I nodded, not trusting myself to speak. Outside the kennel was bad enough. Inside, it was appalling. The room we'd entered was a small office, but beyond that I could see the area where the dogs were housed. I'd expected pens like at Aunt Peg's, but instead I saw crates, dozens of them, stacked from floor to ceiling. Although it was a sunny day, inside the building was dark and airless, with a damp, musty smell.

"Wait here," said Turk. He walked into the kennel room and pulled the door shut behind him.

He was gone only a few moments, but I used the time to walk over and have a look at his desk, whose surface was a jumble of bills, premium lists, and pink-slip phone messages. On top was a bill that looked as though it was ready to be sent out. Three columns listed the shows attended, the charges, and the name of the Poodle shown: Baytree's Mood Indigo.

I loved the name. That's why I remembered so quickly where I'd seen it before. The blue bitch Randall Tarnower had been winning with for the last month was Baytree's Mood Indigo. How could two handlers be showing the same dog? I wondered.

As the door to the kennel room opened, I slid my gaze quickly to the top of the page. The bill was going to Richard Beck in Wellesley, MA. I turned away from the desk, but I wasn't fast enough.

"See anything interesting?" asked Turk. He released a huge black Standard Poodle into the room, then closed the door behind him.

Since I'd already been caught, I figured I might as well brazen my way through. "I didn't realize you handled Richard Beck's Poodles."

"Used to, don't anymore. You want to see any of Beck's dogs, call Randy Tarnower." Turk crossed the room and shoved the bill away beneath some papers. "Maybe he'll have time to talk to you, maybe he won't. He's pretty busy these days, stealing everyone else's clients."

"Stealing them? How does he do that?"

"It's easy," Turk snapped. "When you've got his connections. Now are you going to look at this dog or not?"

"Sure," I said, but I'd already seen enough. The Poodle in question was in continental, which ruled him out immediately.

Still, I waited while Turk snapped his fingers, and said, "C'mere, Joe, show the lady what you look like."

Joe, however, had no intention of obliging. Now that

he was free, he dashed back and forth across the room, careful to keep himself just beyond the handler's reach.

"This dog's owner spoiled him. When he's been here a little longer, he'll learn some manners." From the intent look in Turk's eyes, I had little doubt he meant what he said.

"Maybe he doesn't get enough exercise," I suggested pointedly. The handler just shrugged. Either he was too dumb to realize that his operation had been insulted, or else he didn't care.

Abruptly the side door opened and Beth entered the room. Careening around the desk, Joe took a running leap into her arms. I probably would have been bowled over by having sixty pounds of flying Poodle hit me at that speed, but Beth must have been accustomed to such exuberance, because she recovered nicely, hardly missing a step.

"Joe baby," she crooned, scratching the dog's muzzle. "What are you doing loose?"

Then she noticed us and her smile faded. She dropped Joe to the ground and led him by the muzzle to where Turk was waiting, hand outstretched.

"Sorry, Barry," she said as though the Poodle's behavior was all her fault. "I didn't know anybody was in here."

Turk took the dog without a word and posed him for my inspection. Unable to come up with a quick excuse, I made the expected show of going over him, placing my hands in all the appropriate spots and nodding every so often as though I was making mental notes about the dog's conformation.

"So?" said Turk.

In the short time I'd been going to dog shows and studying the winners, I'd developed an idea about what a proper Poodle should look like. That, combined with Aunt Peg's coaching, had given me a basis against which to make comparisons. Although I probably couldn't have chosen the better between two very good Poodles, I could certainly tell a good one from a bad one.

It was easy to decide which category Joe fell into.

He was big and coarse and overdone. His expression was totally devoid of the ready intelligence so typical of the breed. Tired by his exertions, he was panting heavily, his tongue lolling out of the side of his mouth. To someone whose knowledge of the breed had been fostered by Poodles with the style and elegance of Aunt Peg's, this dog was an anathema.

"Very interesting," I said. It was better than the other alternatives I'd come up with. "Do you have any others I can see?"

"A bunch." Turk nodded, and Beth did, too. Monkey see, monkey do, I thought none too kindly. He handed Joe back to his assistant and said, "Come on this way."

We left the building and went around the back, where the runs were slightly larger. The first four were filled with Standard Poodles. The two nearest us I rejected on sight as one was white and the other was still in show trim. The other two, however, were definite possibilities, and I moved in for a closer look.

Turk began to expound on the Poodles' good points and I nodded as though I was listening. That was enough to keep him occupied while I examined the dogs themselves. Aunt Peg had warned me not to be fooled by the length or condition of the coat itself. Bearing that in mind, I ignored the fact that these two Poodles looked like a pair of woolly, unkempt sheep. From what I'd seen, it seemed reasonable to assume that six weeks under Turk's supervision could do the same for any dog.

A closer inspection, however, proved disappointing. One dog had much too common a head; and his eyes were several shades lighter than the deep mahogany of the Cedar Crest Poodles. The other was long and low. Either he had too much body or else not enough leg; but the end result was that he lacked the square proportion so integral to a correct Poodle outline.

Satisfied that neither one was Aunt Peg's missing stud dog, I turned back to Turk, who, incredibly, was still talking. "Is this all of them?"

"Yeah," said Turk. "All that are here right now. It's a pretty good selection, if I do say so myself. I imagine one of them would suit your needs."

I turned to head back toward the house. Much as I hadn't wanted to find Beau in this situation, the disappointment I felt was acute. "Thank you for taking the time to show them to me. I'll let you know as soon as I've made my decision."

"Do that," said Turk.

As we reached the front of the kennel, he sketched a wave then veered off into the office, leaving me to find my own way out. On the other side of the building, Beth was hosing down runs. I strolled over to say goodbye.

"Did you see everything you wanted to?" she asked. When I nodded, she added, "Barry can be kind of a pain to deal with, but he means well."

A man who meant well wouldn't keep his dogs packed into a dark, airless room like sardines, I decided, but I kept the thought to myself. "You're great with the dogs. They really seem to like you."

Beth looked up and smiled. "Hey, thanks."

"So what are you doing here?"

"It's a job."

"So's McDonald's."

"At McDonald's I wouldn't learn anything." Beth finished the run she was working on and moved on to the next. "Here I'm picking up plenty. Another year or so and I'll be able to go out on my own."

"So you want to handle dogs professionally?"

"Sure."

"Is there money in that?"

I'd slipped the question in casually, but still it made Beth stop and think. "You'd be surprised," she said finally.

Turk knocked on the office window and gestured irritably. Quickly Beth turned off the spigot and began to coil the hose. "I gotta go. He hates it when I keep him waiting."

I left Beth to her work and climbed gratefully into the cool, clean interior of my car. Had Turk really needed her? I wondered. Or had he just not wanted us to talk?

Davey and I spent the afternoon at the beach, building sand forts and splashing in the mild waves of Long Island Sound. Even wearing sunblock, his skin still turned golden. With his blond curls and chubby thighs, he looked like a cherub, racing down the beach to chase a receding wave.

He'd used up so much energy, I knew an early dinner was called for. We grilled hot dogs on the hibachi out back, then toasted marshmallows when the coals died down. Sometimes it's nice just to kick back and be a mother.

I called Aunt Peg while Davey was in the bathtub, rinsing off the last of the sand from every crack and crevice. She listened as I described Barry Turk's operation, then asked several pointed questions about the dogs I'd been shown. I knew she was frustrated at receiving the information secondhand, especially from someone whose knowledge of dogs couldn't begin to rival her own.

"Was there more to the kennel than you were shown?" she asked.

"A whole other room. I looked in, but that was all."

"So Beau could have been there."

"Well yes, but . . ." I dragged a stool over to the counter and sat down. "The whole point is to get Beau bred, isn't it? I can hardly be bowled over by the dog's potential if I don't see him."

"Hmm." Aunt Peg was thinking about that.

I took the opportunity to change the subject, telling her what Turk had said about Randall Tarnower. "Why do all the other handlers seem to hate him?"

"Jealousy, mostly. He's new to the East Coast and hasn't had time yet to pay his dues. Worse still, from their point of view, he's good. Really good. Ever since he got here, he's been beating them at their own game and they don't like it a bit."

"Turk said he steals other handlers' clients."

"That's how Barry Turk sees it, but I'm sure Randy would say there's another side to the story. He's offering a superior product. His trims are better than everybody else's, and he has a wonderful way with a dog. Watching him show his Poodles, you get a sense he really enjoys what he's doing. No doubt his kennel is cleaner than Turk's, too. If you had to choose, where would you go?"

"Not to Barry Turk, that's for sure."

"You see? There it is. Turk says he's stealing clients. From Randy's point of view, he's simply offering better value for the client's money."

When I got off the phone with Aunt Peg, I called and left yet another message on Will Perkins's answering machine. Then I tried Jack Berglund. He was in, and we made an appointment for the end of the week.

Energy restored, Davey was up by six the following morning. I hoped he'd climb into bed with me, but he had other ideas. After two hours of nonstop activity, I put him in the car and headed to camp early. Let someone younger chase him around for a while.

Famous last words. Not only had Emily forgiven me for running out on her the day before, she was thrilled to see me. Both counselors in charge of Davey's group, the Sunfishes, had called in sick. I couldn't turn Emily down two days in a row. Besides, I needed the money.

Try supervising twelve four- and five-year-olds for four hours sometime. It's enough to make you doubt your own sanity. At least at that age the boys and girls don't hate each other. Of course they don't want to play the same games either. Emily helped out when she could, but by one o'clock I felt as though I'd spent the morning going in a dozen different directions at once.

Finally I oversaw the last of the pickups and got Davey back in the car. Still raring to go, he bounced in his seat all the way home. He was angling for another trip to the beach. I was hoping for a nap. Neither of us got our wish.

When we came in the back door, the first thing I saw was the blinking message light on the answering machine. I hit the button, and Aunt Peg's voice filled the room.

"Melanie dear, come over as soon as you get back. Somebody's broken into my house."

⌘ ❀ *Eighteen* ❀ ⌘

The Poodles announced our arrival. Aunt Peg had the front door open before we'd even had time to get out of the car.

"What happened?" I cried as she came down the steps. "Are you all right?"

"I'm fine, just a little shaken."

The herd of Poodles shot past her. By now Davey was used to them. He giggled with delight, found a tennis ball in the yard, and gave it a toss. Bedlam ensued as each of the six Poodles decided it belonged to her.

"Come inside," said Aunt Peg. "Let's get Davey settled, and then I'll tell you everything."

In the kitchen, I saw she'd laid in some supplies. She'd fixed a peanut butter and jelly sandwich for Davey, and beside the plate was a pad of paper and a brand new box of sixty-four crayons. The combination would probably keep him occupied for at least half an hour.

On the counter were tuna fish sandwiches for us. I've never particularly liked tuna, but Aunt Peg serves food the way she does everything else, without options or apologies. We carried our plates into the living room where we'd be out of earshot. The Poodles, ever hopeful, arranged themselves on the floor around us.

"Somebody broke in last night," she said. "It happened

sometime after I spoke with you. I went out with some friends and didn't get in until almost one. I was tired and went straight to bed. It wasn't until this morning that I realized something was wrong."

"What was taken?"

"That's the odd part. As far as I can tell, nothing's missing at all."

I set my sandwich aside on an end table. "Then what makes you think someone was here?"

"For one thing, there's a broken pane of glass in the back door. For another, even though nothing seems to be gone, everything's been just the tiniest bit disturbed. Nothing, from the papers on my desk to the furniture in the living room, is quite exactly where I left it. It's as though someone was searching for something."

"What?"

"I have no idea. You know me, Melanie, I don't wear much jewelry. And it's not as though I'd leave important papers lying around. The most valuable things in the house are the dogs."

"Speaking of the dogs." I reached over and pushed my plate beyond the reach of a particularly inquisitive nose. "Where were they?"

"Right here, just as they always are." Aunt Peg frowned. "All six of them, loose as can be. I suppose that's why I've never worried too much about security before. Of course they're harmless, but the average burglar certainly wouldn't know that."

No, he wouldn't. Besides, though they might be harmless, the crush of Poodles could be intimidating. I'd seen that for myself. They must have made a commotion if someone had come into the house. They'd barked just now when I'd driven in the driveway. It all struck me as very odd.

"What did the police say?"

"I haven't called them."

I stared at her, perplexed. "Why not?"

"Because I didn't want to look like an idiot," Aunt Peg said crisply. "That's why not. With nothing missing, I wasn't at all sure what I was going to say."

"You're going to say you had a break-in. And let them send someone out to have a look."

Back in the kitchen, Davey had finished his peanut butter and jelly and was happily drawing pictures on his new pad. I stood beside Aunt Peg while she made the call, then carried my plate with its unfinished sandwich over to the sink.

"If you're right about the house being searched, then somebody must have been looking for something. What could it have been?"

"I've thought and thought about that," said Aunt Peg. She rescued my sandwich before I could put it down the disposal and set it on the floor. There was a brief flurry of activity among the Poodles at her feet—rather like sharks feeding, I thought—and a moment later the sandwich was gone. "I haven't any idea."

We'd come no nearer to figuring that out when the doorbell rang ten minutes later. The Poodles raced to the front hall. I had to push them aside just to get the door open.

Officer Decker was short and sturdy. I'd have guessed his age at twenty-five, but he had the dour expression of a man much older. He eyed the Poodles without enthusiasm and asked Aunt Peg to put them away before he came in.

When she returned from locking the dogs in the bedroom, he asked enough questions to get the story started, then let Aunt Peg finish it herself. There wasn't much to tell, but Officer Decker seemed neither surprised nor skeptical about what he heard. He followed us through the kitchen to the back door. Davey took one look, hopped down off his chair, and joined the procession.

Aunt Peg showed the officer the broken pane of glass, which he spent only a moment examining. He rattled the flimsy lock in its casing and gave her a stern look. "Not much security here."

"Dogs," she said, returning the look in full measure. "There are six of them in the house. They pretty much do the job."

"They didn't this time, did they?" Decker dusted off his hands and headed back through the house. "I'll make a report for you. But to be perfectly honest, nothing's going to come of it. We're seeing a lot of this type of thing—a quick hit on an empty home. It's kids looking for drug money. They'll go anywhere that looks like an easy target. These aren't sophisticated thieves. I've been to houses where they've walked right by a chest filled with silver. All they're after is cash."

Aunt Peg and I exchanged a look. I knew we were both thinking the same thing. How many kids would consider a house filled with big black dogs an easy hit?

We showed the officer out and got Davey resettled with his crayons.

"What do you think?" I asked when that was done.

"I think I'll have the locksmith out." She headed straight for her bedroom to free the dogs. "Poodles or not, I can see we could use a few sturdy deadbolts around here."

"What about what Officer Decker said? Do you really think it was kids?"

"No." The answer came without hesitation.

"Then someone's been here twice," I said quietly.

"It looks that way." Aunt Peg frowned. "I guess we're going to have to hope that the best defense is a good offense. Find my Poodle, Melanie. Then we'll know who's at the bottom of this."

———

Friday morning I dropped Davey off at camp, then followed Jack Berglund's concise directions northward to the beautiful old New England town of Litchfield. Stately older homes fanned out from the green in the center of town. The surrounding land was filled with farms and estates. I guessed Berglund's house to be in the latter category and was proved correct when I came to the pair of stone gateposts that marked the end of his long gravel driveway.

The house was built of stone as well. Ivy climbed the walls; a large leafy elm shaded the front door. Gravel spun as I rounded the circular drive that looked as though it had been freshly raked that morning. Across a huge expanse of lawn, the kennel building was visible out beyond the pool, the whole place shining with the look of no money spared.

In such a setting, I'd expected a butler, or at least a maid to answer the door, but when it drew open, there was my host himself. He was dressed casually in a button-down shirt with the cuffs rolled back and a pair of well-worn khakis.

"Ms. Travis," he said. "How nice to see you again."

"It's Melanie, please." I wiped my feet before stepping into the circular front hall whose floor was made of Italian tile. At the back was a wide wraparound staircase with a bay window on the upper landing. Lord, it was gorgeous.

"Would you like to have a drink first, some coffee perhaps? Or are you anxious to get on to the dogs?"

"The dogs please. If you don't mind?"

"Not at all." Jack smiled broadly. "Actually I'd have been disappointed if you wanted it any other way."

Even after the house, the kennel managed to hold its own. Though much grander in many ways, the setup was reminiscent of Aunt Peg's. The first room we entered was filled with trophies and show pictures, and I stopped to look and admire.

"Isn't that Crawford Langley?" I asked, surprised to see him handling the Shalimar dogs in virtually every photograph.

"Yes, it is."

Berglund didn't elaborate, and we moved on to the display of trophies. Their dates spanned the last thirty years, highlighting a long, unbroken chain of winners. I congratulated him on his success.

Jack accepted the praise as his due. "I've been breeding since 1962," he said proudly. "I had my first champion in '64. That's her there." He pointed to one of the older photographs. "Champion Shalimar Showgirl, and what a Poodle she was. Most of my present stock traces back to her in one way or another. Come on, I'll introduce you to the gang."

We passed through a grooming room, then on to the actual kennel. Like Aunt Peg's, the Poodles were housed in large pens that opened out into individual runs. Jack whistled shrilly, though it hardly seemed necessary as most of the Poodles had already scrambled inside to greet us.

"You have browns, too," I said, surprised to see that the occupant of one pen was a light russet color rather than the deep, rich black I'd been expecting.

"I do. At one time, I was very interested in the color. Now though, I've gone over to blacks almost entirely. A brown will occasionally pop up in the line, and I have one young bitch that I use for breeding, but that's about it."

We started at one end of the room and worked our way around, going from pen to pen. Berglund paused at each, giving the show statistics and pedigree, from memory, of every Poodle we visited. He truly seemed to love the dogs, and they were equally delighted to see him.

Aunt Peg had warned me about Jack Berglund, but seeing him with his Poodles, I realized she couldn't possibly have known him well. He felt every bit as strongly about his dogs as she did about hers. In other circumstances, they certainly could have been friends.

The first block we passed were the old campaigners. Eight champion Poodles in a row, all cut down and past their prime, but still glorious nonetheless. Of those, two were dogs, but it wasn't hard to tell from their advanced ages that neither one was Beau.

The other side of the room contained the current show stock. There, many of the pens were empty. Only three bitches and a young male puppy were presently in hair. Nothing of interest there either.

"I see you keep mostly bitches," I commented.

Jack nodded. "I don't believe in keeping a dog to offer at stud unless he truly has something special to offer the breed. Ranger is the first stud dog I've had in several years. I think he fits that bill."

After a buildup like that, I couldn't wait to see the Poodle. I pushed on ahead impatiently to the last pen in the row.

"That's him," Jack said with a smile. He unlatched the door and freed the Poodle into the aisle. "Shalimar Showdown. I think you're going to like him."

I was certainly prepared to. That's probably why I felt so let down. At first glance, the dog wasn't terribly exciting. He seemed to be fairly well made, but without any of the spark or fire I'd been prepared to expect. He wasn't a bad Poodle, just an ordinary one. Still, it wouldn't hurt to have a closer look.

"Can we take him outside so I can see him move?"

"Of course." Berglund produced a leash from deep within his pocket, formed a loop, and slipped it over the Poodle's head and behind his ears. As the other dogs barked their protest at being left behind, he opened the back door and led Ranger outside. "Wait until you see him in motion. I haven't seen anything prettier in a long time."

Jack trotted the Poodle across the lawn. The first time out and back was enough for me to see that he was narrow behind and cow-hocked besides. A nice-enough Poodle, but not the one I was looking for. Berglund brought Ranger to a dramatic stop and baited him with a squeaky toy to show off his alert expression.

"He's very nice," I said politely.

"I knew you'd like him. You're one of the first people who's seen him, and I'm delighted to be getting his stud career off to a good start."

Good start? *What* start? Not with my bitch.

But I seemed to be the only one who realized that. Jack chucked Ranger under the chin and the dog leapt up into the air. Together, they spun around in the lush grass, playing with the squeaky and dancing a dance of anticipation. The two of them looked so happy that my first impulse was to find a bitch, any bitch, and go through with the mating. My second was a bit more rational. I'd have to find a way to let him down gently.

I waited outside and enjoyed the view while Jack took Ranger back into the kennel. "How about if we go in and have something to drink now?" he said when he emerged.

"Sure. That sounds nice."

"I'm sure you'll want a copy of Ranger's pedigree to take with you. I have some in my files."

Inside the house, Berglund poured each of us a glass of chilled Chablis, then ushered me into the beautifully understated room he called his office. A Bokhara rug covered the center of the hardwood floor, and a dark cherry roll top desk dominated one wall. There were shelves of leatherbound books, a heavy Travertine marble coffee table, and two overstuffed leather chairs. Berglund motioned for me to have a seat.

He opened a file cabinet behind the desk and pulled out a folder, then came around and emptied the contents onto the table. Pictures, pedigrees, and AKC registration slips spilled out.

"Some day I'm going to have to find a better system," he said, sorting through the papers. "Ah, here it is." He came up with a sheaf of pedigrees bound together by a large clip, peeled one off the top, and handed it over.

The leather chair was plush. The wine was a fine dry California white. I wasn't in any hurry to move on. Idly I skimmed through the document. Nearly all of Ranger's ancestors were printed in red, an honor accorded to those dogs which have finished their championships. Sprinkled among the listings were several Canadian champions, one from Mexico, and one from Sweden. No doubt it was an excellent pedigree.

Looking incongruous among all the red was the black entry for Ranger's untitled dam, Shalimar Solitaire. There were all sorts of reasons why a dog might not finish its championship. I sipped at my wine and made conversation by asking what hers was.

"Solitaire was a pretty bitch," said Jack. "But unfortunately she was only shown once. I could see she was going to be a late bloomer, so I let her have an early litter. That's where Ranger came from.

"Six months after the puppies were born, she was ready. Crawford Langley was showing my dogs at the time, and he had another bitch ahead of her. While she was waiting her turn, I took her to a small show nearby for experience. I'd never taken a dog in the ring before, but she went Best Of Winners, and believe me, I was thrilled."

He paused for a drink that drained a third of his glass. "Two weeks later she got out of her run and was killed by a car on the road out front. It's too bad. She was a nice bitch who deserved better. I'm glad I'm finally getting the chance to do right by her son."

I folded the pedigree and slipped it into my purse. No

way was I going to tell him that the Poodle he obviously adored just wasn't the right one for me. At least not now. I had another sip of wine instead. Its smooth dry taste didn't assuage my guilt in the slightest.

⌘✻ *Nineteen* ✻⌘

As silly as it seems, when I started this project I'd thought of it as a few weeks' diversion during what promised to be a dull summer. Now it was August, and if there'd been one dull moment so far, I'd have liked to have known when it was.

On the plus side, Davey was doing great at camp and I was making enough money, if barely, to keep our heads above water. I was learning about Poodles and dog shows and enjoying my education. The Volvo was still holding its own and last, but certainly not least, Bradley Watermain had left a message on my answering machine saying he'd made a big mistake.

With all that going on you'd think I wouldn't have much to complain about, but I did. In the first place, Aunt Rose wasn't speaking to me and I was none too pleased with her. In the second, there was Sam Driver, who was making his presence felt among the coterie of northeast Poodle breeders. That didn't bother me at all. But at the oddest moments I found him floating around the periphery of my imagination. That did.

And then there was Beau. If we were any closer now to finding the dog than we had been in June, I wasn't aware of it. In fact if it weren't for the recent break-in at Aunt

Peg's, I would have been tempted to decide that we were going about things all wrong.

It's a sad state of affairs when it takes something like a burglary to cheer you up and let you know you're moving in the right direction.

So that's the frame of mind I was in when Sam called. He'd been to some shows and thought that the three of us should get together and discuss what, if anything, we'd learned. Obviously the man had never heard of a conference call. But Aunt Peg was all for the idea, so who was I to complain?

We picked a time in the early evening when Sam was finished working for the day and Joanie's services were available. The more I thought about the idea, the better I liked it. It wasn't that I didn't trust Sam; just that I didn't want to follow Aunt Peg's example and leap into an unquestioning endorsement based on good looks and an agreeable personality. After all, I'd seen pictures of Ted Bundy. He'd fooled a lot of women in his day, too.

Aunt Peg had said that a man who had something to hide would hardly be likely to invite us to his house. But that made me wonder, too. Because if I wanted to appear innocent, that's exactly what I'd do. By issuing the invitation, he would control the visit since anything he didn't want us to see would be tucked neatly out of sight.

Or maybe I was overanalyzing.

Maybe I didn't want to spend several hours with a man who put all my senses on red alert.

Or maybe I did, and that was precisely the problem.

I was thirty and a mother with the stretch marks and sweat pants to prove it. I was under employed and my car had last been new when I was in college. Which is not to say that I had nothing to offer a man. Just that someone a little easier than Sam Driver would have been nice. After all, I'd never particularly considered Bradley Watermain a challenge and look what happened there.

Or maybe I was overanalyzing.

Sam's house was in Redding, a community just far enough beyond easy commuting distance to New York to have escaped the hustle and bustle that characterizes much of Fairfield County. The open land was beautiful; the town itself, unapologetically tiny. Sam's mailbox was made of battered red metal. It sat at the end of his driveway on the stump of a small tree.

The driveway itself was unpaved and climbed sharply upward through the trees. It was going to be the devil to plow when winter came. I've lived in Connecticut all my life; I think of things like that.

But oh, when I reached the house, the view was worth it. Built of weathered shingles and big windows, it perched on the side of the hill and looked out over a panorama of gorgeous New England countryside. The car parked next to the garage was a four-wheel drive. So at least he was prepared.

I'd aimed to be a few minutes late, but still I seemed to have beaten Aunt Peg. When Sam let me in, he told me why.

"She called half an hour ago. Something came up and she isn't going to be able to make it. She asked me to give you her apologies."

Apologies, my foot. "What came up?"

"I don't know, she didn't say." Sam saw the look on my face. "Is something wrong?"

"She set us up."

"Excuse me?"

"You and me," I told him. "She set us up."

"To do what?"

I threw up my hands. The gesture was as eloquent as any comment I might have made.

Sam peered around behind me. "Where's your son? I thought you'd bring him with you."

"Aunt Peg asked me to get a baby-sitter. So we could concentrate better, she said."

Finally he began to realize what was happening. Sam looked somewhat bemused. "We've been had, haven't we?"

I nodded.

"Well, that doesn't have to stop us from putting the evening to good use. Come on in and let's compare notes. I've spoken to a few people, and I'd like to get your input."

The living room had a high ceiling where a fan turned lazily, stirring up just enough of a breeze. A Palladian window in the south wall made the most of the view. The room was furnished in muted shades of peach and hunter green. A faded Persian carpet covered the middle of the floor. Two chintz-covered love seats flanked a brass-screened fireplace.

A Standard Poodle, more gray than black, was draped languidly across one of the love seats. As we entered, she opened her eyes and wagged her tail in greeting, but didn't get up.

"This is Charm," Sam introduced me as I took a seat opposite. He settled himself carefully on the cushion, and she lifted her head just enough for him to slide his lap underneath. "She's fifteen, which is ancient for a dog this size. She runs the place and always has."

Charm's tail thumped up and down in acknowledgment.

"Is she related to Casey?"

"Great-grandmother. Actually they have a good many traits in common. That's one of the reasons I'm so fond of Casey." His fingers massaged behind the Poodle's ears, and she leaned into the caress. "One day she's going to have to replace Charm around here. It won't be an easy job to fill."

First Jack Berglund, now Sam Driver. Obviously there

was something about seeing men with their dogs that placed them in the best light. If Aunt Peg had been here, she'd have been drooling. It was time to get down to business.

Sam was happy to lead off in sharing the information he had gathered. Maybe that was because he didn't have much. Like me when I was starting out, he'd already been referred right back to Aunt Peg more times than he liked to think about. But beyond that he'd also managed to meet Will Perkins and make an appointment to see his dogs the following week. When my turn came, I was torn. For all of Aunt Peg's trust, I simply couldn't see the point in revealing everything I'd done. In the end, I settled for giving him heavily edited versions of my visits to Barry Turk and Jack Berglund's kennels and let him draw his own conclusions.

As we spoke, the light outside faded. By the time I'd finished telling him about Ranger, the living room was almost completely dark. While I'd been speaking, Sam had sat forward in his seat, fingers tangled absentmindedly in Charm's topknot, but his gaze and his focus centered solely on me. Now as I wrapped up the story, he put Charm gently aside, got up, and turned on some lights.

"Gut feeling," he said. "You've met most of the people now. You've been to some of their kennels. Where's the dog? Who else wanted him—or needed him—that badly?"

"I don't know. In the beginning, it all seemed so straightforward. But now . . ."

"You're beginning to doubt that you'll ever find him."

"Yes." If Aunt Peg had been sitting there, I'm not sure I'd have admitted that. With Sam, it came easier. "I keep wondering if there are things I should be noticing, clues I've overlooked. So much about these dogs shows seems foreign to me. Aunt Peg's taught me a lot, and I know I'm picking up stuff on my own, but at times it still seems like I could be fooled pretty easily."

Sam strolled into the kitchen, nudging aside the louvered partition so he could continue to hear. He opened the refrigerator and pulled out a couple of beers.

"At one of the first shows I went to, I saw a Poodle in the ring that I thought was magnificent. He had a huge, profuse coat that was really eye-catching, and I couldn't understand why he didn't win. Then later after the judging, I was back in the grooming tent and I saw his handler removing pieces of hair from the dog. It wasn't his own, it was all a fake."

"Switches," said Sam. He brought in the cans and handed one over. "That's what those hairpieces are called. People make them from the coats of other dogs they've cut down."

If Sam had offered me a drink, I probably would have refused. But my throat was dry after all the talking I'd been doing and the thought of an ice-cold beer seemed just about perfect. I popped the top and took a long swallow. "Is that allowed?"

"Not at all. According to A.K.C. rules, it's totally illegal. But so are half the other tricks that people use, from coloring the dogs to changing their pigment. Bathing, trimming, plucking, clipping, things like that are acceptable. Any artificial additives are not. But when was the last time you saw a Poodle walk into the ring without hair spray?"

"But if it's all illegal, why do people do it?"

"Because they want to win." While he spoke, Sam never stopped moving. Now he was out on the deck that opened off the living room, fiddling with a gas grill. "In the beginning, everyone's a purist. Usually they get started in the sport because they truly love their dogs and want to show them off. But then other people whose dogs aren't any better keep beating them, and they decide that the way to win is to play the game."

He passed through the living room on the way to the kitchen. I stood up and went after him. "What are you doing?"

"Cooking." Sam opened the refrigerator and pulled out a shrink-wrapped package. "Chicken okay?"

"Fine," I said. "But I'm not staying."

He tossed the package onto the counter and went after the makings for a salad. "You're hungry, aren't you?"

"Well . . . yes."

"See?" He came up with two tomatoes and a head of lettuce, then nudged the refrigerator door shut with his hip. "You're hungry, I'm hungry, it's dinnertime. You have to admit there's a certain logic there."

"Aunt Peg set us up," I mentioned again.

"You told me." Now he was shredding lettuce into a colander. I'd never seen a man that was so at home in the kitchen. Bob could barely make his own coffee. "Don't worry, once the grill gets going, it's a quick meal. Do you need to call your sitter?"

"No." Joanie would cope. Probably better than I was, I reflected. "The least I can do is help."

"Cutting board," he said, pointing. "Knife. The tomatoes are all yours."

The tomatoes were plump, dark red, and beautifully ripe. Produce like this never passed through my super-market. "If these are from your garden, I'm leaving."

"Nope." Sam arranged the chicken breasts on a plate and poured a marinade over them. "A farmer near town sets up a stand by the side of the road."

Thank God for that. I watched as he carried the chicken out to the grill. It was heartening to know he wasn't perfect.

Since it seemed to have come about that I was staying

for dinner, I finished putting the salad together while Sam was grilling the chicken. We ate at a small glass-topped table outside on the deck. The moon was huge above us and there was a bowl filled with peonies in the center of the table.

Charm stirred enough to get herself outside, and Sam made the trip well worth it, surreptitiously slipping her pieces of chicken under the table when he thought I wasn't looking. At first we talked mostly about dogs, but then the conversation shifted. I found out that Sam had recently gone into business for himself, designing interactive software. He told me he'd grown up in the East, but school and jobs had taken him to Michigan. Now he was happy to be back.

In return, I regaled him with thrilling tidbits from the life of a Connecticut schoolteacher and single parent. That took about thirty seconds. Then he asked about Davey and managed not to look bored when I went on a bit. Maybe he was a good actor.

Sam didn't inquire about Bob at all. The omission pleased me.

When we finally brought our plates back into the kitchen, Sam took over the scraping and rinsing, carefully setting the leftovers aside. "Where are the rest of your Poodles?" I asked as he opened a cupboard and got out a stack of five stainless steel bowls.

"My office is downstairs, and I've got some crates down there, too. I figured they'd be just as well off sleeping through our meeting. They're show dogs, don't forget. When they're up here, they want to be the center of attention."

"You only have bitches, right?"

"Right." He half-smiled. "Would you like to see them? Maybe count noses or check for testicles?"

I hadn't realized my thoughts were so transparent. "If

you did have Beau, Sam, I doubt that he'd be here to-night."

"Quite right. But since I keep only bitches, unless I bought a dog legitimately I'd have an awfully hard time explaining where he came from, wouldn't I?"

"I don't know. You seem pretty clever to me. I imagine you could figure something out."

All right, so I was being mean. I admit it. Sam had fed me, entertained me, and how was I repaying his kindness? By treating him like a suspect.

"Your aunt trusts me," said Sam.

"Yes, I know."

"Then why don't you?"

Because it scared the hell out of me, I thought. Because I'd trusted Bob and look at where it got me. Obviously I was a lousy judge of character when it came to men. It would be one thing if I only had myself to worry about. But I didn't; I had Davey. I simply couldn't afford to make any mistakes.

"Maybe I don't know you well enough," I said. Though it was the truth, it came out sounding disgustingly like a come-on.

"We can do something about that."

Were we reciting dialogue out of a bad movie or what? That was enough for me. Using the sitter as an excuse, I cut and ran. I got out of there so fast there was barely time to give Charm a pat and say thanks for dinner. Sam stood in the doorway and watched me drive away.

I knew because I looked back.

It wasn't until later that night when I was lying in bed that something occurred to me. For some reason, I was having trouble falling asleep. After I'd pummeled the pillow into a ball for the sixth or seventh time, I remembered what Sam had said about the company he'd worked for having its home office in Detroit.

Detroit was just a short hop across the lake from Ontario.

Ontario, Canada, that is.

Now that was interesting, wasn't it?

⮞❋ *Twenty* ❋⮜

The next time I saw Aunt Peg, Davey was at camp and she was blow-drying a Poodle. It's the sort of thing you have to see to believe. She'd entered her puppy Lulu in a show that weekend, which meant that the preparations had started on Wednesday. The face, the feet, and the base of the tail had to be clipped, the ears cleaned, the toenails shortened.

Friday was bath day. Aunt Peg had a separate room in the kennel where a tub with special hoses had been built at waist height. Even though Lulu was only seven months old, she seemed to know the drill and stood quietly for a shampoo and cream rinse.

Then they moved on to the grooming table for the blow-dry. The objective, Aunt Peg explained, was to take that huge mass of naturally curly hair and dry it so that it was perfectly straight. I understood the theory: I'd been doing it to my own hair for years. What I didn't understand was why one had to do that to a dog.

"It's the only way to get that really thick, plush look," said Aunt Peg. "Otherwise the hair will never stand up."

She wheeled over her dryer which stood as high as my shoulders and looked capable of blowing pictures off the walls at twenty paces. Lulu was unfazed. As Aunt Peg directed the hard stream of hot air and began to brush, she lay down on the table and went to sleep.

"I want to hear all about your meeting with Sam," said Peg. "But first you have to guess who was here yesterday."

I hate to guess. I never do it. I waited, but Aunt Peg held firm. "The Fuller Brush man?" I said finally.

"You're no fun. No, Frank."

"Frank, my brother?"

"Of course, your brother. Who else would I be talking about?" She finished blow-drying the short hair in front of the tail and began to move up along the back toward the neck. "He dropped by to see how I was doing."

I was surprised but also pleased. My brother wasn't known for his thoughtfulness. Then again, maybe he'd reconsidered his skepticism about Aunt Peg's Poodle business. Frank could smell financial gain a mile away, especially if he thought he might somehow get in on it.

"Of course I told him that the police had been here. He was very concerned."

"So am I," I said. "You're the only one who isn't worried."

"I'm realistic," Peg said firmly. "There's a difference. Anyway, Frank said that if being here now all alone made me uncomfortable, I could certainly come and stay with him."

"In his apartment?" The thought made me laugh. "Aunt Peg, have you ever been there?"

She shook her head. "Where does he live?"

"A one bedroom in Cos Cob. He's got a yuppie couple upstairs and a garbage man next door. It's a very democratic building. Frank's place is a typical bachelor pad— cable TV and nothing in the refrigerator. And there's no yard for the dogs."

"I didn't get the impression they were invited."

I was laughing aloud now. "Did he simply think you'd leave them behind?"

"I don't think he thought at all. When I declined the offer, he had the temerity to suggest that perhaps, at my advanced age, I might not know what was best for myself."

"I suppose you let him have it with both barrels?"

"I was tempted." Aunt Peg grinned. "But he meant well. And besides, if the boy's a little short on tact, I'm afraid I know which side of the family he gets it from." She'd finished drying a wide strip up the middle of Lulu's back and neck. Shifting the puppy around, she went on to topknot and ears. "Now then, tell me what Sam had to say."

Because I knew how badly she wanted details, I glossed over the meeting, offering only highlights. I thought of it as self-defense. If I'd given her the satisfaction of knowing her plan had succeeded, who knew what she might try next?

I did mention what I'd learned about his having worked in Detroit. Aunt Peg dismissed the information with a wave. I wasn't that ready to count him out.

"I wonder where Sam was the evening your house got broken into," I said.

"Don't be ridiculous. What on earth could he have been looking for here?"

"We don't know, do we? That's precisely the point. I didn't mention it to Sam the other night. Now I wish I'd thought to. It would have been interesting to see what kind of a reaction I'd get."

"None at all," Peg said calmly. "Sam knows all about it. I told him myself."

"Aunt Peg, you've got to stop telling him everything!"

"How do you expect him to help us if he doesn't have all the facts?"

"That's just it," I said. "I'm not sure I do."

At quarter to one I left Peg to her blow-drying and drove over to Davey's camp. Emily does her best, and some days pickup goes smoothly; but on others, it's chaos. Picture fifty campers and as many parents. Fifty backpacks, fifty wet bathing suits . . . well, you begin to get the picture.

I knew as soon as I arrived that this was not going to be one of the good days. The line of cars stretched all the way down the driveway and out to the street. I pulled out of line, parked over by the curb, and walked in to see what I could do to help.

"Melanie, thank god!" Emily grabbed me as soon as I came within view. "Have you got a few minutes?"

"As long as you need."

"What I need is twenty extra pairs of hands. Not to mention a bucket of cold cream."

"Cold cream?"

"We were putting on a skit today—you know, the older kids entertaining the younger ones? It seemed like a great idea. The theme was the first Thanksgiving—I know it's August, don't even ask. Anyway, all the kids wanted to be Indians. While I was trying to drum up a few more Pilgrims, someone went a little wild with the war paint."

"I don't think the Indians would have worn war paint to Thanksgiving dinner."

"Don't be literal with me, Melanie. I'm warning you."

I wanted to laugh but didn't dare. As the story unfolded, we were hurrying back to the communal locker rooms where the kids stashed their things and grouped before leaving. Inside, it looked even worse than she'd warned. Red grease paint, applied liberally, has a very dramatic effect. The counselors were scrubbing vigorously, faces and walls alike.

"We were going to just send the kids home with the makeup on," said Emily. "But then the first two mothers saw their children and began to scream. I guess they thought it was blood. It's been all downhill from there."

I spotted Davey almost immediately. He'd gotten into the paint along with everybody else and seemed delighted by the effect. A mother's eye told me his yellow shirt would never be the same, and there were streaks of green in his hair. He was playing happily with a blond girl whose name I seemed to remember was Jennifer Reavis. For the time being, I left him where he was and went to work on those who needed me more.

Within fifteen minutes the chaos had begun to subside. After twenty-five, we were clearly heading toward normalcy. I knew my time was up when Jennifer's mother appeared. Once his source of entertainment went home, Davey would be ready to do the same.

Jennifer was one of those pristine little girls to whom dirt doesn't seem to stick. Nor war paint either, apparently. Her mother had dressed her for camp in pink shorts, a white tee shirt, and white frilly anklets to wear with her sneakers. Amazingly, the entire outfit was still intact. On Davey, everything would have been gray, not to mention streaked with green and red.

Janet Reavis gazed at our two children with a smile. No doubt she was heaving a mental sigh of relief over which one was hers. Then she came over and introduced herself. "You're Davey's mom, right? Jennifer has told me all about you. You're the one who has the Poodles."

"Almost," I said, knowing Davey had to be the source of the misinformation. Sometimes his stories got a bit carried away. "My aunt is the one who has the Poodles. Standards actually, the big ones."

"Perfect," said Janet. "That's just what we're looking for. I hear they're great dogs. My pediatrician said that even kids with allergies can have them. I've been meaning to call you. Do you have time to talk now?"

I looked around. The room had all but cleared out. "Sure."

"Jennifer's been dying to get a puppy, and I started looking around a couple of weeks ago. I wanted to do it right. You know all that stuff you hear about how bad it is to buy from a pet store, that you should get your puppy from a breeder? Well, a friend of mine knew about a Poodle breeder who lives up north of here. I called, and he said he did have a litter of puppies, so I made an appointment to go have a look.

"Jennifer was all excited, and frankly so was I. But after an hour and a half drive, when we got there the man was just leaving. He'd had a fight between two stud dogs and had to rush to the vet. There was nothing for us to do but come back home. Jennifer was crushed. Of course he called back later and apologized, and he's invited us to come back again, but I'd really rather find something closer if I can."

"You should talk to my Aunt Peg," I said. "I know she had a litter in May. I'm not sure whether all the puppies are spoken for, but even if they are, she could probably refer you to someone else."

I found an old shopping list in my purse and wrote Aunt Peg's name and phone number on the back. As I saw Janet and her daughter out, Emily came walking back in.

"Just Jennifer and Davey, and then that's all of them." She flopped down onto a bench, lay on the hard seat, and closed her eyes. "My god, I thought this morning would never end."

"Serves you right, turning kids loose with grease paint like that."

"The counselors were supposed to be in charge."

"The counselors are fifteen and sixteen. They're the kids I mean."

Emily opened one eye. "Talk about poor judgment. I should be disbarred."

"From child care? Don't bet on it. Nobody else wants the job."

"I know." Emily sighed. "Sad, isn't it? Even the kids who are working for me just figure they're passing time and making some money. They all want to grow up to be lawyers or rock stars. Teaching? No way."

"We're a dying breed."

"An underpaid, underappreciated, undervalued, dying breed."

I sank down beside her. "God, now I'm depressed."

"Welcome to the club," said Emily.

"Look, Mommy!" cried Davey.

I turned around to find he'd written his name on the wall. In grease paint. In triplicate.

I searched hard, but finally found a bright side.

At least he's not illiterate.

People who show dogs travel a lot. Every week of the year except Christmas there are dog shows somewhere, usually clustered together in groups of two or more. The northeastern states are a virtual cornucopia of opportunity; and on any given weekend, there are decisions to be made. Where are the best judges? Which shows are most likely to draw the points? What are the facilities like?

In June and July there'd been lots of shows in Connecticut. Now things were beginning to move a bit farther afield. Aunt Peg thought nothing of driving to Cape Cod or Maryland if the judges suited her. So when she told me she'd entered five days on the Saratoga circuit in northern New York state, I wasn't terribly surprised.

"Who takes care of the dogs you leave behind?" I asked.

"I'm getting to that. In fact that's why I called."

Oh.

"You see in the past, Max and I have always taken turns. It's not like I could board them in a kennel. They *are* a kennel. I guess I could find somebody to come in, but you know it takes time to find just the right person."

Why did I suddenly feel the fickle finger of fate pointing my way?

"So I was wondering if perhaps you could do me this little favor?"

When Aunt Peg lowered the boom, she didn't mess around. Nor did she take no for an answer. Which is how Davey and I came to find ourselves living in Greenwich for a week.

Davey, of course, was delighted by the adventure. Aunt Peg's house was a child's delight, filled with nooks and crannies just waiting to be explored. When he had a friend over on Thursday after camp, their game of hide-and-seek lasted most of the afternoon. The fact that the action was supervised by a herd of Standard Poodles only added to the excitement.

As to the Poodles themselves, they seemed to be faring pretty well. With regard to my contention that I'd never even had one pet much less a dozen, Aunt Peg had left behind copious lists of instructions, complete with diagrams and arrows pasted onto the cupboards. Coat care wasn't required, thankfully; only feeding, cleaning up, and general in and out.

In no time at all I had the routine down pat. The Poodles were smart enough to make the adjustment easily. Aside from a constant need for human companionship, they pretty much took care of themselves. After a day or so I'd sorted out the different personalities and found myself growing rather fond of the group.

None of which I had any intention of telling Aunt Peg. As far as I was concerned, she owed me big time.

Friday morning I'd dropped Davey at camp and was

just returning from a stock-up trip to the supermarket when the telephone rang. I'd been taking messages all week. The pad and pencil were sitting on the counter ready.

"Hello?" said a voice when I picked up the phone. "Is this Margaret Turnbull?"

"No, she's not here. Can I take a message?"

"It's very important that I speak with her. Urgent, actually. Do you know where I can reach her?"

"She's gone to Saratoga for the weekend—"

"Damn! I was hoping she'd chosen the New Jersey shows. I need to talk to her about her husband—"

"What about Max?"

There was silence on the other end of the line.

"Look," I said quickly. "I'm Margaret Turnbull's niece. I'm sure I can help you. Who is this I'm talking to, please?"

I could sense his indecision and sweated out a long moment before he finally said, "My name is Randy Tarnower. I'm—"

"I know who you are. I've seen you at the shows." To hell with my cover. If Tarnower had information about Max, I wanted to know what it was.

Then he told me and I nearly fell off my stool.

"Your uncle," he said. "I think he was murdered."

⊷❋ *Twenty-one* ❋⊶

I'd never known before that it was possible to feel both hot and cold at the same time. Simba, sensing my distress, came over and pressed a wet nose into my hand.

"Hello? Are you there? Maybe I'd better wait for Peg—"

"No!" I cleared my throat and got the quaver out of my voice. He'd said that his information was urgent. Aunt Peg wouldn't be back until after the weekend. The earliest I could reach her would be tonight. Even then, she'd be six hours away.

"Please," I said, "talk to me. I want to hear about Max's death."

"I don't want to do this over the phone."

"I'll come to you," I decided quickly. "Just give me directions."

He lived, I discovered, forty miles beyond Newark. Midday, if I didn't hit traffic on the George Washington Bridge, I could make the trip in an hour and a half. I told him I'd be there as soon as I could and set about making arrangements for Davey. Joey Brickman's mom, Alice, was home on the first try. She and I have saved each other often enough in the past that she didn't even ask any questions.

"Take all the time you need," she said, probably imagining a midday tryst in the city. "When you get back, you know where he'll be."

That cleared away one problem. Another presented itself as I was rushing around dog-proofing the house before leaving. This time when the phone rang, it was Sam Driver. He'd been trying for Aunt Peg. It took him a startled moment to realize he had me.

"I've been to see Will Perkins," he said.

"Good. I'd love to hear all about it. Just not now, okay?"

"You're in a hurry?"

"One foot out the door."

"When will you be back?"

There was just the briefest flash of something—intuition maybe—and I almost asked him to come with me. But I didn't and then the chance was gone. Instead I told him Peg was away for the whole weekend and that I was off to Randall Tarnower's and expected to be back by mid-afternoon.

There was construction on the George—of course I *would* pick the lower level—so I made up for the time I lost by speeding on the New Jersey Turnpike. Nobody noticed. It's a road where seventy is considered base speed and eighty is required for passing. By the time I reached Tarnower's, the Volvo had blown clean all its cylinders and was chugging along nicely.

His kennel was set in the midst of farm country. Open land, tall corn, and herds of black-and-white cows filled the eye. I felt as though I stepped back a hundred years in time. The impression was reinforced by the small tidy stone house set up close to the road, with neat cream-colored shutters and window boxes filled with impatiens. There was a big red barn out back and an array of large paddocks bounded by dog-proof fencing.

The whole place looked neat, well kept, and modestly prosperous. Someone here was paying attention to details. It was probably that same skill that had Tarnower's Poodles winning so much in the ring.

I knocked on the front door and heard the usual cacophony within. A moment later a slender brunette dressed in cut-offs and a tee shirt drew the door open just a bit. She brushed a fall of long hair back out of her face and wedged herself into the crack so that none of the dogs who crowded behind her legs could escape. I'd seen her at some of the shows, brushing out, spraying up, and ferrying dogs to Tarnower at the ring. The number one assistant.

"Hi, can I help you?"

"Yes, I'm here to see Randy Tarnower. He's expecting me."

"Sure." She smiled easily. "Randy's back in the barn working on his specials dog. I'll show you the way." She slithered through the small space and shut the door firmly behind her. "I'm Kim. Sorry, I don't know your name?"

"Melanie Travis."

"Nice to meet you," said Kim, heading off around the house. "I'm glad you're here. Randy's been all over the place today. I mean, he's usually jazzed before a weekend, but this morning it's been wild. I got two Toys and a Mini bathed, but then I had to have a break, you know what I mean?"

I nodded, but it was hardly required. She simply kept talking. "Randy's a perfectionist. He works himself and everyone else around the clock. And then he has these moods. It can drive you nuts, let me tell you. Before I got here, he went through assistants like crazy."

"Is the kennel in the barn?" I asked. That's the direction we were heading.

"The barn *is* the kennel. We converted the whole thing. It's pretty great. Wait til you see." Kim, it seemed, was happy to expound on almost any subject. She pulled the door open and we went inside.

Pretty great was an understatement. Big rooms, lots of light, and what by now I'd come to think of as the usual accompaniment: barking dogs.

"Randy! Your visitor's here!"

There was no response, but Kim didn't seem to expect one. Somewhere, deep within the barn, music was playing. Glenn Miller's "In the Mood." We walked through the empty office area into a second room filled with grooming tables and pens. Every available surface held a Poodle, all of them up now and barking at us.

"Quiet!" Kim yelled in a voice louder than seemed possible from so slender a frame. Miraculously, the noise ceased. "He's got to be around here somewhere. Probably next door in the grooming room. Come on."

The Poodles all eyed me with curiosity. They danced on their tables and hopped up and down in their pens. I was fascinated by the fact that although none were tied, they all stayed where they'd been left. I wondered if Randall Tarnower could be interested in a career in child care, preferably in Fairfield County.

"Aha!" said Kim, striding through the doorway. "Hey Boom, what's the matter?"

I followed her into the next room. It held two bathtubs, four grooming tables, and a whole wall full of supplies. On one of the tables stood a large, very hairy, Standard Poodle. Though the dogs in the first room had been excited by my presence, this Poodle was clearly agitated before we even arrived. He was pacing back and forth on the rubber-topped surface and whining audibly.

"That's Boomer, our specials dog," said Kim. She quickly crossed the room to his side. "What's the matter, boy? You're okay."

With Kim, like so many of the dog people I'd met, the crooning just seemed to come naturally. Boomer pricked his ears in response but didn't calm down. When she placed both her hands on his front puffs and pulled forward, he lay down as she'd asked him to. But the moment she released his legs, he sprang back up, still whining.

"Sorry," Kim apologized. "I think everybody's wired today. Why don't you stay here and I'll see if Randy's out back in the pens. I know he was expecting you, and with Boomer on the table, he wouldn't have gone far."

As it turned out, she was right. He'd gone almost nowhere at all. Passing an open closet door on her way out of the room, Kim reached automatically to shut it. Then stopped.

"Oh," she said, and I heard the horror in her voice. "Oh no."

Hands over her mouth, Kim was backing quickly away. I skirted around the table to have a look. I shouldn't have, but I did. It was one of those scenes that in the space of seconds etches itself within memory forever.

It was a big, walk-in closet, and Randall Tarnower was lying on the floor. For the briefest of moments I thought he had spilled something and slipped. Then I realized that the thick dark pool on the linoleum underneath him was blood. Tarnower's blood. His eyes were open, the pupils opaque. He'd fallen on his side, and I could see his back. The handle of a pair of grooming shears protruded from between his shoulder blades.

The mind is an interesting thing. Stressed, it processes that which it has to deal with and filters out the rest. It took me a while to realize that someone was screaming. For a moment, I thought it was me. Then Boomer joined in, his howl raising the noise level another notch, and I realized it was Kim.

Well, you couldn't blame her. But we had to think of something better to do than stand around and scream.

"Where's the phone?" I asked.

Kim gestured into the closet. It was a sure bet neither one of us was going in after it.

"Besides that one."

"In the office." The screaming had stopped; now she was hiccuping. "He's dead, isn't he?"

"I think so." I didn't see how he could look that bad if he wasn't. I guess I should have felt for a pulse; but this was the first dead body I'd seen. I wasn't about to go any nearer.

"Go call 911," I said. "And try not to touch anything."

Kim hurried out the side door as the back one opened. Her screaming had summoned another assistant. A chunky young man in his early twenties called out Randy's name, then stopped dead at the sight of feet protruding out of the closet.

"I don't think you want to come in," I said. "There's been . . . an accident." All right, so that wasn't strictly accurate. I wasn't about to go into details.

"Who the hell are you? Where's Randy? Where's Kim?"

I ignored the first two questions and answered the last. "She's gone to the office to call the police."

Behind me, Boomer began to growl. His agitation had been growing by leaps and bounds. Now he was pacing like a caged panther. "Can you take him out of here?"

The assistant nodded. As he sidled past the closet, he had a good look inside. What he saw made him run to the nearest bathtub and throw up. He couldn't say he hadn't been warned.

"Damn," he said when he was once more upright. "The Japanese scissors." He hopped Boomer off the table and left. I followed him out and shut the door behind us.

I found Kim in the office. She was slumped in the corner of a tattered couch, pale and sobbing.

"Who else was here this morning beside you and Randy?" I asked.

She looked up, thought for a moment. "Just Ben."

"He's the other assistant?"

"Yes."

"No other visitors? Deliveries?"

"No."

"Phone calls?"

Kim lifted her shoulders in a shrug. "This place is like Grand Central Station. The phone rings all the time. Sometimes I pick up, sometimes Randy does. I don't really pay attention."

"But you knew that I was coming this morning?"

"Yeah, Randy said so."

"Was he expecting anyone else?"

"Not that I know of."

"Would he have mentioned it if he was?"

She thought again. "I guess. I mean, he told me about you."

"Do you know what he wanted to see me about?"

Kim shook her head and lapsed into silence. I could hear sirens in the distance. The police were on the way. Maybe their questions would shed some more light. All I knew was that Randy Tarnower had had something important he wanted to tell me about Max's death. Something urgent, he'd said.

And someone had stopped him before he'd been able to.

The police and paramedics arrived in a flurry of flashing lights and blaring sirens. The coroner's van slipped in silently twenty minutes later. Kim, Ben, and I were fingerprinted and questioned at length. I told the police what I knew, which wasn't much and didn't impress them at all.

The only new bit of information I picked up was that Kim was separated from her husband and had moved in with Randy six months earlier. She insisted their relationship was platonic, but I saw the two officers exchange a look.

Finally they decided I could leave. Up at the house, I spent ten minutes in the bathroom washing my hands.

Though I hadn't touched anything, the smell of blood still lingered. Or maybe it was my imagination.

Kim walked me out. "What will you do now?" I asked her.

Only a couple of hours had passed, but I could tell she'd been pondering the question. "Ben and I will have to talk. We might be able to make a go of it on our own."

"I thought people sent their Poodles here for Randy to show."

"They did. And we'll probably lose a few clients right off the bat. But I bet we'll be able to convince the others to give us a try." The look in her brown eyes was shrewd. "It was Randy's operation. That didn't mean he was the only one around here with talent."

Yes, well. I was glad I wasn't the one standing between Kim and something she wanted.

There was little traffic on the drive home. That was good because the trip passed by in a daze. I needed to pick up Davey, but Aunt Peg's was on the way, and I decided to stop there first. I could let the Poodles out and make sure they all had fresh water. Even more importantly, I could use the time to wind down and try and clear my mind of all that it had seen.

I wanted the comfort of holding my child in my arms, but not until I was clean, fresh, ready. Even half an hour could make a big difference. But when I pulled up to Aunt Peg's house, I saw that I wasn't going to be able to put the whole thing behind me just yet. Sam's Bronco was parked in the drive. The car was empty, but then I spotted him.

He was lying in the hammock Uncle Max had hung from the limbs of a Japanese Maple. His eyes were closed, but he opened one as I approached.

"It's about time," he said.

❧❀ *Twenty-two* ❀❧

"If I'd known you were coming, I might have tried harder to be here."

Then again, maybe not. He was wearing jeans so old the denim was soft as tissue. His topsiders were scuffed and worn; his tee shirt was plain heather gray. I've seen men who don't look that good in Armani. I know I'm in trouble when I notice a man's hands. Sam's were large and strong, long fingers tapering to blunt-cut nails. I'd seen him use them to stroke the dogs. It wasn't hard to imagine . . .

Well, you get my drift.

I strode past him, up the walk, and into the house. There was no point in closing the door behind me, so I didn't. The Poodles escaped, and I let Sam round them up. That kept him busy while I saw to the dogs out in the kennel. All too soon, we both ended up in the kitchen.

Sam had already put on a pot of coffee. I'm barely at home in my own kitchen. How did he function so well in someone else's?

"Want to tell me about it?" he asked.

"About what?" I was staring out the window over the sink. It overlooked the fenced backyard where the Poodles were now gamboling happily.

"Whatever's bothering you."

"No." Eventually I supposed I'd have to. But I wasn't ready to relive the whole thing just yet.

"Okay. Want to hear about Will Perkins?"

"Sure."

We filled two mugs with coffee, added milk for me, sugar for Sam, then sat down at the kitchen table. I tried to pay attention to what he was saying, I really did. But I kept seeing Randy's face with its chalky skin and blank, staring eyes.

Sam finished telling me about the Poodles he'd seen at Will Perkins's, then paused, waiting for my response.

"Randall Tarnower's dead," I said.

His mug came down on the table hard. Coffee sloshed up and over the side. *"What?"*

"He's dead."

"I heard that." Sam grabbed a napkin and mopped up the spill. "How? When?"

"This morning—"

"While you were there?"

God, what a thought. And one I hadn't even considered until now. I'd been assuming that the murder had happened before my arrival. But maybe not. Maybe while Kim and I had been calling around the front of the kennel, the killer had been slipping out the back. I wrapped my fingers around my mug and began to shiver.

Sam took one look and left the room. He returned moments later carrying a thick cardigan sweater of Aunt Peg's, which he wrapped securely around me. "Did you see him?"

I nodded.

"Do you want to talk about it?"

I did and I didn't. But not talking about it wasn't helping. Maybe this would.

I told him the story from start to finish, no editing, no glossing over. Aunt Peg would have said I was finally beginning to trust Sam. I'd have told her I was merely desperate.

"So you have no idea what it was Randy wanted to tell you?" he asked at the end.

"No. He said he wanted to talk in person. How was I to know an hour and a half would make such a difference?"

"You weren't," Sam said firmly. "And you saw nobody else there but Ben and Kim?"

"Right."

"How about cars?"

"What about them?"

"You said it was farm country, isolated. So the killer must have had his own transportation. I would think an extra car would have stuck out."

I knew he was trying to work out the details in his mind. I'd been doing the same thing myself ever since. Applying logic to the situation was a much better alternative than sitting there and wallowing in shock.

"Not necessarily. I looked around on the way out and lots of the fields were bounded by dirt tracks. If I'd wanted to slip into Randy's kennel without being seen, I probably would have parked behind the neighbor's corn field and hiked in."

"You have to wonder . . ." Sam said thoughtfully.

"What?"

"Was Tarnower killed because of what he knew about your uncle, or was it something else? It's not as if he didn't have enemies."

"I know. I've been wondering about that, too. In the few shows I've been to I've seen him fight with everyone from other handlers to the animal-rights protesters. And yet, he'd just tried to call Aunt Peg. You can't discount that."

Sam frowned. "What a choice, coincidence or conspiracy. Damn it, you're sure he didn't give you a clue?"

"Nothing."

We sat in glum silence for what seemed like a long time. Whichever way I approached the problem, there simply wasn't enough information.

"I wonder what his clients will do," Sam said finally.

"Kim said something about carrying on herself."

"She can try certainly, but she doesn't have Tarnower's skill. That kennel will be largely empty within a month."

"Too bad," I said, picturing the big clean rooms and skylighted ceilings. "It's a beautiful setup."

"Somebody will snap it up, don't worry. Places like that with room for the dogs, plus zoning permits already in place are really at a premium these days. I've heard of grandfather clauses that upped the price of kennels by as much as a hundred thousand dollars. There are probably half a dozen handlers with their eye on Tarnower's place already."

I went out back and opened the door so that the Poodles could come in if they wanted to. Of course, they did. Poodles are people dogs. Roughhousing in the yard is fun for a while, but basically they want to be where their people are. According to Aunt Peg, that's why they make such great pets.

I counted noses as they came in. By now I knew them well enough to greet each one personally. Simba would push to the front, while Chloe always hung back. Gracie had her nose on the floor looking for food. Watching them race into the kitchen and line up next to the counter in the hope that biscuits would be offered, it was hard to think of these playful pets as being part of the big business Sam had been talking about.

Not that I was skeptical about what he'd said. Once you've accepted the possibility of Poodles wearing makeup, mascara, and wigs to be shown, I guess you'll believe almost anything.

"Where's your son?" Sam asked as I handed out treats all around.

"At a friend's house. I'm about to head over and get him."

"I'll come with you."

I was fitting the lid back on the canister, but that stopped me. "Why?"

"Because I don't think you should be alone."

Half of me was surprised, and maybe even a little pleased, that he would care enough to make the offer. I hadn't known a lot of men whose strength I'd been able to lean on. For a moment I was almost tempted to let myself be taken care of.

Then I gave myself a mental shake and got real. I was an adult and I'd been running my own life—quite handily—for years. Who was Sam to say whether or not I ought to be alone?

"I don't recall asking what you thought," I said, scooping my car keys up off the counter.

"All right, here's the deal. Does Davey like pizza?"

"Do pigs fly?"

Sam stared at me, perplexed. "Actually, no."

Unexpectedly I felt like laughing. "I can tell you haven't been around enough four-year-olds."

"Precisely my point." Sam and I were walking out the door together. "Here's your chance to remedy that. We drive over to . . . ?"

"Stamford."

". . . right, Stamford, and pick up Davey. There's a pizza parlor on Hope Street that makes the best sauce you've ever tasted."

He was smooth, I had to give him that. Even more amazing, he was right about Hope Street. "What if I'd said Darien?"

"Then we'd be heading for the Post Road."

Right again, I thought. Damn. "You've only been here

a couple months. How have you managed to scope out the best pizza parlor in every town?"

"I work fast."

That's what I was afraid of.

Sam opened the car door, and I slid behind the wheel. I know when I've been outmaneuvered. I also know when I've allowed it to happen. But I've learned the hard way that sometimes it's best just to go with the flow and not agonize over every little eventuality.

Besides don't forget, he was still wearing those jeans.

Davey is my litmus test. Any man who doesn't get along with him is history. But when he and Sam got together after our stop at the Brickmans', I was the one who never stood a chance. Before we even arrived at the pizza parlor, they were well on their way to being best buddies.

Not only that, but I couldn't even fault Sam's methods. He didn't take credit for the pizza, nor the ice cream sundaes that followed. He didn't attempt to be current on silly riddles or cartoons. Nor did he slip my son a five dollar bill when I wasn't looking.

Instead he simply treated Davey as a somewhat younger, and slightly smaller, friend. He asked his opinion on dinner and listened carefully while Davey listed the eight most important reasons why he didn't like mushrooms. They discussed baseball and dodge ball with equal solemnity and included me in the conversation as often as they remembered I was in the room.

And I'd said Sam didn't spend enough time around four-year-olds.

After we drove back to Aunt Peg's and I snuggled my sleepy child off to bed, I asked Sam what his secret was.

"Brothers, younger. Two of them. Both married now and both with sons of their own. I have a nephew almost Davey's age, and two that are younger. Unfortunately one brother lives in San Francisco and the other, Atlanta. I don't get to see either of them as often as I'd like."

We were having the conversation on the doorstep. Sam had seen us inside, then waited while I put Davey in bed. I was feeling pretty mellow. Now that it was just the two of us again, I'd been hoping he might like to stay around for a little adult conversation. But as soon as I returned from tucking Davey in, Sam was on his way to the door.

"You ought to go to bed, too," he said to me. "After the day you've had, you look like you could use the sleep."

I don't think he meant to be insulting. At least I hope not. But I have to admit, I did check out my reflection in the mirror by the door as he left. I probably would have stood there watching him start his car and drive away, but the telephone rang.

Of course since it was her house, the call was for Aunt Peg. But when I took the caller's name, I found out I was talking to Janet Reavis. Quickly I identified myself and told her she could reach Peg after the weekend.

"I've been wondering about something," she said. "And maybe you'll give me your opinion. As I told you, when Jennifer and I went to Litchfield, the breeder was rushing off to the vet because two of his dogs had gotten into a fight. Is that the norm for Standard Poodles? Are they very aggressive? Because I'm looking for a family dog . . ."

"Not at all," I reassured her. "Standard Poodles have wonderful temperaments. They're smart, they're funny, and they're incredibly eager to please. But you shouldn't take my word for it. Talk to my aunt next week and come and meet her dogs. They're their own best advertisement."

I wrote a note about the call for Aunt Peg and left it along with all the others, then devoted half an hour to feeding the Poodles and getting them all outside. I hated to admit it, but Sam had been right. I *was* tired.

Tired enough that as soon as I climbed into bed, I dropped into a fitful sleep. I'd been afraid I'd have nightmares about Tarnower, but his image never appeared once. Instead the man I saw had tousled blond hair and incredibly blue eyes.

And he wasn't wearing any jeans.

⊃⸻❋ Twenty-three ❋⸻⊂

When Aunt Peg finally returned late Sunday night, I told her what had happened to Randall Tarnower. News travels fast on the dog-show circuit; it turned out she already knew. What she hadn't known was that I was there, or that Tarnower had tried to reach her on the morning that he died.

I could see how shocked she was by that information. "I don't think Max even really knew Randy," she said. "Oh, they may have chatted occasionally at the shows, but nothing more than that. As to Randy having information for us, I find that hard to believe."

"I'm only repeating what he told me."

"Which wasn't nearly enough." Peg was clearly irritated. "And he never mentioned Beau at all?"

"No, only Max. I wish you'd been here. Maybe he would have told you what it was about over the phone."

"Possibly. Or maybe the only difference would have been that I was the one to get to New Jersey too late. I have to tell you, Melanie, I don't like the direction things are heading."

Well, that was a news flash.

"Beau may be a valuable dog, but nobody in his right mind could think he's worth the price of two lives."

"My thoughts exactly. So either something else is going on around here . . ."

"Or we're dealing with someone who's crazy."

"Or desperate."

Just another cheery thought with which to begin the week.

I moved our things back home Monday morning while Davey was at camp. The Poodles had been plenty of work, but now I was surprised to find that I missed having them around. A memorial service was held for Randall Tarnower at the end of the week in New Jersey. Aunt Peg went. She came back wearing a frown and carrying one of Kim's newly printed business cards.

I thought about everyone I'd spoken to so far and realized that one person I'd missed was Tony Wasserman. Now that there'd been two break-ins at Aunt Peg's, I began to wonder if Tony was any more observant than his wife.

I dropped Davey at camp and drove over to Greenwich. Most businesses downtown don't open until nine-thirty or ten. With luck, I'd be early enough to catch him at home. There were two cars parked in the Wassermans' driveway: the Taurus I'd seen on my first visit and a late model burgundy Jaguar sedan. Having met Doris, I could guess which car Tony drove.

Once again the chimes played through the house. I got to listen to them twice as nobody was in any hurry to open the door. Finally Tony appeared. He drew open the door and stood there staring at me. He was dressed for work in suit pants, a cotton tab-collar shirt, and a multihued Ferragamo tie. One hand held a piece of whole wheat toast; the other, a section of the *New York Times*.

"Well?" he said. Definitely not a morning person.

I began by introducing myself. By the time I finished

explaining why I was there, Tony was warming up. I accepted his invitation to come in and soon found myself ensconced at the sunny kitchen table with a tall glass of orange juice.

"You don't know how sorry we were to hear about Max," Tony said. "He was a fine man."

Doris, standing by the counter, dropped a pot and swore under her breath.

Tony didn't even glance her way. "I told Peg and I'll tell you, if there's anything we can do . . ."

"Actually there is. I don't know if Mrs. Wasserman told you, but I was here before."

"She might have mentioned something," Tony said vaguely. I got the impression these two didn't talk about much.

"The night my uncle died, one of his Poodles was stolen from the kennel. My aunt would like to get the dog back."

"Can't see why." Tony's tone was jovial, but lines tightened on either side of his mouth. "She's got plenty of others."

"The one that was taken was the most valuable and the most important to her."

"Like anyone could even tell those dogs apart," said Doris. "I told you before, we didn't see anything important."

"Sorry," said Tony. "Wish we could have helped."

"Maybe if I reminded you which night it was—"

Tony shook his head. "If Doris says we didn't see anything, we didn't. Believe me, she keeps track of everything."

For two people who supposedly wanted to help, the Wassermans were pretty obstinate. I hadn't wanted to prompt Tony, but it was beginning to look as though I didn't have a choice. "Doris mentioned that the Poodles were barking a lot that night. They woke the two of you up, and she said she saw a car leaving—"

"Driving by on the road," Doris broke in, looking disgusted. "That's what I said." She glanced at her husband. "You know the night. It was hot and we had the windows open. Those Poodles were howling for what seemed like hours. You went downstairs to your office."

"I guess I did. So what?"

"Maybe you saw the car too," I said.

"Maybe I did." Tony shrugged. "Seems to me I was staring out the window. We don't get much traffic around here at that hour of the night. Usually, everyone's asleep. We would have been to, if it hadn't been for those damn dogs."

"What did the car look like?"

"It wasn't anything in particular," said Tony. "Just some white sedan. It came flying around the corner from Peg's place going like a bat out of hell."

White sedan? Doris had seen a dark station wagon.

"Are you sure?"

"What's to be sure about? Like I said, it was just any old car. A generic sedan. Ford, Chevy, something like that. You know, like the kind of car the rental agencies use. They all look the same."

"I believe your wife said she saw a station wagon."

Doris was standing at the sink. She had her back to us and didn't bother to turn around. "So there were two cars," she said. "Who cares?"

I care! I wanted to shout. Maybe this makes a difference. Was it possible there'd been two cars at the kennel that night? Or was it just that there'd been two cars on the road? On the other hand, maybe one of the Wassermans was mistaken. If so, neither seemed to care.

There had to be some way to get past their indifference. I tried appealing to Tony's chivalrous instincts.

"Since that night, there's been another break-in. My aunt is concerned about security—"

He snorted under his breath. "I guess maybe she should be. Sounds to me like all those dogs aren't good for much. If a whole gang of them can't even keep people out of the house . . ."

"The Poodles annoy you, don't they?"

"Hell, yes."

Again, a pan clattered by the sink. The tension in the room was so high even I was beginning to feel jumpy.

"Look at them," said Tony. "All that hair going every which way. They're a joke. And how many does she have over there anyway? Twelve? Fourteen? Who needs that many dogs?"

"Aunt Peg breeds her Poodles," I reminded him. "And she exhibits them at shows."

"Well, la-di-dah."

That editorial comment came from Doris. I swiveled around to face her. Earlier in the year I might have felt the same way. But now I'd been to enough shows to see that beneath the surface glamour there was a great deal of hard work going on. The dogs that won had to be physically fit and mentally sound. Any dog whose structure or temperament wasn't up to the rigors of life on the circuit got weeded out pretty quickly. It wasn't a perfect process, but I'd developed respect for the people, and the dogs, that were involved.

"Have you ever been to a dog show?" I asked.

"Who me?" Doris laughed. "Not one. Never will either."

"Why not?"

"It's the people," she said firmly. "They're not my type."

I still had more questions, but the telephone began to ring. Tony immediately stood. Just as quickly Doris said, "Just let it ring. It won't be anyone important."

Tony glared at her before turning to me. "Would you excuse me for a minute?"

"Sure."

He left the room with Doris staring after him. She and I both pretended not to notice that there was a wall phone near the door. I sipped my orange juice and waited to see what would happen next. In another part of the house the phone was picked up after the third ring. Doris stood there frowning. Finally she dried her hands on the front of her apron and left the room as well. I guessed I'd been invited to leave.

When I reached the front hall, they were both coming down the stairs. "It was work, Doris," Tony was saying. "Now leave it alone." He saw me and smiled. "Sorry about the interruption. I've got to get to the office, but listen, you tell Peg to let us know if she needs anything."

Sure, I thought. Right.

The Volvo started up on the second try, but by the time I'd driven around to Aunt Peg's the engine was making a plinking noise that couldn't possibly have been good news. I don't know a whole lot about engines, but I figured it couldn't hurt to take a look. I'd lifted up the hood and was wondering what to poke first when a burgundy Jaguar sedan shot past the end of the driveway going like the wind.

That got my attention fast. Doris had told me that Tony had an insurance agency in town; but downtown Greenwich was the other way. Whatever had Tony speeding through the back country now, it wasn't a need to get to work. The Volvo could plink until it gave out. I was going to follow.

The current rage in Greenwich is Range Rovers. Tony's Jag stood out pretty well, and it wasn't hard to keep him in sight. Ten minutes after we set out, we crossed the border into New York state. Tony kept right on going. After twenty minutes I was trying to decide how foolish I'd feel if he was on his way to inspect a claim.

Then his blinker came on, and I eased my foot off the gas pedal. Tony turned down the entrance of a long, wooded driveway. I let his car disappear before driving up closer to read the wrought-iron sign that was hanging at the end.

Even before I could make out the lettering, I saw the framed silhouette of a Poodle and began to smile. I pulled over to the side of the road and read: BEDFORD FARM, DOGS BOARDED. PROFESSIONAL HANDLING. CRAWFORD LANGLEY, PROP.

What an interesting destination for a man who didn't like Poodles or dog shows, a man whose wife claimed that show people weren't their type. I wondered what Aunt Peg would have to say about that.

As it turned out, I didn't have a chance to ask her. She wasn't home when I called, and then it was time to pick up Davey at camp. By the time we got back, we had a visitor of our own.

"Uncle Frank!" cried Davey, launching himself out of the car and into my brother's arms. "What did you bring me?"

"Davey!" I protested, but Frank was already pulling a plywood airplane out from behind his back and shooting it across the yard. Davey squealed with delight when it crash-landed in the azaleas.

"Now you try," said Frank. Davey scrambled after the toy. I unlocked the front door, and my brother and I walked in the house together.

"What a nice surprise," I said.

"I was hoping you'd think so."

"Of course, why wouldn't I?"

"I haven't told you why I'm here yet."

"Oh, Frank." I grimaced. Why couldn't we ever just enjoy each other's company without there always having to be a catch?

"Hey, it's not as bad as all that." He followed me into the kitchen where I unpacked Davey's backpack, throwing out a soggy, uneaten half sandwich and tossing his wet bathing suit and towel in the dryer. "In fact, you might even be pleased."

I sent him a narrowed glanced. "By what?"

"I'd like to invite you and Davey over to my apartment this afternoon."

"That's sounds nice." I was still bracing for the worst. "What's the occasion?"

"Think of it as a family get-together."

"Okay." I could guess what was coming, but I still had to ask. "Which part of the family?"

"You and me and Davey . . ."

"And?"

"Aunt Rose and her fiancé."

"I don't want to see her."

"Mel, come on."

I turned and faced Frank squarely. "She and I have nothing to say to each other."

"You can't go blaming Aunt Rose for something that wasn't her fault," said Frank. "She didn't make Dad's problems, she only told you about them."

I'd gotten over the shock and the worst of the hurt, but I still wasn't ready to forgive. "She used that information like a club, Frank. She wanted to break down the relationship I'd built with Aunt Peg, and she very nearly succeeded. She forced me to choose between them, and I did."

"Fine." Frank walked over to the refrigerator and helped himself to a cold soda. "So now what?"

"What do you mean?"

"She's our father's sister, but you're mad, so okay. Are you planning never to see her again, or what?"

"Of course not . . ." I stopped, confused.

Frank let me think about that for a moment. "This meeting wasn't my idea," he said finally. "It was hers. I got the feeling she wanted to call you herself, but she was afraid."

Aunt Peg had wanted Frank and called me. Rose wanted me and called Frank. I suppose there was a circuitous logic in that somewhere.

"Turnbull women aren't afraid of anything," I said.

"Except maybe rejection from someone they really care about."

Well, that hit me just about where he figured it would. I pulled in a breath and let out a sigh as Davey came running into the kitchen. Somewhere he'd managed to lose his sneakers, and his new airplane had a bent tail. Neither fact seemed to concern him in the slightest.

"I want to go to the beach!" he announced.

"Can't," I said, scooping him up. "We're going to go see Aunt Rose and meet the man she's going to marry."

"Holy cow!" said Davey.

I couldn't have put it better myself.

❧✷ *Twenty-four* ✷❧

Frank lived on the second floor of a big old Victorian house that had been subdivided into four apartments. The rooms weren't large, but they were beautifully crafted, with carved moldings, bay windows, and a view of Long Island Sound, only a few blocks away. He paid for part of his rent in cash and the rest in odd jobs: painting, mowing, helping to keep the place up. The owner was an elderly woman who otherwise would have had to hire someone to do the work, so the arrangement suited both of them.

Aunt Rose and her fiancé, Peter Donovan, were already at the apartment when we arrived. I supposed that said something about how certain Frank had been of his persuasive powers.

Rose performed the introductions, and there was an awkward moment while we all tried to figure out where to sit. Obviously the money my brother saved in rent had not been applied to the purchase of furniture. Davey ended up on a window seat, and Frank on a stool he'd dragged in from the kitchen. Finally we were all settled.

"Melanie, I want to apologize for my behavior the last time we were together," Aunt Rose said as soon as we were seated. "I have no excuse except to say that there's been so much turmoil in my life recently, it's obvious I wasn't thinking clearly. I do hope you'll forgive me."

"I'll think about it," I said and got a glare from Frank, which I returned in full measure. Aunt Rose displaying humility? That had to be a first. And knowing our family, there was probably a catch.

Aunt Rose nodded, not satisfied but willing to let it go for the moment. "Now the other reason I wanted us to get together today was so that you could have a chance to get to know Peter. He and I are in the process of finalizing our plans. There will be a small wedding ceremony in the chapel at Divine Mercy on September thirtieth. Of course we hope you can all come."

"So soon?"

"Melanie, what possible reason would there be to wait?"

I didn't have an answer for that. Since opening my mouth wasn't helping matters any, I decided to keep it shut for a while. As Frank and Peter began to sound each other out and Davey climbed up into Rose's lap, I studied the man my aunt had left the convent for. But as soon as the thought presented itself, I knew that Rose would have corrected me. She'd left the convent for herself; Peter was just the icing on the cake.

He was about her age, give or take a few years, with thinning gray-brown hair that receded sharply at the temples. I wouldn't have called him handsome, but he had a very comfortable face. When Davey was rude enough to stare openly, he beckoned, then patted his own lap.

"Come here, son. Why don't you climb over here and check and see what I've got in my pockets?"

Davey considered the offer. "I'm not your son," he said finally.

Peter Donovan smiled. "No, but you're going to be my nephew."

"Do you have kids?"

"No."

Davey inched closer across the space that separated them. "How come?"

Nothing like four-year-old candor to get right to the heart of the matter. "Davey, Father Donovan . . ." I stopped, looking for guidance. "Mr. Donovan?"

"Mr. Donovan is fine," he told me. "Uncle Peter's even better."

"Honey," I said to Davey. "Uncle Peter was a priest." I hoped that might put an end to the matter, but of course it didn't.

"So why didn't you have any children?"

"I had a whole congregation full of them," Peter said, patting his pockets. "But I wasn't married, so I couldn't have any of my own."

Davey watched in fascination as Peter withdrew a cherry lollipop from inside his jacket. "But I bet I probably have a pretty good idea of what kids like. Now would you like to have this?"

"Yes, please," Davey said firmly.

At least he'd remembered to say please. I held onto that thought as Davey snatched the lollipop out of Peter's hand, ripped off the paper, and retreated to the window seat with his prize.

"You're a hit," I told Peter, and his smile was genuine.

"I like kids. They're usually pretty direct about how they feel. I like that, so I'm going to try some directness myself."

Frank and I shared a glance, wondering what was coming.

"I love your Aunt Rose," said Peter. "Now as I'm sure you can see, neither one of us is as young as we used to be. We saw what we wanted, and we're going to go after it. I hope you approve of that. If you don't, I hope you keep your objections to yourself. We're not hurting anybody, and we're making each other happy."

He paused to drape an arm around Rose's shoulder fondly. "It's great if you can share in that happiness with us. If not, don't rain on our parade."

Well, that laid it on the line. By the time the sermon was finished, I was having trouble keeping a straight face. Even Aunt Rose was looking a bit nonplused. Maybe she hadn't known until that moment just how well she'd chosen.

"Jesus!" Frank said under his breath, then we all were laughing together.

I stood up, went over, and gave Peter a hug. "Welcome to the family. I can see it's going to be interesting having you around."

"Around," Aunt Rose clarified, "but hardly underfoot. Peter's been offered a teaching post at Connecticut College. We'll be moving to New London before the start of the new fall term."

Rose gave her fiancé's arm a squeeze. She was glowing, she was so proud. And of course that had to ease the financial worries as well.

"I think this calls for a celebration," Frank said, rising. "I don't have any champagne. Will wine do?"

We decided it would.

"Beer," said Davey. "That's what I like to drink."

Peter had the startled look of a man who's just discovered he doesn't know children nearly as well as he thought he did. Rose merely lifted a complacent brow.

"It's a long story," I told them.

"You'll have grape juice," Frank said to Davey, and the two of them headed off to the kitchen to negotiate.

When they were gone, I turned to Aunt Rose. "Would you answer a question for me?"

"I'll try."

"Why do you and Aunt Peg hate each other so much?"

She was surprised by the question, I could tell. But that

didn't hurt her ability to block and parry. "Hate is a very strong word—"

"Call it what you will," I interrupted. "But as someone who's gotten caught in the cross fire, I think I deserve to know."

Rose was wavering. It was Peter who tipped the balance. "I think I'll go join the men in the kitchen," he said, dropping a quick kiss on Rose's cheek. "Take all the time you need."

Both of us watched him leave. "He's a special man," I said.

Rose nodded. "I'm very lucky. Blessed, in fact. So maybe it is time to put all this other unpleasantness behind us once and for all. Peg and I first met under what I would not have called the best of circumstances."

"Was this when she was engaged to Uncle Max?"

"Yes," said Rose, then dropped the bombshell. "And pregnant."

Pregnant? I'd never had a cousin, never even heard of one.

"In those days what they were doing was called living in sin. I'm afraid I was a bit rigid in my thinking then, as the young often are."

"But what happened . . ."

"She lost the baby in childbirth," Rose said quietly. "And with it her ability to have any other children. I said some things then that I never should have. My only excuse is youth, and perhaps an overabundance of religious zeal. I told her that what had happened was a sign of God's displeasure. His revenge, if you will, for the immoral way she had conducted herself."

No wonder mayhem ensued every time these women were in the same room. If words were daggers, they'd have killed each other long since.

"Peg thinks you were jealous of her," I said.

"Perhaps I was, a little. I do know I didn't think she was

good enough for Max. Of course I've grown up since then. I've even made some efforts at rapprochement. But Peg is a hard woman."

"So are you."

Rose gave me a mild look. "Need I say it runs in the family?"

I swallowed heavily, remembering the way I'd put her off earlier. There were enough rifts in the Turnbull family without my adding to them. I moved over and sat next to her on the couch.

"I'm outspoken," she said firmly. "It's the way I am. Peg hasn't forgiven me after all these years. If you have the same capacity for carrying a grudge, please bear in mind I'm not getting any younger."

"All right," I said, laughing. "I forgive you."

"That's better." She sat up and looked around. "Now didn't someone promise me some wine?"

We talked the rest of the afternoon away, then all went out and took a walk around the beach at Todd's Point. Frank ordered Chinese food for dinner, and the evening's entertainment evolved into a wicked game of Charades. Davey was on my team. His enactment of *Cat on a Hot Tin Roof* was the hit of the evening.

If only the rest of my life could go as smoothly. The next morning the first thing I did was call Crawford Langley. No one answered, and I didn't leave a message on the machine. Aunt Peg had told me that this was a big weekend—four prestigious dog shows in a row, culminating in Westchester on Sunday. Everyone who was anyone would be there.

The Friday show was in Tarrytown. I decided to drop Davey at camp, then drive over and see if I could talk to Crawford in person. It was a good idea in theory, except that as soon as I got to camp, Emily grabbed me to sub.

After camp we had a birthday present to shop for. Joey Brickman was turning five, and his mother had planned a late afternoon party including a movie with pizza and cake afterward. I tried Crawford again before taking Davey to the party, but he wasn't back yet.

I suppose I could have gone home and tried again after dropping Davey off, but to tell the truth, I just didn't feel like it. Alice Brickman expected me back at seven-thirty. Until then I was on my own, with nothing planned and nowhere I had to be. It was a beautiful late summer evening—much too nice to be indoors. I decided to take a drive.

Ever since I got my license as a teenager, I've loved to get in the car and just go. The experience is part escape, part pacifier. I can make plans, daydream, or simply drift. I never start with a destination in mind. Sometimes I drive in a big circle and don't go anywhere at all. And sometimes my subconscious takes over and pilots me exactly where it wants to go.

At least that was the only way I could explain how it was that I happened to find myself in Redding.

Once I was there, it was pretty obvious what I was going to do next. If I'd had a phone in my car, I might have called and announced myself. But I didn't; so instead I simply drove up Sam's driveway, parked my car, walked up to his front door, and made a fool of myself.

It didn't start out that way. I knocked and Sam answered the door. The jeans, unfortunately, were gone. Instead he was wearing twill slacks and a chambray shirt the same color as his eyes. I wondered if he'd shown one of his Poodles over in Tarrytown earlier and figured eventually I'd get around to asking. For the moment, I was happy just to stand there and smile.

"Melanie, hi." His gaze darted back over his shoulder, then returned. "What a surprise."

"I was in the neighborhood," I said brightly. "I hope this isn't a bad time?"

There was just the slightest moment of hesitation before he answered. "No, of course not. Come on in."

I'd started to when a woman's voice came floating out of the kitchen. "Sam, where do you keep the basil?"

"Bottom drawer in the refrigerator, on the left."

I hate it when I blush. I don't do it often, and when I do, it annoys the hell out of me. Now, in an instant, I could feel the heat coming on.

"I'm sorry," I said, fumbling. "Obviously, you're busy—"

"No, it's all right—"

"Sam, I can't find the fresh stuff. How about dried?"

The woman I'd heard came walking out of the kitchen. She was tall and blond with drop-dead legs and the kind of knit jersey dress they sell in the Victoria's Secret catalogue.

I had a small dab of finger-paint on the front of my shirt, courtesy of camp, and was wearing shorts from L.L.Bean. Just so you get the picture.

"Susan Lewis," said Sam. "Meet Melanie Travis."

Susan flashed me a friendly smile and something clicked in my mind. I'd seen her before, though I had no idea where.

"Nice to meet you," she said. "Don't mind me. I'll be in the kitchen, making do."

Before Susan had even left the room, I was already backing toward the door. At some point Sam must have closed it behind me because now I ran right into it. I reached around and fumbled for the knob.

"Look, I'm really sorry. I never should have stopped by like this. It was a stupid idea—"

"It wasn't a stupid idea." Sam followed me out onto the step. "And you don't have to leave."

I stared at him as if he were crazy. "Of course I do."

"First, tell me why you came."

What was I supposed to say to that? Because I was hoping we might spend some time together? Hardly.

"Your water's boiling," Susan called from the kitchen. "Do you want the pasta in?"

It's too bad I was one of the involved parties. Otherwise I might have found the expression on Sam's face to be almost comical.

"Look," I said firmly, "I didn't mean to intrude and I'm out of your hair, right now."

If I'd gone down those steps any faster, I'd have fallen on my face. Then it would have had a reason for being so red.

"I'll call you," said Sam.

Yeah, right.

❧❖ *Twenty-five* ❖❧

I could have headed home, but then I would have had plenty of time to dwell on what had just happened. Distraction seemed like a better idea. I drove west instead and made my second unannounced visit of the evening at Bedford Farm, Crawford Langley, Prop.

Langley seemed just as surprised to see me as Sam had been. But at least he was alone. He opened the door in stocking feet, carrying a glass filled with two fingers of scotch, neat. The nightly news was playing in the background.

Before I could introduce myself, he cocked his head slightly to one side and said, "Travis." Then a moment's thought produced a first name. "Melanie. You're the lady with the bitch."

"Yes. How nice of you to remember."

He frowned slightly, peering around behind me. "Don't tell me she's in season now."

"Oh no, nothing like that. Actually I've been trying to reach you on the phone. I was hoping we could talk."

"I guess." He stepped aside so I could come in. "But I've just gotten back from a show, and I have another tomorrow, so it can't take long."

Langley switched off the television set, then paused

next to a bar cabinet holding a selection of tumblers and bottles. "Can I get you something to drink?"

"Coke?"

While he was pouring, I got straight to the point. "The last time we met, I wasn't entirely honest with you."

"Oh?" He handed me the glass and we both sat.

"I *am* looking for a stud dog, but I had a particular dog in mind. My aunt is Margaret Turnbull. I've been trying to track down the whereabouts of her dog, Beau."

For the second time, I'd succeeded in surprising him. "And you suspected *I'd* taken him?"

"At the time, I thought there might be a possibility. Of course as soon as I saw your dog, I knew I was wrong."

"About that dog. I have others as I'm sure you know. Is that why you're here?"

"No." There didn't seem to be any way to say this nicely, so I didn't even bother to try. "I'm here because I want to know what your relationship is with Tony Wasserman."

"I don't see that that's any of your business."

"You're right," I admitted. "It isn't. But I've spent the last two months trying to find a dog that doesn't seem to be anywhere, and one of the few things I have managed to discover is that Peg's next-door neighbor, who claims to have neither seen nor heard anything the night Beau was stolen, is very probably hiding something. If you know what that something is, I want you to tell me."

Crawford stared down at the tumbler in his hand, shifting it from side to side so the amber liquid swirled in the light. "I've always admired the Cedar Crest Poodles," he said finally. "Your aunt is a fine woman."

"Then you'll help me?"

"I couldn't help you even if I wanted to. I'd heard that one of Peg's dogs was missing, but I have no idea where he is." He stood up and walked over to the bar. "I'm afraid you've come here for nothing."

No, I'd gone to Sam's house for nothing. Perhaps if that experience hadn't been so fresh in my mind, I would have backed down. But that would have meant that my entire evening had been a waste of time; and I was just irritated enough by the way things were turning out not to let that happen. I had a hunch about what the two of them were hiding, and I played it.

"You and Tony are . . . involved, aren't you?"

Langley turned slowly to face me. "What a quaint way of putting it."

"All right then." If he wanted me to spell it out, I supposed I could manage. "Having an affair."

Crawford sipped at his drink. A smile played at the corners of his mouth. "It was much more than that."

"Was?"

"Was . . . is. Who knows? I've never been one for static relationships."

I thought back furiously. "Doris said she and Tony had never been to a dog show."

"Quite right, I'm sure."

"Then how did you meet?"

"At Max and Peg's, of course. Isn't it ironic? They had a party several summers ago, and fate stepped in. Tony took one look at me and fell like a ton of bricks."

"What about Doris?"

"Ah yes." Crawford sighed. "There was that little complication. At first it didn't seem to matter. Tony was . . . motivated, shall we say, and he proved very adept at juggling."

"And now?"

"Now it's gotten to the point where Doris barely lets him out of her sight. I can't imagine why he puts up with it, but *I* certainly don't have to. I've told Tony it's over. Several times, in fact. But then he pleads for another chance and, well . . ." His voice trailed away as he readdressed his scotch.

I thought about what he'd said. It answered everything except what I needed to know. "What does this have to do with Aunt Peg's dogs?"

"That's what I've been trying to tell you. Nothing. The only reason Tony is so angry about those Poodles is because when he's sitting at home with dull, stolid Doris, their barking reminds him of me." Langley smiled. "It's not hard to imagine where he'd rather be."

He stood, and I figured my time was up. On the way to the door, I tried one last question. "I heard that you do some showing in Canada. Were you up there this year?"

"No. I used to go because one of my clients enjoyed it. Now that his account is gone, I don't bother."

"Which client was that?"

"A man named Jack Berglund." He drew the door open, and I found myself being inched out. "You may have run into him at the shows."

"I have. Do you know if he went up north this year?"

"You'd have to ask him," Langley said shortly. "I don't keep up with anything Berglund does anymore."

I started to thank him, but the door closed in my face. Obviously it was not my night for graceful exits.

Back in the car, I drove like crazy and managed to get to Stamford just as the birthday party was ending. Alice Brickman was standing at the front door, greeting the returning parents with palpable relief. She had green icing in her hair and a pizza stain on the front of her shorts. Her front hall was mostly intact, but the family room looked as though Sherman's army had marched through recently.

"How'd it go?" I asked when the rest of the group had gone.

"It's over," Alice said with a survivor's grin. "That's all that matters."

"Do you know you have icing in your hair?"

She stopped at the hall mirror, poking at the sticky

clump with a shrug. "That's the least of my problems. I also have an exploded juice box in the microwave and Legos in my VCR. None of which I plan to worry about in the immediate future. After running around nonstop for the last three hours, I think I've earned a cigarette and a cup of coffee."

Joey and Davey were in the family room with a pile of new toys which was big enough to keep them occupied for at least a while. Alice and I went into the kitchen. She lit up and I started the coffee maker.

We'd met at a neighborhood play group when our sons were less than a year old and formed an immediate bond. Alice's husband, Joe, was a lawyer in town who worked long hours and left the child raising to her. Joey's fourteen-month-old sister, Carly, was upstairs asleep. Not unexpectedly, Joe was nowhere in sight. The thought of twelve four- and five-year-olds taking over his home had been enough to keep him in the office until after everything was finished.

"I should be cleaning up," Alice said as I poured the coffee and served us each a cup. Good intentions notwithstanding, she made no move to rise.

"Later." I sank down beside her. "I'll help. It'll only take half the time."

"You don't have to—"

"Of course not," I agreed. "Just like you didn't have to drive to White Plains to pick me up the last time my car died."

That shut her up. We'd been covering each other's backs for years. Now Alice needed some time to sit and unwind, and I was happy to do the same. After the evening I'd had, almost anything would have seemed like an improvement.

We drank two cups each before deciding we were fortified enough to tackle the mess that awaited us. Alice scrubbed the microwave while I put the family room back together. I only had to shake the VCR twice to know that it was beyond my help. I unplugged it and recommended a trip to the repair shop. Joey and Davey both fell asleep in front of the TV.

By the time I got Davey home and snuggled into his own bed, it was almost ten. Of course, thanks to those two cups of coffee, I couldn't fall asleep myself. I put on my pajamas and climbed into bed, but the book I'd left on my nightstand didn't hold my interest. Instead I found myself thinking about Crawford Langley and Tony Wasserman. Then I added Randall Tarnower to the mix. And Jack Berglund, who liked to show his Poodles in Canada . . .

I thought about them all for a good long time and finally the pieces began to fall into place. It was like a crossword puzzle; one right answer made the next one come that much more easily. And when I remembered the phone conversation I'd had with Janet Reavis, I knew I was headed in the right direction.

She'd told me she'd gone to visit a breeder, but hadn't been able to see any puppies because two stud dogs had gotten into a fight. She wanted to find someone closer so she wouldn't have to drive all the way to Litchfield again.

Jack Berglund lived in Litchfield.

When I'd visited him, he'd told me he only had one stud dog—Ranger, the Poodle I'd come to see. A Poodle he was very high on. A Poodle he'd just acquired and couldn't wait to breed. So where had the second dog come from?

I reached for the phone and dialed Aunt Peg.

It rang three times before she picked up, and then she didn't sound too happy about it. "Do you know what time it is?" she demanded.

"No."

"Well then I'll tell you. And bear in mind that I'm reading from the clock beside my bed. It is after midnight."

"Aunt Peg, listen. I'm sorry I woke you up, but there's something we need to talk about. I think I might know where Beau is."

"Where?" Aunt Peg was instantly awake.

I told her about my visit to Langley's place, the conversation I'd had with Janet and the connections I'd been making since. This was good stuff; the first real lead we'd had. I thought she'd be thrilled, but when I finished speaking there was only silence.

"Aunt Peg, are you awake?"

"Unfortunately. Melanie dear, am I getting this straight? You got me up in the middle of the night to tell me that you think Jack Berglund might have had a dog fight and by the bye, he's the type of person who could conceivably have Canadian change in his pocket?"

Put that way, my ideas didn't sound nearly so impressive.

"Yes, I guess so."

"That's what I thought. I'm going back to sleep, and I suggest you do the same." The telephone clicked down with finality.

All in all, it was just not my day.

❦❖ *Twenty-six* ❖❦

Aunt Peg showed up on my doorstep at eight o'clock the next morning, carrying half a dozen cinnamon buns as a peace offering. Davey, who loves surprises, launched himself into her arms and asked if she wanted to see his new pet frog. They trooped upstairs together while I put the cinnamon buns on a plate. Upon their return, Davey helped himself to two, one for his mouth and one for his pocket, then went outside to play.

"That child needs a proper pet," Aunt Peg said.

"Like a puppy?"

"Precisely."

No surprises there. "Aunt Peg, why are you here?"

"We have to talk. Last night I was asleep when you called, and the whole point you were trying to make went right by me." She eyed the buns for the moment, then made her selection. "But you know how it is when you start thinking about a problem just before you fall asleep? Your mind works on it the whole night. When I woke up this morning, I realized that not only has Jack Berglund seen and admired Beau, but he also might have a motive for wanting to acquire him."

Even though I'd just finished a bowl of bran cereal and skim milk, watching her tuck into that cinnamon bun made my stomach grumble. I gave in and went and got another plate.

"That's the part I don't understand. Jack's obviously got money. And more importantly, he has a top winning line of Poodles himself. Why steal from yours?"

Aunt Peg took her time breaking off a piece of roll and buttering it. "Did he tell you he's no longer with Crawford Langley?"

"Both of them did. I gathered there was no love lost either way. Is that important?"

"I think so. And if you don't mind waiting while I make some phone calls, I'd like to check it out."

I went outside and found Davey in the backyard. We kicked around his soccer ball for almost half an hour before Aunt Peg came to the door and called me back in. She was holding a pad of paper on which she'd taken some notes. From the look on her face, I'd say their content pleased her quite a bit.

"I've been talking to Anna Barnes," she said. "I was going to call Crawford directly, but of course he's off at the shows. Anna did just as well. She may not be much of one for gossip, but she knows everything. Crawford's handled her Poodles for years, and once I explained what we were after she was happy to help out."

We both found seats at the table. Two sticky buns remained on the plate in the middle. I figured we'd split them before long.

"One thing I didn't need Anna to tell me," Peg began. "It's common knowledge that the Shalimar line has been going downhill for quite some time. Too much inbreeding I would suspect, or perhaps just not enough thought going into the choices he's made.

"At any rate, Crawford Langley had been handling Jack's Poodles for almost twenty years, up until last summer. According to Anna, his account had always been a bit behind. Sloppy bookkeeping, he blamed it on."

I nodded, picturing the all-but-useless filing system.

"But things had been getting worse and worse, and a year ago they came to a head. The account was way over-due, and when Crawford demanded to be paid, Jack said he wanted to dispute some items on the bill. He claimed that the charges were entirely too high, and Crawford blew his top. You know how he is, he takes himself very seriously.

"The next thing Anna knew, Jack's dogs were gone. Everyone just assumed that he'd move them to another handler, but he didn't. Instead he took them home, and he's been showing them himself ever since. And doing a godawful job of it, if you ask me."

"Are you trying to say you think he didn't have the money to go to another handler?"

"I'm considering the possibility."

Even though Jack Berglund had been my idea in the first place, I still found myself shaking my head. "It doesn't make sense. There's got to be money there. The house alone must be worth a fortune."

"It could be mortgaged," Aunt Peg pointed out. "And maybe more than once. I've heard that Jack's money came from family wealth, and not anything he was smart enough to earn on his own. Oh, he made a stab at work-ing for a while. I told you, he and your father were at the same firm at one point."

"Yes, you did." I frowned, remembering. "You also said there'd been some sort of a problem. Something about junk bonds?"

"I never knew the details, but I did know that Michael and Jack went in together on some sort of scheme. Jack promised your father it would go through the roof, but instead the opposite happened. I believe a good deal of Nana's money was lost on just that one deal."

A deal that had precipitated my father's decline. Jack

Berglund had succeeded in taking advantage of my family once. Had he now returned to try it again?

"By taking Beau," Aunt Peg continued, "Jack could kill two birds with one stone. First, the dog's stud fees generate a healthy income. And second, and perhaps just as important for a man who enjoys winning the way he does, on the strength of Beau's producing ability his line's reputation is restored."

"I have to go back to Shalimar," I decided.

Aunt Peg nodded. "You need to see the dog there. Either that or we've got to come up with some solid proof that he *is* there."

"What if I call and ask to see Ranger again?"

"You've done that already. We need something else."

"How about puppies? Didn't you tell me that the value of a stud dog is determined by what he produces? Suppose I ask Jack if his dog has sired any litters yet, and if he has, can I see them?"

"Perfect," Aunt Peg agreed. "Go call."

I did and found Jack Berglund at home. He told me that Ranger had sired one litter so far, which was now three weeks old. I set up an appointment to see them at the first mutually convenient time, which was Thursday afternoon.

When I hung up, Aunt Peg was counting something off on her fingers. "Beau has been gone just long enough to have sired that litter. Oh, how I'd love to come and see them for myself."

"Could they be the proof we need?" I asked. "Are there any identifying characteristics I could look for in the puppies?"

"If they were older, we might have a chance. But at three weeks they're just too young for that sort of evaluation." Aunt Peg popped the last piece of bun into her mouth. "Something we might do, though, is call Sam. I'd feel a whole lot better about this if he went up there with you."

The thought had crossed my mind, too, but I'd rejected it for all the obvious reasons. None of which I had any intention of telling Aunt Peg.

"I'd feel better, too," I said honestly. "But how would we explain what he was doing there? Jack would be bound to be suspicious, and then there's no way I'd get anywhere near Beau."

"I guess you're right," Aunt Peg said unhappily. She hated having her plans fiddled with. "At least there's one bit of good news."

"What's that?"

"It didn't seem important until now, but I remember distinctly that the morning Randall Tarnower died, Jack Berglund was up on the Saratoga circuit showing his bitch."

"You saw him there?"

"Saw him? I lost to him. I'd hardly be likely to forget that."

Well, that was heartening. I wasn't confronting a murder, only a con man and a thief. What a relief.

Thursday was a dismal, gray day. Rain, punctuated by the occasional grumble of thunder kept the Graceland campers inside all morning. I'd booked Joanie's services early in the week, but her mom called at noon to tell me that my baby-sitter had the flu.

I picked Davey up at one. After four hours of confinement, he was delighted by the prospect of heading off on an adventure. The ninety-minute car ride delighted him less; and it wasn't long before he decided that a song was in order. He was on his twenty-third chorus of "Row, Row, Row Your Boat" when we arrived.

Despite the dreary backdrop of steady rain, the great

stone house looked just as imposing as ever. Jack Berglund greeted us warmly at the door, looking only slightly askance when he saw Davey in his yellow slicker, standing beside me. To his credit, he recovered quickly. He asked how the ride had been and offered something warm to drink.

Last visit I'd been content to linger in Jack's company. This time I wanted to do what I'd come for and be gone. The manners that had seemed so charming before, I now found cloying. Jack didn't frighten me, but he did make me angry. The less time Davey and I spent in his presence, the better.

Of course knowing how I felt was all the more reason to watch what I did and said. If I was going to learn anything about Beau's whereabouts, Jack had to be convinced that my motives were pure. Politely I declined his offer of refreshments. He donned his own slicker, and we headed out the back door and across the rain-drenched lawn.

"Hey!" cried Davey, looking at our host with new respect. "You have you own swimming pool!" He slipped out of my grasp like a wet snake and ran on ahead.

"Don't go too close," I called after him. The tiles around the pool looked slick and slippery. Davey stopped just short of the edge. He leaned over and peered down into the deep, clear water.

"Back you go," said Jack, grasping him firmly by the shoulder. "We wouldn't want you to fall in."

"I can swim," Davey told him proudly.

"Of course you can," I said. "But we're here to look at Poodles." He'd been carefully coached that he wasn't to mention Aunt Peg or her dogs, and now I held my breath, praying that he'd remember. But Davey only shrugged, and we continued on to the kennel.

Just inside the door, Jack paused. "Would it be all right with you if Davey waited out here? He could look at the pictures on the wall or go through and visit the older dogs, but I'd really rather he didn't come into the nursery."

"Of course." I understood his hesitation. Baby puppies were fragile. Aunt Peg hadn't let him play with hers either. Besides, from my point of view, the less time he and Jack spent together, the less chance there'd be for any slip-ups. I looked at my son pointedly. "You'll be happy here, won't you, Davey?"

"Sure." A pile of brightly colored leashes caught his eye, and he wandered over to investigate.

Jack went on ahead into the nursery to remove the dam so that she wouldn't be upset by having a stranger in with her puppies. A moment later when he told me to enter, I caught only a glimpse of a chocolate brown hindquarter disappearing through a small door to the covered pen outside. He locked the door behind her, then motioned me over to a large, low-sided box in the corner of the room.

Inside, ten tiny black puppies, with eyes just open, were scrambling over a furry sheepskin rug. Their source of warmth had just been removed, and it took them a moment to find another—the heating pad that lined one end of the box. Finally they all did, and piled in a heap.

"They're adorable," I said softly, sinking down beside the box. "Can I hold one?"

Jack reached in to disentangle one puppy from the heap. "Just be careful to support both ends."

I cradled the baby against my shirt, and it made a low, throaty rumbling sound before snuggling into the crook of my arm contentedly.

Jack joined me on the linoleum floor, and together we leaned over the box. He scratched an ear here and tickled a tummy there, and pretty soon they were all up and moving around. Given the perfect opportunity to study the litter, I found out nothing except that Aunt Peg had been right. They were little and they were black. At that age, I couldn't even have sworn they were Poodles.

"It's a very pretty litter," Jack said, beaming like a proud father. "I'm sure Ranger will do just as well by your bitch."

"Speaking of Ranger, where is he? Doesn't he ever get to come in and have a look at his kids?"

Jack shook his head firmly. "In the first place, he wouldn't realize they were his. And then there's always the chance he might try to hurt them. Don't worry, he's perfectly happy back in his pen."

I laid my sleeping puppy back in with the others. "Ranger might not know what he's done, but I think he should be very proud. Can we stop and give him a pat?"

"Certainly."

We left the nursery and found Ranger in the same pen where he'd been before—the last one on the end. He leapt up to welcome us happily, and his excitement infected the rest of the kennel. Inquiring heads popped up on both sides of the aisle. I scanned the group quickly and felt a stab of disappointment. Ranger was the only young male dog in the room.

Stalling for time, I leaned down to say hello to the stud dog. Just because Beau wasn't in the kennel didn't mean he wasn't at Shalimar. Jack didn't have any Poodles running loose in his house, but I supposed Beau could have been crated. And what about the garage? Perhaps now would be a good time to take Jack up on his offer of a warm drink. Once inside the house, I could plead the need to take Davey to the bathroom, maybe even convince him that now would be an excellent time for a game of hide-and-seek. All right, so I was planning to use my son shamelessly. What other choice did I have?

Then Davey, in his own inimitable way, took the whole thing out of my hands. Jack and I heard the thin, high-pitched scream at the same time. It was followed by a loud splash.

"Mommy!" Davey wailed as only he could. "Mommy, help!"

⌀❧ *Twenty-seven* ❧⌀

Davey, of course, had gone head over heels into the pool. What else would a four-year-old boy do for entertainment on a rainy afternoon? I was across the room and out the door in two steps. But despite my haste, I fully expected to see him paddling around happily. Davey makes his share of outrageous claims, but he does know how to swim.

Unfortunately, I saw as I sprinted across the lawn, that knowledge wasn't doing him any good. His arms had become entangled in the slicker's wide sleeves, and now the cumbersome coat was filling with water, dragging him down. The water rolled around him as he thrashed in vain, trying to free himself. He wasn't panicking yet, but it wouldn't be long.

I hit the water with a clean, flat racing dive which shot me straight across the surface and into my son's arms. Judging by the look on his face, he was very glad to see me. He opened his mouth to speak, took in water, and began to cough.

"Hang on," I said, grasping him under the armpits. Not satisfied with that hold, Davey wrapped his short arms tightly around my neck and nearly took us both under. I kicked hard to keep us on the surface and hugged him to me. It wasn't the best life-saving technique, but it was good enough to get the job done. With Davey clinging like a leech, I gave two good kicks to bring us within range of the pool's concrete lip.

Jack was pacing back and forth on the tiles, and I hoisted Davey up into his arms. "Are you okay?" he cried.

"He's fine." I gasped, still lying half in and half out of the water as bursts of unused adrenaline shot through my body.

"I held my breath," said Davey, looking rather pleased with himself. "Just like Uncle Frank taught me." He took off his slicker and dropped it on the ground, then began to check through the ample contents of his pockets.

Looking at the two of us, Jack shook his head in bewilderment. It was easy to see he'd never had any children of his own. Compared to some of the stunts Davey had pulled in the past, this was a relatively minor incident.

"You're sure you're both all right?"

"Positive," I said firmly.

I sat up and hauled my feet out of the water. We were wet, but at least it wasn't cold. Davey and I were in for an uncomfortable ride home, but I doubted we'd catch pneumonia. I pulled off my flats and dumped them out. Davey followed suit with the red sneakers.

It was all too much for Jack Berglund. Clearly our little adventure had violated his notion of proper etiquette for social occasions. Visibly upset, he tried to salvage the situation by hovering over us solicitously.

"What can I do to help?" he asked as I picked up Davey's slicker and shook it out.

"How about a towel?" I suggested, mostly just to give him something to do.

"A towel, of course. Two towels even." Still brimming with agitation, he strode over to the pool house and yanked open the door. My attention was on Davey, so it was a moment before I realized that a black Standard

Poodle had shot out through the open doorway and into the yard. Jack's yelling, however, was hard to miss.

"Hey there! Come back!"

The dog ignored him and galloped away. Shrugging, Jack continued after the towels. The Poodle danced around the yard, delighted.

"Come back! Come back!" yelled Davey, getting into the spirit of things. The Poodle ignored him also.

I stood and stared, but I didn't say a word. I didn't have to. It was Beau; it had to be. Who else would Berglund have stashed away inside the pool house? The Poodle's coat was long and shaggy, and his face was unclipped; but there was something about him that was immediately arresting—the way he carried himself, perhaps, or the assurance with which he moved.

Quickly I tried to remember everything Aunt Peg had told me to look for. It was no use. I'd gone totally blank. The Poodle skidded past us, racing around the pool. As he galloped by, so close that I could have reached out and touched him, I realized with a small sense of shock that he looked familiar. But that was impossible, wasn't it?

The kennel dogs, hearing the commotion in the yard, burst out into their runs and began to bark. The Poodle skidded to a stop and stiffened. His head and tail snapped up at attention; and suddenly I had my answer. It wasn't one dog he reminded me of, but rather a whole group. Standing alertly with his neck arched and his tail high, this dog was the very image of a Cedar Crest Poodle.

The hair on the back of my neck began to tingle, and the sensation worked its way down my spine. After three long months, I'd finally found the dog I was looking for.

"Beau?" I called the name as loudly as I dared, but the Poodle was too far away to hear me. Then Jack emerged from the pool house, towels in hand, and the dog took off toward the kennel.

"There he goes!" Davey cried gleefully.

Jack tossed the towels to me, then went after the Poodle. I wrapped Davey up warmly in plush yellow terry cloth and went to join in the chase. Unfortunately by the time I reached the kennel, Jack had already caught the collarless dog and was leading him inside by the muzzle. Davey flopped into a chair in the front room, but I followed them on inside.

"What Poodle is that?" I asked as he released the dog into an empty pen.

"His name's Scotty. He belongs to the neighbors."

"What's he doing here?"

Jack reached in to ruffle the dog's topknot. "They dropped him off yesterday before they left on vacation. I'm looking after him while they're gone."

He had to be lying. But how could he have come up with a story like that so quickly? And why didn't he look even the tiniest bit nervous?

Unsure now, I moved in for a closer look. Deftly, Jack angled me away. Outmaneuvered, I gave ground and asked casually, "Is he a stud dog, too?"

Bad question, if the look on Berglund's face was anything to go by. "No, he's not. The problem is, he thinks he is. He and Ranger have been driving each other crazy. That's why I had to put him in the pool house."

Standing as we were in a room full of strong, high-walled pens, that sounded like a terrible reason for locking a dog in a pool house; but I nodded as though it made perfect sense. "He seems to have a good temperament. Was he one of your puppies originally?"

Even as Jack answered, we were already moving away from the pen and back to the outer room. "No, they bought him before they moved in. I never asked where he came from and they never said. He's just the children's pet."

I guess Davey had had enough excitement for one day, because for once he was actually waiting where I'd left him. Thoroughly damp and grinning happily about it, he jumped up when we appeared. Jack escorted us out to our car.

"I'll be in touch," I said, and he nodded.

We parted the best of friends.

Davey napped on the ride home, and I spent the time back trying to decide how I was going to present what I had seen to Aunt Peg. Though I was just about certain that I'd found Beau, I had no proof. The farther away I got, the more I began to worry. What if the visit had been nothing more than a self-fulfilling prophecy? Maybe the reason that Poodle had looked like Beau to me was because I'd expected him to.

By the time we reached Greenwich, I'd decided to aim for cautious optimism—I would describe the visit as it had gone and see if a recital of the facts brought her to the same conclusion I'd reached.

Davey was still asleep when we arrived, so I parked in the shade and left him in the backseat. I'd barely climbed the steps when the front door flew open. The herd of Poodles surged out, but I barely spared them a glance. One look at Aunt Peg's face and I knew how anxiously she'd awaited my arrival. Everything she was feeling was right there: impatience, frustration, but most of all, a naked yearning for wonderful news.

"Well?" she demanded, and I couldn't disappoint her.

"He's there."

For a moment I almost thought she was going to cry. But of course, she didn't. Instead she practically ran me into the living room and shoved me down on the couch, damp clothes and all. She wanted news, and she wanted it fast. Quickly I told her about our visit, glossing over the details until I came to the part about the mysterious Poodle in the pool house.

Aunt Peg listened with remarkable patience as I described the scene down to the last detail.

"Of course I asked who the Poodle was," I told her. "But Jack had a perfectly reasonable explanation for everything."

"So what makes you think that the dog was Beau?"

"He didn't look like someone's pet, for one thing. No matter what Jack said. And besides, he reminded me of your dogs."

Her brow lifted. "You mean he resembled them?"

"Yes." I wished desperately that I had more to offer. "The way he held himself made me think of them."

"Well, I suppose that's something," Aunt Peg said. "Did he look like the pictures I showed you?"

I honestly didn't know, and I admitted as much. "When you come right down to it, there's not all that much difference between one black Standard Poodle and another."

At least not to me, I thought. Aunt Peg could sort out a dozen or more at twenty paces. How she managed it, I had no idea. My damp clothing was itching like crazy, and I sat back on the couch with a frown. Aunt Peg had spent the whole summer coaching me on how to develop an eye for a dog. I hated having to tell her that just when I'd needed it most, my knowledge had proven inadequate.

"I suppose the hair was different, too," she said with a sigh.

I nodded.

"You didn't get a chance to call him by name, did you?"

"I tried, but outside I was too far away. And then once we went into the kennel, Jack was all over me."

We sat in silence for several moments, considering.

Finally Aunt Peg spoke. "Give me your gut reaction."

She'd already had it, earlier. But now that she'd heard

how nebulous my evidence was, I couldn't blame her for asking again.

"It was Beau."

Unexpectedly, she grinned. "I think so, too."

"So now what?"

"I'm not sure."

That was hardly the decisive response I'd been hoping for. "Shouldn't we call the police?"

"It's not that simple," Aunt Peg said slowly. "Don't forget, I spoke with them before. In order to get a search warrant, they're going to need proof—something nice and solid—which is precisely what we don't have. The problem is not in proving Beau's ownership once we get our hands on him. It's in getting the police to go out there in the first place."

I had thought that the hard part would be finding Beau. It had never even occurred to me that once that happened, we might be stymied all over again by the process of trying to reclaim him.

"Tell me about the puppies you saw," said Aunt Peg. "Was there anything worth discussing there?"

I related what little there was to tell. They were ten black, furry little balls, as indistinguishable from each other as if they'd been made from a mold.

Aunt Peg nodded as though she hadn't expected anything else. She had to be feeling just as frustrated as I was, but she was doing her best not to let it show. "Never mind," she said. "Let me work on it overnight. I'll think of something."

I could only hope she was right.

⌥❖ *Twenty-eight* ❖⌥

I took Aunt Peg at her word and gave her overnight to think. But she didn't call on Friday morning or the rest of the day either. It was Davey's last day of camp and all the parents were invited to the closing festivities which included several skits, an arts-and-crafts display, and a parent-child kickball game.

Emily Grace pulled me aside at the end and handed me an envelope containing a fifty-dollar bonus. "Thanks for everything," she said.

"Thank you." I tucked the envelope away. "I can't believe the summer's just about over. School starts in two weeks."

"Real school." Emily reached down and tweaked the brim of Davey's baseball cap. "You're going to be in kindergarten. Wow!"

"I'm going to ride the bus," Davey told her proudly. "It's going to stop right on our block."

"We'll miss you at Graceland." Emily looked up suddenly. "Just because he's graduated, let's not lose touch, okay?"

"Okay." I grinned. "We'll do lunch."

"You're on," she said, and we hugged to seal the deal.

———

I probably forgot to mention that Sam had left a message on my answering machine at the beginning of the week. That's because I was trying not to think about it. I hadn't returned his call, though I'd started to several times. The problem was, I couldn't quite think of what I was going to say. So like a coward, I said nothing.

Aunt Peg did call Saturday morning, but it wasn't to offer any solutions. Instead she said she was on her way to a dog show in Danbury. "I'm still hoping for a brainstorm. But in the meantime I've got a puppy entered and ready to go. Why don't you and Davey meet me there?"

The idea had merit. Not the least of which was the possibility that I might run into Sam at the show. The meeting would be casual and uncontrived. And Sam would start right off by telling me that the blonde was really his sister . . .

Right. And maybe Jack Berglund would bring Beau along and deliver him into Aunt Peg's outstretched hands. Nevertheless the schedule wasn't exactly full and the forecast promised a beautiful, sunny day. The Volvo performed like a champ, and we arrived at the show ground an hour before the start of the Poodle judging.

The first thing I saw, upon checking the catalogue, was that Sam wasn't even entered. So much for Plan A. Plan B consisted of simply enjoying the day with my son. And that was nice, too. Without a mission to accomplish, we approached the show as spectators, wandering wherever Davey's whims took us.

Back in the grooming tent, voices were subdued. Predictably, the conversation centered around Randall Tarnower's murder, and the talk was rife with speculation. Kim was there to show several of Randy's dogs, and it was clear she relished the attention she was receiving.

The Poodle judging came and went with little fanfare. The entry wasn't large. Aunt Peg won the puppy bitch class with Lulu, and I could sense her displeasure when

Jack Berglund won the Open class and they went head to head for Winners Bitch. Lulu was probably the better Poodle, but the Shalimar bitch had her beaten on coat, maturity, and training. The judge took no time at all in making his decision. Jack won the points, and Peg's puppy was reserve. No champions had been entered; the Winners Bitch was awarded Best of Variety, too.

After the Poodles were finished, the Chow Chow judging began. Davey was delighted by the bushy orange dogs, and we lingered for a bit to watch. Unfortunately the routine wasn't nearly so interesting without the added spice of caring about the outcome, and we soon strolled on to see what the other rings held.

First Scotties, then Basset Hounds caught Davey's eye. When we came to the Chinese Crested ring, however, I was the one who stopped and stared. The toy dogs were small and entirely bald, except for a profuse tuft of fluffy hair that sprouted from the top of their heads.

"Look, Mommy," said Davey, giggling. "Cartoon dogs."

The judge was making his selection for Best of Breed from a large group of champions, which he sorted through with deft authority. He looked familiar, and after a moment, I figured out why. He was Aunt Peg's friend, Carl Holden.

Davey was enthralled, so we watched until the end. Carl handled his ring like a master, and the funny, playful Chinese Cresteds drew a large gallery of spectators. Among them, I saw to my surprise, was the blond woman I'd met at Sam Driver's house. I stared for a moment, but she was intent on the drama being played out in the ring and didn't look back.

At least now I knew why she'd seemed familiar. Though she didn't have Poodles, she must have exhibited another breed, for I was sure I'd seen her at the shows.

Carl made his selection for Best Of Breed. Pictures

were taken, and then the ring was opened up so the group judging could begin. All of the breeds recognized by the American Kennel Club are divided by seven groups, according to common heritage or function. Standard and Miniature Poodles are in the Non-Sporting group. Toy Poodles are judged with the Toy Group. Each Best of Breed winner is eligible to compete in its group. The seven group winners then go on to vie for the title of Best In Show.

The Toy Group was scheduled first, and once again Carl was judging. More than a dozen Toy breeds filed in and took their places. Even to my admittedly untrained eye, there were several outstanding specimens in the ring, and I was pleased when my favorites, the Shih Tzu, the Chihuahua, and the Toy Poodle all made the cut.

In the end, however, the group was won by a rather lackluster Maltese. I wasn't the only one who was disappointed. The knowledgeable spectators ringside showed their displeasure by giving the winner no applause at all. Carl handed out the ribbons and quickly left the ring. Wondering, I watched him go. Then Davey reached over and tugged on my hand, and the thought that had been forming was lost.

"Hey, Sport," I said, "you've been very patient. I think you deserve a treat."

I had ice cream in mind, but Davey's eyes immediately lit up. "Wow," he said. "Anything I want?"

I may be a pushover, but I'm not that dumb. "Anything within reason," I qualified.

"Come on." Davey grabbed my hand. "Let's go."

"Where are we going?" I asked as we skirted around the group ring and cut across the field.

"To the parking lot. You said I could do anything I want. I want to see the big rigs."

Big rigs. I had to smile. He had a book by that name at home. It was filled with construction vehicles and heavy machinery. I doubted that the trailers and motor homes he'd find at the dog show were big enough to qualify, but if he was happy, I supposed I could humor him. We could always go for ice cream later.

Most four-year-olds have short attention spans, and Davey is no exception—unless cars and trucks are involved. Then he's happy to look for hours. We strolled up the first row of vans, trailers, and motor homes, then back across the second. They were long rows; my own attention was wandering when Davey ran on ahead.

The object of his fascination was a shiny silver behemoth of a motor home. Before I could catch up, he bounded up the steps and tried the door. To my surprise, it opened easily.

"I like this one. Let's go inside."

"Davey, wait!" As I snatched him off the step and swung him to the ground, I heard dogs barking within, but no irate human appeared to ask what we were doing.

"Honey, we can't go in there. It belongs to someone. It's like their house."

"Oh." Only momentarily deterred, Davey tried the next door. It, too, was unlocked. Obviously Aunt Peg wasn't the only one who relied on her dogs for security.

"Come on," I said, taking a firm grip of Davey's hand. "I think we've seen enough big rigs for one day."

We were almost back to the show when a familiar blue and white motor home with a striped awning caught my eye. Neatly lettered on the cab were the words, "Shalimar Kennels."

I stopped. I had to. Davey was eager to move on, and I probably should have let him lead me away. But if God wanted to drop a golden opportunity like that into my lap, who was I to pass it by?

I strolled over and tapped casually on the door. Nobody answered. My hand was shaking as I reached for the handle, but I grasped it firmly and flipped the latch. Like the others we'd seen, the door was unlocked.

"Jack?" I called, poking my head inside. "Are you home?"

Apparently not. My heart was beating so fast I was surprised I could still think clearly. Group judging was going on. The Shalimar bitch had won the variety and qualified for the Non-Sporting group. That had to be where Jack had gone.

The choice was now or never. I opted for now.

"Come on, Davey," I said, sprinting toward the grooming tent. "Quick. I'll race you."

That did the trick, and we reached Aunt Peg in no time. I hopped Davey up onto the top of her crate. "What group is in?"

Aunt Peg looked up from wrapping Lulu's ears. "Non-Sporting."

"How long have they been judging?"

"I think it just started. The judge is going over the Dalmatian."

Davey attended to, I turned to have a look. Jack Berglund was standing second in line. He couldn't leave the ring until the judging was over. That gave me at least fifteen minutes.

"Will you watch Davey?"

"Where are you going?"

"I'll tell you later. Just don't let him out of your sight, okay?"

I didn't wait to hear her reply because I was already running back in the other direction. I've never been one for gratuitous bravery, but what choice did I have? I'd found Beau only to discover that I needed proof to get him back. If Jack Berglund's motor home might offer up anything in the way of evidence, I was going to find it.

I looked both ways, then opened the door and slipped

inside. I was ready for anything; except, as it turned out, the actual reality.

Inside, the motor home was perfectly ordinary in every way. A row of empty crates lined one wall and a narrow bed and a built-in set of drawers filled the other. The whole space was uncommonly neat; there wasn't a leash or brush out of place. Obviously Jack wasn't the sort of man who left anything, much less incriminating evidence, lying around.

I opened the drawers in turn and found only a selection of grooming supplies and several changes of clothing. The countertops were mostly empty; the cupboards above them held some canned food and a bag of dry kibble. Suddenly my wonderful opportunity wasn't looking nearly so opportune.

On one end of the counter, several books were stacked in a tidy pile. I'd passed them by the first time, but now I went back for a closer look. That's when I discovered that the one on the bottom wasn't a book at all, but rather a photo album. I held it up to the small bit of light that filtered in through the windows and flipped through the pages.

Not surprisingly it held show pictures, no different than any of the dozens I'd seen before. Jack had written the name of each Poodle across the top of his picture. I was skimming through them quickly when I saw the name Shalimar Solitaire.

Ranger's dam. That alone was enough to make me pause; but a closer look revealed nothing of consequence. Solitaire was a small, nondescript brown bitch, presumably shown winning her first and only points shortly before her death. It was just a show picture, the same as any other.

I heard the quiet click behind me, but in the time the sound took to register it was already too late. I dropped the album onto the counter, but there wasn't time to close it. Then Jack was there in the doorway, his voice loud and angry. "What the hell do you think you're doing in here?" he demanded.

Good question.

Twenty-nine

Too bad I didn't have a good answer.

I turned around slowly, and as I did so the light, shining through the open doorway, revealed to Jack who his visitor was. "Oh it's you," he said, sounding considerably less angry, but still pretty curious. Perhaps there was a way to salvage the situation after all.

"Hi," I said brightly as though the fact that he'd found me poking around inside his motor home was nothing unusual. "I thought of a couple more questions I wanted to ask you. I hope you don't mind if I waited in here."

"I guess not." Jack climbed up the steps and closed the door behind him. "I'm free now. Ask away."

Ask what? The only question I had was how I was going to get Aunt Peg's dog away from him, and that wasn't a suitable topic of conversation. Instead I began to babble. "I was wondering about your puppies. I told a friend of mine how cute your puppies were, and she said she might be interested if you had any available . . ."

Jack was looking around the interior of the motor home, and I realized suddenly that he was just as unsure of the situation as I was. Disaster hadn't been averted, only postponed.

Of course the first thing he noticed was the open photo album on the counter. As I edged past him toward the door, Jack moved in for a closer look. Something he saw there was cause for alarm because even in the half light, I could see his tan pale.

It was, I decided, a very good time to leave. "I've got your number," I said. "I'll have her give you a call."

Jack turned and caught my arm. His grip wasn't painful, but it was tight enough to get its message across. "Who are you really?"

I tried for a surprised laugh which ended up sounding slightly hysterical. "You know who I am, Jack."

"I doubt that." The strength of his grip grew. "Let me tell you something," he said. As if I had a choice. "Every once in a while a truly exceptional dog comes along, one that can do a great deal of good for the breed—if he survives to produce. It's happened before that such a dog is cut down in his prime. It could happen again."

He was holding tightly enough that he must have felt me shudder. Then suddenly his fingers were gone and I was free to go. I scrambled out of the motor home before he had a chance to change his mind.

Back at the grooming tent, Davey and Aunt Peg were eating chocolate ice cream cones and awaiting my arrival. "We have to talk," I said grimly to Aunt Peg. "But not here. I'm going to take Davey to a friend's house. I'll met you back at your place, okay?"

One look at the expression on my face and Aunt Peg knew not to ask any questions. She delivered Davey into my arms, and we drove straight from the show to Joey Brickman's house. I cited emergency and Alice, bless her, promptly asked him to stay the night. Then it was back to Aunt Peg's.

She'd arrived home before me but not by much. We went out to the grooming room in the kennel, where she used her big hair dryer to blow the hair spray out of Lulu's coat while I told her what had happened in Berglund's trailer.

"I don't have even the slightest idea what it was that set him off," I said at the end. "One minute I thought I'd be able to bluff my way through. The next, he saw the open album and was furious."

"Obviously something about the pictures you saw upset him," Peg said, brushing through a tangle. "Describe them to me."

"There's nothing to describe. They looked just like everyone else's pictures. I was just flipping through quickly. The only name I even recognized was Shalimar Solitaire, Ranger's dam."

"Tell me about her picture." Aunt Peg redirected the flow of hair, and Lulu, lying quietly on the table, shifted sides. "What did she look like?"

"Not particularly pretty. Lots of coat, and not much leg. Nice-enough head, but terribly light eyes. In the picture, they looked almost yellow."

"Yellow eyes?" Peg looked up. "What color was she?"

"Brown. Could that be important?"

"I don't know," Aunt Peg said thoughtfully. "But it's the only new fact we've learned. Let me think about it. I'm almost done here. Why don't you go up to the house and start some tea? I'll be along in a minute."

Her one minute turned into ten, but in that time I'd made both tea and instant coffee, and managed to find a box of Mint Milano cookies she'd squirreled away in the back of the cabinet. She came in the back door, sat down at the table, and took up where we left off.

"Tell me again about those puppies you saw. What color were they?"

"Black. I told you that before."

"All of them?"

My mouth was filled with cookie. I settled for a nod.

"How about the bitch? Did you get a chance to look at her?"

"Only for a moment. She was brown like Solitaire. But

you told me yourself that the different colors could produce one another—"

"That's it!" Aunt Peg cried.

"That's what?"

"That's what Jack didn't want you to see. Black Poodles *can* produce all the other colors, if the correct recessive gene is carried. If Ranger's dam was brown, then he would have to carry the brown gene. Bred to a brown bitch, that litter you saw—if it was Ranger's—should have been mixed, some black, some brown. You're working on statistical averages, of course, but in a litter of ten not to find a single brown puppy coming from those two parents? That's highly unlikely."

"Jack told me himself that a number of his Poodles carried for brown."

"*His* do," Aunt Peg said emphatically. "But mine don't. Jack might have guessed that, but he wouldn't have known for sure. Once he had Beau, however, he had to be certain. That's probably why he bred the dog to a brown bitch right off the bat."

"He told me that Solitaire had only been shown once at a very small show. There weren't many people there to see her, and even those who did probably wouldn't remember."

Aunt Peg nodded. "If Jack let it be known that Solitaire was a black bitch, who would have been able to contradict him?"

"Nobody but me," I said slowly. "He must have forgotten that the picture was there. No wonder he was so upset."

Aunt Peg stood. "It's time to call the police. Frankly I'd hoped to have more evidence than this to offer, but if we don't get Beau away from there soon, it may be too late."

She dialed the state police emergency number, then cocked the receiver away from her ear so that I could listen in. After a minute or two, I'd heard enough. The offi-

cer who answered had no concept of dominant and recessive genes and no desire to learn about them over the
phone. He did not view the situation as an emergency and
was not at all pleased by what he saw as Aunt Peg's abuse
of the special number. If she wished to come down and
make a complaint in person, the sergeant would be happy
to listen; but no immediate action could be promised until
the police were fully cognizant of the situation.

"You don't understand," said Aunt Peg. "Two men
have died because of this dog."

That got his attention, but only briefly. Uncle Max's
death wasn't listed as a homicide; Randall Tarnower's
had taken place in another state. Once again the officer
reiterated that Aunt Peg would need to come down in
person.

"That moron has all the brainpower of a shoe horn!"
she said, fuming, as she hung up the phone. "Now I have
to go down there and explain everything all over again."

Already I was on my feet and dumping our dishes in
the sink. "We don't have time for that. Jack has got to
realize that the dog is the link that ties him here the night
that Max was killed. If I were him, I'd get rid of Beau first
thing."

"What choice do we have? We need to have the police
with us, or what's the use? Jack would have every right to
turn us away at the door. And especially after the threats
he made to you, we can't afford to force his hand."

"We'll split up," I said. "You go see the police. I'm
heading up to Shalimar."

"No." Aunt Peg was firm. "I don't like that idea at all."

"You said it yourself just a minute ago. We don't have
a choice. I'm going, and that's that. So hurry, okay?"

She considered for a minute, then finally nodded.
"We'll be right behind you."

If I'd known how wrong she'd prove to be, I would have been very worried indeed. But I had every faith in truth, justice, and the American way, and was fully convinced that the police would come roaring to the rescue as soon as they understood the facts. They'd be fifteen minutes behind me. Twenty, tops.

I managed the trip in just over an hour, which meant that I broke the speed limit all the way. That was more than enough time to think about what I was going to do. As I saw it, the trick was to avoid a confrontation. I'd simply slip in quietly and keep an eye on things to make sure that Jack didn't do anything clever before the police could get there.

It was dusk when I arrived and getting darker by the minute, which suited my purposes perfectly. I drove past the Shalimar gateposts and left the Volvo parked by the side of the road ten yards farther on. Two long minutes at a rapid jog left me utterly winded, but within viewing distance of the huge stone house and kennel beyond.

Breathing heavily, I leaned against a tree at the top of the driveway and studied my approach. A small light glowed softly above the front door, but other than that the front of the house was unlit. The kennel and the pool house were both completely dark. Beau could be in any one of those three places. I would have had the dog inside with me, but since I'd never seen any Poodles in Jack's house, I guessed he was more likely to choose the kennel.

Stealthily I crept around the side of the house. A light was on in the library window, and as I drew near I could hear someone talking. I dropped to my hands and knees on the soft turf and covered the remaining distance at a crawl. From beneath the sill of the open window, Jack's voice was clear. He seemed to be speaking on the telephone.

"What do you mean you haven't left yet?" he was saying furiously. "I expected you to be here by now." He listened briefly, then said, "Do you think I care if it's your anniversary? The woman's been here twice already; who knows who she's filed a report with? I don't think anything could happen this quickly, but just to be on the safe side I want the dog moved. Tonight. No, I can't bring him to you. If there are questions to be answered, I want to be here. How would it look if I weren't?"

I'd heard enough to realize that just keeping an eye on things wasn't going to be good enough. If Jack succeeded in getting Beau away from us a second time, he'd make sure we never found the dog again. Whoever he'd been speaking to might arrive in five minutes or in half an hour. I couldn't take the chance that he might beat the police. I had to find Beau first and get him out of there before it was too late.

Still on my hands and knees, and giving thanks to Berglund's gardeners every inch of the way, I continued around the house until I was clear of the windows. Then I pulled myself up into a low crouch and dashed across the darkened yard.

I reached the pool house and flattened into the shadow of its walls, waiting for the outcry I was half sure would follow. My heart was beating loudly enough to feel like a tangible presence on the still night; but as the moments passed and no one charged out of the house in outraged pursuit, it slowly settled and I was able to get on with the job at hand.

Cautiously I pushed my face up against the nearest window. It was too dark inside the pool house to make out anything, much less the shadowy presence of a black dog. The door was on the side of the building that faced the house, but there were two windows in back. The first held firm, but the second grated open grudgingly, making far more noise than was prudent under the circumstances.

Immediately I stopped tugging, settling for a crack merely an inch wide. It was enough for what I needed to do. I knelt down and applied my lips to the opening, then softly called Beau's name. There was no welcoming bark, no answering whine. No one was home.

So much for simple solutions, and on to round two.

The kennel—my next conquest—presented a whole new set of problems. Chief among them was how to get into the building without setting off the inevitable noisy chorus. And then secondly, once inside, how to determine quickly and in the dark which of the dozen or so black Standard Poodles housed there might be Beau.

Aunt Peg, I thought, I hope you're hurrying.

From the pool house it was only a matter of yards to the bushes beside the kennel. I raced across the dark expanse, then stopped to listen. So far, all was quiet. Sneaking like a thief, I made my way around the building to the side farthest from the house, then stooped down and groped around until I found a large flat rock. I reached back and lobbed it upward in a high, soaring arc. The rock flew over the runs and landed on the roof of the kennel with a satisfyingly loud thud.

The response was instantaneous. Immediately the night was filled with the clamor of a dozen outraged, awakened Poodles. It was all I'd hoped for and more. I leaned back against the darkened building to await Berglund's reaction.

It didn't take long. At once the kennel lit up like a torch. Floodlights illuminated all four sides of the building and spread out over the lawn beyond, illuminating with equal clarity just how stupid I'd been. I'd expected Jack to march out and have a quick look around with a flashlight. Instead, he had the whole place covered like Fort Knox.

Before there was time to say much more than, "Oh damn!" Jack appeared at the back door. Maybe he'd be satisfied to look around the yard from there, I prayed.

He wasn't.

When he pushed the screen door open, I jumped back

behind the cover of the kennel and sprinted with all the speed that panic could induce. Thirty feet of open lawn ended at a belt of woods that separated his house from the next. Scrambling for the nearest cover, I lost the sleeve of my shirt to a bush full of thorns as I dove headfirst into a prickly nest of pine needles and twigs.

I got myself turned around and peered out through the bushes, waiting for Jack to come storming around the side of the kennel. He never did. Instead he'd gone inside, and I was able to follow his progress though the building by the lights that switched on and off in the various rooms.

All my instincts told me to stay put, forget the dog, and never venture out again; and for a full five minutes, I listened. By that time I was cold and damp, and both legs had gone to sleep. Movement of any sort had begun to feel inviting. Staying just inside the strip of trees, I crept along the ground until I was able to see the front of the kennel.

Only a moment later the door to the building was yanked open, and Jack emerged. He was carrying a powerful, high-beam flashlight in one hand and something small and shiny in the other. It took me a moment to figure out what it was, or maybe my brain simply didn't want to process the thought. Finally it did.

Jack Berglund had a gun. Oh great.

∾❋ *Thirty* ❋∾

He gazed out over the yard and for a moment seemed to look right at me. Hurriedly I dropped from knees to stomach and took in a mouthful of dirt for my trouble. Jack swept the beam around the area at waist height, and it passed harmlessly over my head. Apparently he was satisfied by what he saw, for he turned back to the kennel and switched off the inside lights, then strode back across the lawn to the house.

Lots of people keep guns for protection these days, I told myself. It didn't mean he'd be willing to use it. And over a *dog?* Get real. No doubt the gun was a scare tactic. All right, so I was scared. But I wasn't about to give up.

I gave him two minutes. This time I knew what to expect and had almost made it back to the trees by the time the rock hit the roof and started the dogs off again. This time I could almost smile as he came flying out the back door at a dead run.

The second time around, his inspection was much quicker; and on the third, when the Poodles began to howl, he simply stuck his head out the back door and bellowed "Shut up!" in their general direction. That was the response I'd been waiting for. One problem down and one to go.

You'd think it might have occurred to me that the back

door to the kennel would be locked, which it was, quite securely. The front door was open. I knew that for a fact because Berglund had been in and out twice in the last fifteen minutes and I hadn't seen him stop to fumble with any keys. But it also faced the house squarely; and with the floodlights still on and doing their job, I couldn't chance using it.

Then I remembered Beau's innovative thief, who'd gone over the chain-link fence and in through one of the swinging doors. If he could manage it, so could I.

By the time I'd reached the top of the fence and swung over, I'd pinched all of my fingers and most of my toes and was beginning to take a rather dim view of this rescue operation. And where the hell was Aunt Peg anyway? She should have been there with reinforcements ages ago.

I was pleased to discover that my trick with the rocks had paid off handsomely. By the time I arrived in their midst, the Poodles were all barked out. We'd met before anyway, and now they greeted me like an old friend. Even the old matron into whose pen I climbed seemed glad of the company. As I wriggled in through the narrow door, she took the opportunity to clean my face which, considering how much dirt it had been exposed to lately, wasn't an entirely unwelcome gesture.

I let myself out of the pen and felt my way around the room, going from stall to stall and calling out Beau's name softly as I passed each one. Down the first side, I got no response. Ears pricked in curiosity, but no Poodle leaped up and threw himself into my arms, demanding immediate rescue. Maybe I'd been a fool to think that he would.

Then I hit the jackpot. With an excited whine, a big black Poodle bounded up in the air. Balancing his front paws on the top of the gate, he danced up and down on his hind. "Beau?" I said again, this time louder. "Is that really you?"

His tail wagged in affirmation.

My God, I thought. I'd actually done it. Now all we had to do was get out of there.

That was when the lights came on.

"This is getting to be a habit," Jack said from behind me. "And not a pleasant one at that."

There's no doubt that I was as frightened at that moment as I've ever been in my life. As I turned to face him, the first thing I noticed was that he hadn't forgotten his gun. I strained my ears, listening for the sound of oncoming sirens, but the night outside was quiet.

"Please explain what you are doing in my kennel."

There wasn't much point in lying. Bravado wasn't my first choice, but my options seemed to be rapidly dwindling. "I've come for the dog."

"Really?" Jack looked around. "Which one?"

"I'm sure you know the answer to that." My hand strayed back to the latch on Beau's gate. When I flipped it open, he bounded out into the room. "This dog doesn't belong to your neighbors. He's the Poodle you stole from Max and Margaret Turnbull."

Jack leaned back against the doorjamb. Though he was blocking the only way out, he must have decided I wasn't much of a threat because he slipped the gun into the waistband of his pants.

"I haven't stolen anything," he said calmly.

I gave him the look that comment deserved. "Then why were you planning to send him away?"

"That's none of your business."

"Fine. Then you can tell your reasons to the police. They'll be here shortly."

"The police? I thought you worked for the A.K.C."

Why would he think that? Something was definitely wrong. Jack should have been sweating, but he wasn't. In fact he hardly seemed perturbed at all.

"The police won't find anything but a kennel full of

black dogs that all look alike. Besides, no crime has been committed, except perhaps your own trespassing."

"Oh no?" I cried. "What about grand larceny? Or maybe even murder. I'm sure the authorities will have plenty of questions for you to answer."

"Murder?" I'd gotten his attention all right, but now Jack looked perplexed. "What are you talking about?"

"I'm talking about Max Turnbull. The man you stole Beau from. The man you left lying on a cold kennel floor to die."

"That's absurd. You don't have any idea what you're talking about—"

I might have debated the question, but it wasn't necessary. Finally I heard the far-off sound of gravel crunching. Headlights swept across the lawn. Jack turned to look, and in that moment of inattention, I grabbed Beau and the two of us scrambled past him out of the kennel.

We'd crossed the yard and rounded the house before it occurred to me that we might be running straight into the arms of Jack's friend. Then I saw the brace of lights on top of the police cruiser. Relief turned my knees to rubber. As doors began to open and people emerge, I sank down slowly into the soft grass. Unfortunately for Beau, I was still holding his collar. The two of us went down together.

"Melanie?" called a familiar voice. "Is that you?"

I started to rise, but Beau was quicker. With a whine that started deep in his throat, he leapt up in the air, tossing me aside like a bag of old kibble. I recovered in time to see him go tearing across the driveway and straight into Aunt Peg's arms.

She bent low to greet him, and he all but knocked her over. Beau, who was growling and whimpering at the same time, climbed up and down every inch of her, lapping the tears from her cheeks.

Two stern-looking policemen stood beside their squad car and watched the scene with varying amounts of skepticism. Finally one, whose name tag identified him as Officer Denny, moved over into the beam provided by the headlights and began to take notes.

"Is this the dog you told us about?" he asked.

Aunt Peg was clearly in no shape to answer questions, so I did. "Yes, it is. That's her Poodle, Beau. Jack Berglund, who lives in this house, stole him from her three months ago."

Officer Denny looked me over from head to foot, taking in everything from the ripped blouse to the mud that still clung to my clothes in patches. Evidently I didn't suit his idea of a star witness. He sighed as he said, "I take it you're the niece?"

"Yes."

Aunt Peg tore herself away from Beau long enough to perform the introductions. I shook hands solemnly with Officers Denny and Mosconi, but they were not appeased. Some reinforcements. I felt like Custer, longing for a second cavalry, only to discover that more Indians had arrived instead.

"We've heard one side," said Officer Denny, tucking his pad away. "We may as well hear the other. Let's go find Mr. Berglund and see what he has to say."

Together we all trooped back to the kennel, Aunt Peg and I trotting along behind like first graders on a school outing. "Where'd you get these two?" I asked her under my breath.

"They were the best I could do," she whispered back. "They didn't want to come at all. Finally I told them you were in dire danger and kicked up such a fuss that the sergeant made them. That's what took so long."

Jack Berglund greeted us at the kennel door with a convincing mixture of bewilderment and righteous indignation. Gratefully, the two policemen settled upon him as the only rational person they had encountered thus far, and I could see our case unraveling before our very eyes.

"This is all a misunderstanding," Jack told them smoothly. "I'm terribly sorry you gentlemen had to come all the way out here at this time of night for nothing."

"Nothing? Why don't we start with the stolen dog? And by the way," I told the officers, "he has a gun."

"A gun that I have a permit for," said Jack. He pulled open a drawer and indicated the stashed weapon, then took out his wallet and handed over the permit. "The Poodles alerted me to the presence of a prowler on the property. I was merely taking sensible precautions."

Score another for his side, if the look on the officers' faces was anything to go by.

"As to the dog, I'm afraid I don't understand what all the fuss is about. There are no stolen Poodles here."

The two officers conferred quietly. Things were not going well. I looked to Aunt Peg for help, but she was still engrossed with Beau, as though seeing him again was the only thing in the world that mattered.

"Look at them," I said. "Can't you see that the Poodle is hers?"

"So he's a friendly dog," said Jack. "So what?" He chuckled smugly, and I glared in his direction.

"Look, Mrs. Turnbull," said Officer Mosconi. "You told us there was solid proof that the dog belonged to you. Now if you've dragged us all the way up here just to watch a scene out of *Lassie*, I'm not going to be pleased. Do you have the proof or don't you?"

Aunt Peg, as always, rose to the occasion. "Gentlemen," she said grandly, "if you will follow me."

We did, and she led us to the grooming area on the other side of the room. Beau trotted along happily in Aunt Peg's wake. Anybody could tell just by watching that Beau was Aunt Peg's dog. The look on her face was proof enough for me. The long arm of the law, however, wanted more.

Aunt Peg hopped Beau up onto the grooming table,

then gestured for all of us to gather around. She reached into her purse and withdrew a gadget that looked like a small dustbuster with a digital read-out screen near the handle. Beside me, Jack drew in a sharp breath. He knew what she was up to, I realized. I still hadn't a clue.

"This is a scanner," said Aunt Peg. She laid Beau down facing away from us. "All of my dogs have been fitted with microchips for the purposes of positive identification." She passed the scanner over the top of Beau's shoulders, and an eleven-digit number appeared on the screen. Officer Denny copied it down on his pad.

"This number is registered with a national recovery service, Find-A-Chip, in Easton, PA. It identifies this dog as Champion Cedar Crest Chantain and me, Margaret Turnbull, as his owner. They maintain a twenty-four hour toll-free number in case of emergencies. If any doubt remains, I suggest we go inside and give them a call."

I could have kissed her, but of course I didn't. Instead I settled for a wide grin.

Jack was shaking his head vigorously; but at last Aunt Peg and I had the police on our side. "What do you have to say to that?" asked Officer Mosconi.

"You've got this all wrong. Maybe the dog was hers, but I didn't steal him. And I don't know anything about Max Turnbull's death."

"If you didn't take the dog," I asked, "where did you get him from?"

"I bought him."

Sure, I thought. This was almost fun. "From whom?"

Jack waited a beat until he was sure he had everyone's full attention. "I bought him from Max Turnbull," he said. "And I have a bill of sale to prove it."

Thirty-one

He was bluffing, he had to be.

I looked to Aunt Peg for confirmation and saw that her skin was ashen, her mouth slack. She'd sagged back against the grooming table and wouldn't meet my eye. In the wake of that bombshell, she had nothing to say. Jack, however, was talking plenty.

"Max contacted me," he said, folding his arms over his chest calmly. "He told me that Beau was for sale. Of course I was interested, just as he knew I'd be."

"Why did you come for the dog in the middle of the night?" I asked.

"That was his idea, not mine. He said that Peg would never agree to the sale; that he wasn't planning to tell her. I guess he'd made up some story to explain the dog's disappearance. I don't know what it was, and I didn't ask."

To say I was unconvinced by Jack's version of the facts was an understatement. The two policemen were listening; no doubt hoping to hear something conclusive one way or the other. Aunt Peg, who should have been protesting vigorously, was still curiously silent.

Officer Denny had his notepad back out. "If there's a bill of sale that backs up what you've told us, I'd like to see it."

He wasn't the only one. I hoped that the prospect of

producing hard evidence would make Jack back down, but it didn't. Instead he took us up to the house. He and the two officers walked ahead. Aunt Peg, Beau, and I brought up the rear. Her fingers were tangled in the Poodle's topknot, and the grim look on her face precluded conversation.

That left me to my own thoughts, and they weren't pleasant. Aunt Peg should have been blasting Jack Berglund right out of the water. So why was I the only one objecting to everything that he said? Was it possible that I'd devoted three months to looking for a dog that wasn't really stolen? Had Aunt Peg finally recovered Beau only to face losing him again? Maybe she was in shock; maybe she was in denial. Whatever it was, I hoped she snapped out of it soon.

Jack led us straight to the library where he unlocked a lower drawer on his desk. There was none of the fumbling for records I'd seen on my earlier visit. Whatever he intended to produce, Jack knew exactly where it was.

He passed the paper to the policemen first. They read it and handed it to Aunt Peg. I read over her shoulder. It was a bill of sale, all right. It was dated May twenty-eighth, the night that Uncle Max died.

Aunt Peg glanced at the paper for only a few seconds before letting it drop from her fingers. Go on, I thought, tell them it's a scam, a forgery. Jump up and down. Cry foul. Make a scene.

Aunt Peg did none of the above.

"Is that your husband's signature, Mrs. Turnbull?" Officer Mosconi asked.

She nodded, and I exploded.

"It's not!" I cried. "It can't be."

"It is, Melanie," Peg said quietly.

"But how? Why? It makes no sense. You and Uncle Max loved Beau. There would have been no reason for

Max to sell him, especially not to someone like Jack Berglund."

"People have been known to do all sorts of things for money," said Officer Denny.

Aunt Peg shook her head. Her eyes were glassy with disbelief. "It wasn't the money. Max would never have parted with Beau for money."

"Oh no?" Jack snatched up the bill of sale and waved it triumphantly, and I wanted to slug him.

Fortunately I didn't have to. Aunt Peg drew in a deep breath, and I could see her hardening her resolve. Clearly she was struggling with a set of facts she could scarcely believe; but just as clearly, she was finally ready to fight back.

"There isn't enough money in the world to make Max do business with someone like you." Peg took several steps forward, crowding Jack back against the edge of his desk. "Max never forgot what you did to his brother, and he never forgave you either. If he sold Beau to you, there could be only one reason. He intended to ruin you."

"Ruin me?" Jack frowned. "That's ridiculous. He couldn't turn me into the A.K.C. without turning in himself. He knew how the dog was going to be used, he had to have known. In the eyes of the A.K.C., he'd be just as guilty as me."

"The American Kennel Club had nothing to do with what Max must have planned for you," Peg said grimly. "What you don't know—what nobody knows—is that Max and I had punch skin biopsies done on all our Poodles last spring. All the dogs passed but one."

There was absolute silence in the room as Aunt Peg delivered the *coup de grâce*. "Beau has SA, Jack. He can never be bred again."

Thank God there was a couch behind me; otherwise I'd have ended up on the floor. Above me, everyone was talking at once. Jack was insisting that Peg had to be wrong, the two officers were clamoring for an explanation.

I remembered what Aunt Peg had told me about the disease, months ago when Sam Driver had brought up the subject of genetic testing. Any dog affected with sebaceous adenitis would require careful management in order not to develop skin problems. All of his progeny stood a chance of having the disease and were, at the very least, carriers. Once a dog was diagnosed with SA, he had to be totally eliminated from a breeding program. Any ethical breeder would do so immediately.

No wonder Aunt Peg had been frantic to get Beau back. But why hadn't she trusted me enough to tell me the truth? And what about the other Standard Poodle breeders who'd already bred their bitches to Beau? In light of this information, all of the puppies produced would need to be tested. If introducing Beau's genes to the Shalimar line could have ruined it, what did that say for the state of Cedar Crest?

Damn Aunt Peg and her judicious omissions!

I glanced up and found her watching me. She looked worried. Well, she ought to be, because she had a lot of explaining to do.

"You weren't planning to admit it, were you?" I asked quietly.

"Of course I was. Eventually."

"You told me and Frank that Beau was being bred at least once a month."

"Up until the diagnosis, he was. Of course we didn't allow him to be used after that."

"But you didn't tell about the SA, because if you had I'd have heard it from someone else. News like that is big." I was growing angry now. Damn it, I hate to be deceived. "What about the puppies he already had on the ground? They're all carriers, aren't they?"

In spite of everything, Aunt Peg smiled. "You're a quick learner, Melanie."

I didn't want her compliments. Right that moment, I didn't want anything from her at all. Right from the start, she'd controlled my involvement in every facet of the dog game; making me think I was an ally when all I'd ever been was a dupe. Deliberately, I turned my back.

A moment passed, then she went to confer with the police who were taking a statement from Jack Berglund. With my luck, he was probably pressing charges for trespassing. On the wall behind the couch was the inevitable display of dog-show photographs. I let my gaze drift over them.

I wasn't hoping for revelation; I was simply trying to look anywhere but at the gathering of people in the room. But as I skimmed over the pictures and thought back to those I'd seen in Jack's trailer, another missing piece fell into place. Finally, I knew who had killed Uncle Max.

They were all still talking, but when I stood up and cleared my throat loudly, the room fell silent. "You weren't alone when you went to get Beau, were you, Jack?"

"Of course I was. Neither Max Turnbull nor I had any desire to advertise what was going on."

"But you had told somebody what you were going to do."

When he didn't deny it, I knew I was on the right track. The pictures were the key. Once I'd seen enough of them, the pattern was clear. It wasn't the brown bitch he hadn't wanted me to see, but rather the judges who'd awarded his dogs wins. Instead of forming a random selection as should have been expected, one person appeared with unexpected regularity: Carl Holden.

"Aunt Peg told me your line's been going downhill."

"That's her opinion," Jack said stiffly.

"And yet you've continued to win."

"Can I help it if the judges like what I bring them?"

"One judge in particular, isn't it? Someone who was giving your Poodles extra wins they didn't deserve—"

"My Poodles were always deserving. Carl's an excellent judge. That's why he was able to recognize their quality and reward it accordingly."

"And one good turn deserves another, doesn't it?"

"Melanie," said Aunt Peg. "What on earth are you talking about?"

It was nice to be the one with the information for a change. I might have savored the power it gave me a little longer, but the choice was taken out of my hands when the doorbell rang.

Officer Denny was taking notes again. It was left to Mosconi to escort Jack to the door. When they got back to the library, I was surprised to see Sam Driver with them.

"Well, it's about time," said Aunt Peg.

So much for being the one with information. "What are you doing here?"

"Peg left a message on my machine saying there was trouble and that I should get up here as soon as I could."

I gave Aunt Peg a look. And here I thought she'd had faith in me.

"A little extra backup never hurts," she said primly.

Sam glanced around the room. "It looks like you have the situation pretty well in hand." He crouched down and called the Poodle over to him. "This must be Beau."

"It is," I said. "But apparently that's only the beginning."

It took us ten minutes to bring him up to speed. Like all the major players in the room, as the story unfolded, he alternated between elation and looking as though he'd been run over by a bulldozer. By the end he was reduced to shaking his head. "Then you were already onto what Holden was doing?"

"No," Aunt Peg and I said together.

"And I still don't know what's going on," she added.

Jack, who seemed delighted by something that would turn the spotlight away from him, invited us all to have a seat while we listened to what Sam had to say.

"I've been talking to Susan Lewis," he began.

"The woman at your house," I said.

"The A.K.C. rep," said Aunt Peg.

The A.K.C. rep? Oh.

"One and the same," said Sam. For the benefit of the two police officers, who were looking baffled, he explained. "Dog shows are held under the auspices of the American Kennel Club. In order to make sure that everything is running smoothly and correctly, the A.K.C. sends a representative to nearly every show to keep an eye on things. The rep for this part of the country is Susan Lewis."

"What does that have to do with Carl Holden?" asked Aunt Peg.

"The A.K.C. has been conducting an investigation of his judging practices. Early in the year, they were tipped off that he was accepting bribes in exchange for handing out wins."

"I don't believe it," Aunt Peg said flatly.

"Think back," said Sam. "What about that big case only a few years ago where several judges were censured? It wouldn't be the first time."

"Not Carl," Aunt Peg insisted, loyal to her old friend. "He's too good a judge. There's no need for him to be involved in anything like that."

I thought about what Officer Denny had said earlier. People have been known to do all sorts of things for money. But then, I didn't know Carl Holden. To me, he was simply another piece in the puzzle. Aunt Peg, however, looked positively stricken.

Absently she patted her lap and Beau, who been leaning against her legs, climbed up and settled in. He was much too big for the space he was occupying, but neither of them seemed to notice. She circled her arms around the Poodle's neck and hugged him close to her chest.

"There's more," said Sam.

I figured there would be.

"The A.K.C. has been investigating Holden quietly for months. They questioned anyone they thought might have information they could use."

"They didn't talk to me," said Aunt Peg.

"No, but they did speak with Max, and apparently he had more than an inkling about what was going on."

From the look on Aunt Peg's face, I figured she wasn't the only Turnbull who was good at withholding information. Either she was an excellent actress, or Max had never discussed the situation with her.

"And did Max give the A.K.C. the evidence they needed?" she asked.

"He told them he would if it was necessary. But first he planned to confront his old friend and suggest that he turn himself in. Max gave Carl a week to decide."

"And in that time," I said to Jack, "Holden spoke with you and learned of the deal you were about to transact. He followed you when you went to Max's kennel that night."

I was guessing now, but it all made sense. "He waited outside, probably taping what transpired. When you left, he went in and confronted Max with evidence of his own wrongdoing in an attempt to blackmail him into stonewalling the A.K.C. They must have had an argument—probably a violent argument—because whatever happened next was enough to precipitate Max's fatal heart attack."

"Geez," Officer Mosconi muttered under his breath. "You dog people are crazy." Even Officer Denny had stopped taking notes and was simply sitting there listening. Disputes with the American Kennel Club were beyond their jurisdiction.

"The A.K.C. never received the information they'd hoped for," said Sam. "The next thing they heard, Max Turnbull was dead."

I thought about all the people I'd met at the shows over the last few months, and of one in particular, who was relatively new to the game but who had met with immediate success. "If Carl Holden was taking bribes, then I bet I know one of the people who was offering. Randall Tarnower."

Sam nodded. "With all that talent it would have been his turn soon enough anyway. But apparently Randy didn't want to pay his dues. The A.K.C. was investigating him as well. They'd promised him leniency if he'd deliver Holden, and that's exactly what he was about to do."

"Except that he never got the chance."

"Carl Holden had a very busy summer," said Sam. "And for a Texan, he spent an awful lot of time on the East Coast. I went back through the premium lists from May through August. Every time something happened, he was in the area.

"The week Max died, Holden was judging near Hartford. He finished an assignment in southern Massachusetts the day before Peg's house was broken into. And according to the expense report he submitted to the Shoreline Kennel Club, he flew into Newark Airport the Friday morning that Randy was killed, although he wasn't due at their hotel until dinnertime."

"Randy's kennel was only forty miles from Newark."

"Carl Holden had been there before," said Sam. "Apparently he knew that, too."

As we'd moved from dog business to murder, the policemen began to get interested again. "That's it," said Officer Denny. "You're all coming back to the station. We're going to need to get statements from everybody."

Aunt Peg was the last to stand. In order to get up, she had to nudge Beau from her lap. It was obvious she did so with great reluctance.

The bill of sale was lying on the edge of Jack's desk. I'd been to enough Disney movies to know that this wasn't how things were supposed to end. We'd found the dog; now it was time for the joyous homecoming.

Except that what we'd also found was that Aunt Peg didn't own Beau anymore.

Then she turned and faced Jack Berglund squarely. With Aunt Peg's flare for rising to the occasion, I don't know how I ever could have doubted her.

"How much?" she demanded.

"Pardon me?"

"He's no good to you anymore, we've already settled that. If I give you back what you paid, I assume that will be sufficient?"

Berglund sighed unhappily. "The dog's no good to anyone now."

"I think Beau and I would disagree," said Peg. She was already pulling out her checkbook.

All in all, I was glad that summer was over. Davey started kindergarten in the fall, and it seemed like things might finally begin to get back to normal.

The police arrested Carl Holden about the same time the A.K.C. concluded its investigation and suspended him for life. Jack Berglund, who was cited for falsifying a litter registration, was barred from participating in all A.K.C. activities for a period of seven years. Fortunately there was no way to prove what Max did or didn't know when he sold Beau to Jack, and they let the matter drop.

Beau sleeps on Aunt Peg's bed at night now. She's training him to compete in obedience and says there are plenty of useful things a Poodle can do besides siring puppies.

At the end of the month, Aunt Rose was married in a quiet ceremony in the chapel at the Convent of Divine Mercy. Aunt Peg attended. She didn't bring a gift, but I did see her slip Rose an envelope when she thought no one was looking. Frank brought some sort of a huge ceramic soup tureen that nobody in his right mind would ever use; but he'd just gotten a job and was feeling pretty high on himself, so we all made a big fuss over it.

Sam called a few days after that and invited Davey to a picnic on the beach. He mentioned that Davey could bring a friend. My son thought that meant he should ask Joey Brickman, but I nixed that idea myself. I've always been a sucker for a good picnic.

If you enjoyed *A PEDIGREE TO DIE FOR*
then turn the page for an exciting sneak peek of
Laurien Berenson's second Melanie Travis mystery
UNDERDOG
now on sale wherever
paperback mysteries are sold!

⌖ ❋ *One* ❋ ⌖

Bringing a new puppy into the family is not unlike having a new baby. Both cry at night when you wish they were sleeping. Both benefit from being kept on a regular schedule; and both immediately set about demonstrating how little you really know about the job of parenting.

My son Davey just turned five, so he's had plenty of time to acquaint me with the things he thinks I should know. Our new Standard Poodle puppy, Faith, is six months old. One theory has it that the first year of a dog's life is equal to fourteen human years. Each year thereafter is worth seven. That makes Faith and Davey approximately the same age so I wasn't surprised when they immediately became best friends.

At six months, puppies are both hopelessly endearing and full of mischief. In the case of Standard Poodle puppies, they're also smart as a whip. Davey's already got Faith carrying his backpack, sleeping on his bed, and eating the broccoli he slips her under the table.

I should protest, but my son has wanted a pet for a long time. I don't imagine a little over indulgence will harm either of them and I'm a single parent, so it's my call. We had a frog briefly last summer but Davey took it outside to play and lost it in the grass. We're trying hard to take better care of the puppy.

If we don't, we'll have my Aunt Peg to answer to and Margaret Turnbull is not a woman to be trifled with. She's nearing sixty, but she could probably out wrestle a person half her age. I know she could out talk one. She wears her gray hair scraped back off her face and has sharp, dark brown eyes that notice everything. She was married to my Uncle Max for more than thirty years until his death last spring. She is also Faith's breeder, and in the dog show world that counts for a lot.

Aunt Peg can be blunt to the point of pain, which is why she'd be the first person to tell you that her Cedar Crest Standard Poodles are among the finest in the country. Rank has its perogatives and Aunt Peg doesn't sell her puppies to just anybody. Rather, a prospective buyer must deserve the privilege of owning a Cedar Crest dog.

Or, as happened in my case, you can earn it.

Of course nothing is ever as simple as it seems and Faith came with strings, as do most of Aunt Peg's projects. She'd had a litter of puppies in the spring—all black, the only color Cedar Crest Poodles come in—and had run on the three best bitches. That means she kept three girls until they grew up enough so that she could be certain of their potential for the show ring. When the puppies were five months old she did another evaluation and made her decisions. Hope she kept for herself. Charity went off to a show home in Colorado. And Faith came to live with Davey and me.

Aunt Peg showed up one Saturday morning in early October with the Poodle puppy sitting beside her on the front seat of her station wagon. She and I had spent a good deal of the previous summer together and I'd learned enough about showing dogs to realize what a Saturday visit meant: there weren't any good judges at the area shows, otherwise Aunt Peg would surely have been off exhibiting. Instead she sat down at the kitchen table, drank a cup of strong tea and introduced me to the joys of dog ownership.

I've seen Aunt Peg lose her car in a parking lot because she thinks all station wagons look alike, but when it comes to her puppies, she's very thorough. She plunked a ten page booklet down on the table—mine to keep, for easy reference—and worked her way from "b" for bathing all the way to "w" for periodic worming.

By the time she got to the part about how she fully expected Faith to finish her championship in the show ring, then spent an additional half hour outlining the extra time and effort that endeavor would involve, Davey had long since fallen in love. Aunt Peg and I sat in the kitchen and watched child and puppy scamper through the autumn leaves in my small backyard. We both knew it was already too late to say no.

Aunt Peg likes wringing unexpected commitments out of me and she seemed to take great delight in the way she'd managed this one. Even so, she doesn't make things easy. Before she left she pressed the number of a fence builder into my hands. Clearly there was to be no roaming about the neighborhood for any Cedar Crest Poodle.

On my teacher's salary it seemed much more likely that I'd be putting up econo-mesh myself than having someone else install post and rail, but I took the card and figured I'd think about it later. For the first few weeks I solved the problem by walking Faith on a leash. It was not a perfect solution.

Poodles are shown with a mane coat of long thick hair. In order to grow the coat required for competition, the hair must be protected at all times. Show Poodles are never supposed to wear collars except for training or when they are actually in the ring. Then again, I've had a lot of practice with making do in my life and I thought I was managing okay.

Peg apparently disagreed because one day in mid-

October, Davey and I returned home from school to find our backyard fully enclosed.

"Wow!" cried Davey. "When did you do that?"

Like a deer entranced by oncoming headlights, I stared at four feet of post and rail *and* wire mesh that hadn't been there in the morning when we'd left. "I didn't."

"Cool!" Davey still believes in Santa Claus and the tooth fairy. No doubt the image of a fence fairy was taking shape in his mind.

As we climbed out of the car, he grabbed the key from my hand and ran ahead to let himself into the house. With his light hair and laughing blue eyes, my son is the image of my ex-husband. They also share approximately the same level of maturity. Then again I may not be the best judge of that as I haven't seen Bob in four years.

He and I had bought this house together, back when we were newly married and filled with dreams, before he'd decided he was far too young to be tied down by the demands of something as mundane as fatherhood. Putting all the money we could scrape together into a down payment had seemed like a great leap of faith at the time. But then again, so had marrying just out of college. Frankly, the house had turned out to be a better deal.

It's a really cute little cape in a sub-division in Stamford, Connecticut, that was built in the fifties. In step with those times, we got solid construction, an extra half bath and sidewalks on most of the streets. What we didn't get was land, or for that matter, privacy. There isn't much that goes on in Flower Estates that the neighbors don't have an opinion on. I was sure I'd be hearing from mine in due time.

I took one last look, then went inside to call Aunt Peg. The machine was on, taking messages. No doubt she'd guessed I was going to be steamed over her high-handed tactics and made herself scarce. It's hard to work up a good head of anger on a recording and I didn't even bother to try.

She couldn't hide forever, though, because two days later we had breed handling class together. Among the new things I'd discovered since Faith became part of the family is that there are all sorts of classes dog owners can take their pets to: everything from puppy kindergarten, to agility, to advanced obedience training. The purpose of our class is to teach a dog and its owner how to present themselves correctly in the conformation ring.

Class is held at the Round Hill Community House in back country Greenwich. Despite its auspicious address, the white clapboard building is durable rather than pretentious. Things in New England are built to last and the community center has been around for more than a century, serving as a gathering place for several generations of Fairfield County residents. On Thursday nights, it goes to the dogs.

The class is run by a husband and wife team named Rick and Jenny Maguire. Both are professional handlers. Their specialty is sporting dogs and according to Aunt Peg, they maintain a large and successful string serving a variety of clients. Luckily for me, they also like to teach beginners.

Judging by the cars in the parking lot, I'd gotten there before Aunt Peg. Davey was home with a sitter, so that was one less distraction to worry about. I parked just beyond the door, slipped on Faith's leash and collar, then exercised her on the grass for a few minutes before going in.

I had more practical things in mind, but the puppy sniffed, and scampered, and danced playfully at the end of her lead. All Poodles are clowns at heart and Faith was no exception. Of the three sizes of Poodles—Toy, Miniature, and Standard—Standards are the biggest. Faith wasn't going to be large for a bitch, but already her head was level with my hip.

Her ancestors had been bred to retrieve and I could see how that capability had been preserved through the generations. Her beautiful head had a long muzzle, strong underjaw and even white teeth. Faith's dark brown eyes were meltingly expressive, and her compact body was covered with a plush coat of dense, coal black hair.

Poodles are certainly among the most intelligent breeds; but what really sets them apart as companion dogs is their inate desire to please and an almost intuitive connection to their owners' needs. When I glanced at my watch, Faith knew it was time to head inside. Don't ask me how. I'm new to this dog owning business. I gathered the leash in my hand and followed along behind.

Before class starts, Rick gets the room ready by laying down the mats the dogs need for traction, while Jenny takes attendance and collects fees in the lobby. A long line had already formed and Faith and I took our place at the end.

I hadn't known Jenny Maguire long, but already I liked her a lot. She was bright, and funny, and had a wonderful hand on a dog. I was also intrigued by her viewpoint on the sport of dogs since I'm a real neophyte and she's been around forever. I'm not tall, but Jenny is truly petite. She has shiny, seal brown hair and an engaging, dimpled smile. She's the kind of girl I'd spent my high school years envying: the one born to be a cheerleader and have all the boys think she was cute.

She and Rick make a great pair. Even after seven years of marriage, his eyes still follow her around the room. His sturdy build compliments her slender frame and they often teach the class standing side by side, with one of his arms draped protectively over her shoulder. I should be so lucky.

Slowly the line inched forward. Faith was busy touching noses with the Pointer in front of us and eyeing the male Beagle to the rear. She's a natural born flirt and the more I thought about that, the more I realized that maybe I shouldn't be so upset about the fence.

When we'd almost made it up to the doorway, I started looking around for Jenny's dog, Ziggy. Despite her background in setters and spaniels, her pet is a black Miniature Poodle. That's probably one of the reasons why we hit it off so quickly. Jenny was delighted to find two Poodles signed up for her class along with the usual assortment of Cocker Spaniels and Bichon Frises. I told myself that that was why she'd singled me out for extra attention, and not because I'd looked as though I'd needed it so badly. She's also been generous with lots of Poodle specific advice about top-knots and coat care and feeding.

While things are getting organized, Ziggy's usually racing around the room. His favorite game involves tossing his stuffed rat high in the air and catching it on the fly. Even though he's seven—middle age for a dog—he hasn't lost a step. Once the class gets down to business, Jenny settles Ziggy on the stage, where he lies down to oversee the proceedings.

But when Faith and I finally reached the front of the line and I got a look at Jenny, I knew immediately that something was wrong. Her hair was pulled back into a careless ponytail; her eyes were red rimmed and downcast. When I held out a ten dollar bill, she made change without even looking up.

"Jenny?" I said. "Are you all right?"

Wordless, she shook her head.

"What's wrong?"

"Ziggy."

The word was so soft, I could hardly hear it. I looked around the room but didn't see the little black Mini anywhere. "Where is he?"

"He's gone."

"Gone where?"

"He's dead."

"Dead?" As if repeating the terrible news would help. "What happened?"

"It was all my fault." She bit down hard on her lower lip. "He's always so good. You've seen him. He would never run away."

"Of course not." I tangled my fingers in Faith's top-knot, looking for comfort, or maybe just the reassurance that she was all right. Sensing I was unhappy, the puppy pressed against my legs. She tipped her muzzle upward and licked the inside of my wrist with her tongue.

"I was out in the kennel and he was back at the house. I guess the front door wasn't latched securely because it must have blown open. Ziggy got out and he was run over on the road out front."

"Oh Jenny, I'm so sorry." The words were hopelessly inadequate, but I couldn't think what else to say. "Is there anything I can do?"

"No. I'm dealing with it."

I stepped out of line and the Beagle man took my place. He paid for the class and moved on. Two other students followed, then we were alone.

"Where are you and Rick showing this weekend?" I asked.

"Northern New Jersey. Why?"

Good, that meant the shows would be day trips. "Come to my house for dinner tomorrow night. I make a great lasagna. We can drink a little wine . . ."

Jenny smiled wanly. "And forget all about our troubles?"

"Something like that."

She thought about it for a minute. "Sure. Why not? I'd like that."

I scribbled directions down on the back of the sign-up

sheet and we decided six o'clock would work for both of us.

"Come on people!" Rick clapped his hands loudly. "Let's get ourselves into some kind of order or we'll be here all night. Everybody line up along the side. Big dogs in front, please."

I was moving to comply when the front door opened and slammed shut in the outer hallway. "I'm here! I'm here!" called Aunt Peg. She and Hope came barreling into the room and she was shedding her coat as she ran. "Don't start without me!"

Rick grinned and shook his head. Even Jenny managed a small chuckle. Good old Aunt Peg. Never let it be said she didn't like to make an entrance. She stopped grandly in the middle of the mats.

"Where do you want me?"

I'd taken a place about halfway down the line. Aunt Peg purposely avoided looking my way.

"How about right up front?" said Rick.

Some things never change.

Davey and I spent most of the next afternoon after school raking leaves. The yard isn't that big and the job wouldn't have taken so long except that every time I got a decent sized pile together, Davey and Faith dove in. They were so cute together that I had to go into the house and get the camera. Now I'd have to be sure that Aunt Peg never saw the pictures of her show puppy with leaves intertwined through that all important coat of hair.

We finally bagged the last of what was on the ground and while Davey was taking a bath, I brushed through Faith's coat with a pin brush, then took down her topknot which is the hair on the top of her head. If a Poodle is going to be shown, that hair is never cut. Eventually it will grow nearly a foot long. To keep it out of the dog's face, the hair is gathered into a series of small pony tails which are held in place with tiny colored rubber bands. I cut loose the old bands, brushed through the hair, then reset it with new ones. I was just finishing when the phone rang.

It was Aunt Peg. "This is so awful," she said.

"What is?"

"I was just talking to Rick Maguire."

As I waited for her to continue, I slipped Faith a piece of cheese as a reward for being good, then hopped her down off the portable grooming table I'd set up in the kitchen.

"What?" I asked again when a moment passed and she still hadn't said a word.

"I just can't believe it." Peg's voice was oddly flat. "Rick was so upset I could barely understand what he was saying. Melanie, Jenny Maguire is dead."

GET YOUR HANDS ON THE
MARY ROBERTS RINEHART
MYSTERY COLLECTION

__HUS_____   _CAN
  1-5_

__DOG EAT DOG $5.99US/$7.99CAN
  1-57566-227-2

__A PEDIGREE TO DIE FOR $5.99US/$7.99CAN
  1-57566-374-0

__UNLEASHED $5.99US/$7.99CAN
  1-57566-680-4

__WATCHDOG $5.99US/$7.99CAN
  1-57566-472-0

__HAIR OF THE DOG $5.99US/$7.99CAN
  1-57566-356-2

__HOT DOG $6.50US/$8.99CAN
  1-57566-782-7

__ONCE BITTEN $6.50US/$8.99CAN
  0-7582-0182-6

__UNDER DOG $6.50US/$8.99CAN
  0-7582-0292-X

Available Wherever Books Are Sold!

Visit our website at **www.kensingtonbooks.com**